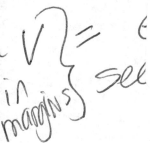

MW01249129

THE RAGMAN MURDERS

ELIZABETH A. MARTINA

Elizabeth Martina

SERRA BOOKS

AN IMPRINT OF

Lanternarius Press

a V² = c
in
margins} see

Customer Reviews
4.6 out of 5!
What?

The Ragman Murders is a novel based on an actual murder. Many of the characters, incidents, and dialogues are based on or inspired by the historical record. The work as a whole is a product of the author's imagination.

Cover by C. Alexander Moore

DEDICATION

When Anna was an old woman, she told her granddaughter, "I once saw the ragman and it was the most horrible thing I ever saw."

To Marianne Amato, the greatest storyteller I ever knew, who introduced me to this story, and to Joseph, her husband, who gave me the one piece of information that gave me the impetus to follow the story to the end. May this book answer the questions they could never tell.

ACKNOWLEDGEMENTS

Throughout the twenty years that I researched this story, many people have helped. A big thank you to all of you. I hope I haven't missed anyone. First to Detective Jose Lopez, of the Hartford, Ct. Police Department who led me to the newspaper accounts of this story. His first words were, "Are you sitting down?" Next to the staff of the Connecticut State Library and the Providence, RI City Library for their helpfulness in finding the details I needed. A big thank you to ancestry.com not only for the genealogical research, but also for the forums which led me to meet the British Columbia segment of the Amato family, especially Cory Dvorak, a wealth of knowledge of the family. I thank Carmen Amato, my sister in writing, and Aron Efimenko who took his summer vacation to edit the book. Lastly, I thank my son, Alex, and step-daughter, Teresa, who spent time with me in the libraries helping research dull directories and microfiche. And, there's my mom, Jean, and husband, Bob, who supported me when I wanted to give up. I could not have achieved this dream without you all.

CHAPTER 1

HARTFORD, CT. MARCH, 1930

"Here, Miss Amato, have a seat." Detective Lieutenant Frank Santoro held the back of a worn wooden desk chair for his guest, then walked around to the other side of his own desk and eased his old frame into the extra-wide leather chair across from the frosted glass door. The only wall hangings were a framed photo of a younger, thinner Santoro accepting an award from William Henney, well-known mayor of the city of Hartford, and a large, well-marked calendar, turned to the correct month of March, 1930.

He quietly studied her as he pulled out various papers from his desk drawer. Anna Amato was obviously uncomfortable being here, for this reason, but had been advised by her family to just do it and get it over with. The young lady demurely looked at the older man across from her. Anyone, even a crotchety old man, could appreciate the chiseled features, the dark bob, the piercing dark eyes, all sitting on top of a well-made mink coat. Her hands, placed lightly on her lap, had fine white gloves. Her cloche was a little out of date, but it looked appealing on her. It was very hard for the detective to believe that such a woman was the little girl he remembered.

"First of all, I want to thank you for coming in here on such short notice. Since you are not in Hartford very often, I wanted to meet with you this week. Your traveling between New York and here is easier for me. I am not one to chase."

Miss Amato watched the detective pull a large white handkerchief out of the pocket of his vest, regarding it as he began to cough. He held it up to his nose and trumpeted loudly. She looked with concern at the face of a supposedly hostile questioner. Santoro then turned to a brass spittoon on the floor beside his desk and nicely aimed into the pot.

The detective began again. "Excuse me, Miss. Allergies."

"Detective, I am married now," she began, turning in her seat to indicate the tall fair man with the glasses. He was sitting on the other side of the frosted windows dividing the questioning room from the main detective bureau office.

"Miss Amato! I have so many names in this file! It goes back eighteen years! And with all the Italians Americanizing their names, I am not going to start adding another generation of married names! DeFrancescos becoming Francises! Amatos not getting adopted but pretending they are! And then Amatos marrying each other! Or Italian women not always changing their names when they do get married! No, I'm sorry but I am not going to fill in any more new last names. We will keep what you got. The others in the squad are going crazy with the names as it is. Besides," Santoro nodded towards the door. "He hasn't got anything to do with this, anyhow." He blew his nose again and breathed in deeply. "And then, I do not want to retype all these pages just to add another name in all the right spots when I am trying to close out this whole thing. So, we will just stick with Amato."

Santoro took another deep breath and smiled to reassure her. "We had to reopen the murder case based on information that your family gave to one of our detectives a few weeks ago."

"Yes. It was my sister Mary," the young lady

interrupted. "And my cousin, Nickie. They came here together. It's about the phone number, isn't it?"

Santoro looked at her impatiently, not appreciating the interruption. He had this all settled in his head and he did not want details where he did not want them. "Chief Farrell wants this file closed. It has been a thorn in his side, and mine, all these eighteen years. He was a detective when the whole thing happened. He and the whole crew were pretty mad that we did not get our man."

"I spent an hour with them and one of the other detectives spent another. We wanted every little detail they could remember," Santoro continued. "But they could not seem to associate the phone number in British Columbia with anyone they know."

He began to flip though the file, looking for something specific. "Yes. Here it is." He looked up at the young lady, simultaneously pointing to the faded typewritten words. "It says here that you and your sister Teresa were eye-witnesses. You two and Mrs. Tassone are the only ones. And Mrs. Tassone disappeared off the surface of the earth a long time ago."

Anna Amato felt a shiver go down her spine. A name she had not heard or thought about in a long time had been bringing back memories these past few days. Bad memories. Santoro watched her hands ball up, gripping the coat. She blinked hard a few times and swallowed. She glanced around the room, apparently trying to get her bearings. The old place had eleven foot ceilings, the paint was peeling at the corners and the wallpaper torn along the seams. The upholstered chairs, sitting against the wall common to the detective squad room, had seen better days. It smelled like dirty shoes and cigar smoke from the old stubs in several ashtrays.

"Your sister, Teresa, hasn't been back to Hartford in

years. And I cannot subpoena her across state lines. So that leaves you. And I am going to sit and have a long talk with you. I want to get every last little memory out of you. The murder investigation has been reopened because of this new information and the chief wants to finalize everything before he retires in June. So I am going to give it one more attempt."

"I was very little then," began Anna.

"Your uncle and aunt must have talked about it." The detective was not taking no for an answer. "I want you to think back. Any detail. Any detail at all may make a difference in how we go about finding this man, picking him up and making him pay for what he did."

"May I have a glass of water before we start?" she asked.

Santoro heaved his arthritic frame out of the maroon leather chair and walked over to the door, opened it and shouted, "Hey! Charlie! Get us some water. A pitcher!" Then, horrifying the witness, he turned to the bespectacled young man who had looked up at the sound of the door opening, and said, "I'm keeping your wife for a few hours. Go back to wherever you are staying. You'll just be underfoot here." Then he shut the door and returned to his seat.

Meanwhile, Miss Amato had removed her coat, revealing a navy blue dress with a dropped waist, pleated skirt and white collar. It was knee-length, a little short for the current fashions, but well-tailored. She had removed her gloves as well, but left on the hat, as was the mode.

A knock on the door was followed by Charlie, an older assistant, bringing in a tray with two glasses and a pitcher of water. He crossed the spacious room, moved papers out of the way, then placed the tray on the old wooden desk. He turned to the lady. "Miss, the man outside waiting said to call him when you are ready to leave."

"Thank you," she replied. He exited quickly, after nodding to the detective. Santoro glanced at his guest and poured some water into one of the glasses.

"There you go," he said, handing her the glass across the desk. He pulled out his fountain pen, filled it from his ink fountain and straightened out some blank white paper, ready for any notes. "Now let's get started. I want everything. Leave nothing out. There has to be a clue somewhere."

After taking a sip or two from the glass, the young woman placed it on the desk. "I do not remember my real mother and father very well," she began. "I was only six and a half when everything changed. But my Papa, who is really my Uncle Ciro, has told me some information. My Aunt Mary and Uncle Dominick Francis have filled in more. My Ma, actually my aunt, my Uncle Ciro's wife, Emelia, gave me the biggest piece of information, probably accidentally."

Santoro rolled his eyes. "Wait. Let me make sure those names are in my file here." He viewed a list of names, making growling sounds as he found each. "Okay. Go on."

"Once, when I was about nine or ten, I had a dream. I dreamed that I woke up and there was a red-headed lady standing at the foot of my bed just watching me sleep. Well, I think it was a dream. It may have been real. At any rate, I was frightened and asked Ma about it. She told me the lady was my real mother and she had come back from Heaven to check on me. That answer made me feel better than I had in a long time. I felt a little of the love that I had lost.

"That is not to say that there is no love for me. My

Papa loves me and spoils me sometimes. Like this mink coat he bought me for my 16th birthday and the beautiful librettos he got me when he took me to the operas in New York. But, Ma, who makes sure I am always aware that she is not my real mother, made life dull as possible. But that is neither here nor there."

"Yes, that's very nice," Santoro scowled, remembering meeting Emilia Capocasale Amato at the funeral and things he had heard about her among the gossipy ladies who lived by the tracks. He had to admit, however, that snippy, formidable woman had done a good job raising this lovely thing sitting before him.

"But how about your real father? What do you remember about him?" He looked at her carefully, trying to catch if she recognized him. But there was no glint of acknowledgement.

"My real mother and father met and married in Italy," the young lady continued. "It was in the small town of Serra San Bruno. Up in the mountains. They had dreams for the future. They were in love, at least at the beginning."

CHAPTER 2

SERRA SAN BRUNO, SUMMER, 1898

It was dark, close to 9:00 pm on a Saturday night. Four young men, two not yet out of their teens, stealthily walked through the woods. The two barely older ones, one wearing a bandana around his neck, were dragging a poorly made straw man clothed in discarded pants and shirt behind them. One of the younger ones had a lantern, with just a stub of a candle, just enough to not stumble over roots. The other was carrying a small drum. The two older ones, the leaders of this band, were talking in very low tones. They had been walking for over half an hour, since their goal was two miles from the town. As they broke out of the woods into open spaces, they saw the large gate which was their intended target. Past the gate, about 100 yards, was the caretaker's cottage.

Giuseppe and Tony, nicknamed "the Mule," dropped their fake man, larger than life, onto the ground to assess the situation. They glanced up at the gate to judge the distance to the lantern swinging twelve feet above the ground. Tony unwound the rope he had carried over his left shoulder for those full two miles. He looped one end and swung it over the lantern, tying it to the gate, pulling it taut. Giuseppe nodded and tied the straw man to the other end of the rope and hauled it up about five feet above the ground.

Salvatore, holding the lantern, walked up to the straw man and lit the straw legs. It burst into flames immediately. And the fourth young man, Carlo, began to beat the drum loudly, in an attempt to awake the caretaker, so he could see the burning figure and, presumably, be scared. Within a minute, the caretaker and his wife came running out of their cottage door, screaming. The four young men laughed boisterously and ran into the woods, leaving the two old people to put out the fire as best they could before the breeze carried it further.

Back in town, the men did not part ways but went to the door of a white stucco house on one of the back cobbled streets. Tony knocked the proscribed tattoo and the door was opened by a wizened old man.

"Is it done?" he asked.

"*Si, capo*," Tony responded.

"Come in for a moment, you four," the man addressed as "capo" ordered. The men stepped aside, allowing Tony to be the first one to cross the threshold, in deference to him as their leader. Tony acted familiar with the surroundings implying that he had been there before. For the others, it was a new experience.

Inside, the house was well appointed with a silk couch against the wall and a cedar buffet serving as a room divider. The old man's wife brought in five glasses of wine on a tray, placed it on the buffet and left.

The old man was bent and gnarled, but his dark eyes did not show his age. They were actively reviewing the four young men and glistening in anticipation of certain answers. He passed out glasses of a better quality wine than the young men were used to. Then he sat on a high-backed wooden chair leaving the others to stand.

"Tell me what happened," ordered the elderly man again after they had all had a sip of their wine.

"It all went as planned, *capo*," addressed Tony. "The caretaker was frightened. I think he will listen the next time you wish to talk to him."

"Good. Good." The old man nodded with contentment. "Maybe we can yet do business with these northerners. They think they can come down to buy our land out from under us and then prevent us from using it. The caretaker is a wimp. He can be made to listen to reason." He rose from his chair with some difficulty and stretched himself as tall as he could to gaze up into the men's eyes. One man, especially, was taller than the rest. The old man knew him to be Giuseppe Amato, the cobbler's son.

"I hope I can depend on you four again. Soon."

"*Si, capo,*" the men muttered in unison. One did not speak out of turn in front of the head of the village. They downed the rest of their glasses and bowed to the old man as they left.

When out of sight of the house, Tony stopped the three others, pointed to their chests with a crooked middle finger and asked, "Did you know that if we do more for the *capo*, he might even pay us? I have worked several times for him. He gives us a free chicken, or some silver. Maybe a cask of wine. If you are in, I would like to work with you. But, you know, there are a lot of men in the village who could use a little something extra."

The two younger men nodded their assent without blinking an eye. Giuseppe looked at Tony.

"You know, my friend, I am working in my father's shop and do not want any problems. You must promise me no problems with his shop."

"I cannot promise," Tony said soothingly. "But we keep a low profile. I do not see that your father's shop will be hurt."

"Well, maybe I can work with you and the *capo* for a while. But I want to go to America in a few years. When I have the money."

"You and everyone else in Calabria, my friend," Tony retorted good-naturedly. "Maybe you can raise money faster this way, eh?"

CHAPTER 3

SERRA SAN BRUNO, SUMMER, 1899

It was getting to be dinner time in the village, although it would be several hours before the sun set on this late summer evening. Mothers were calling their children in from play. Men and young women were making their way home from their various jobs in the olive orchards or the charcoal plants, walking through the narrow cobblestone alleys that comprised most of the streets of Serra San Bruno. The two and three story whitewashed houses with their terra cotta tiled roofs crowded right up to the edge of the cobblestones, without yard or porches, casting the alleys in shadows most of the day. The houses butted up against each other, side by side, making side yards impossible. Old men were sitting on chairs placed, for the afternoon, outside their doors to enjoy the cool mountain breezes that ran through the streets later in the day. They were engaged in smoking and chatting with neighbors. Old ladies could be seen, too, sitting outside their homes, knitting or tatting. There was always a need for some new items for babies, caps, jackets and blankets, who constantly seemed to arrive to further populate the various families. And the grandmothers were also always making new items for the households, anything from tablecloths and bedspreads to pillowcases and collars.

The bells of the three churches simultaneously chimed the Angelus, just at six o'clock, when the chairs began to move indoors and the streets became quiet as the stragglers made it to their houses. Tradition and family time were most important in this region of Italy.

Maria Carmela Amato stood outside her house, talking to her friend, Rosaria Timpano. Her beautiful auburn hair was in braids wrapped high on her head. Tendrils of curls ringed her face and clung to her skin from the sweat of the work day. Carmela was a handsome young woman, with a somewhat stern face masking the humor which often bubbled to the surface. Her heavy eyebrows were a rather dominant feature, belying the delicacy of her lips, which often quivered with excited anticipation. The little gold earrings that had dangled from her ears since before she could remember shook slightly as she shared a few secret words with her friend. After bidding Rosaria goodnight, she walked through the heavy front door of the house she shared with her parents and siblings.

The first floor of the Amato house was all one big room. The center of the room contained ten wooden chairs around a wide, long table, covered with a red and white tablecloth. The scullery and a large cooking fireplace were at the back, where the food was prepared. By the front door were two chairs and a small table, topped with an oil lamp, set to look out the window this time of year. One of the chairs was on rockers and was Mama's favorite chair. Although it was still bright outdoors, the interior of the house was dark. There were only the front windows and the window next to the back door to bring the sunshine indoors. In good weather, the back door was left open for some much needed air, as it was this evening.

Carmela was hungry after working all day. The bread and cheese she had had for lunch had not been sufficient after an intense afternoon. Stepping into the house made her mouth water. The house had that luscious aroma of garlic indicating that it was Tuesday, the day Mama always made sauce and pasta for the week. Wooden racks stood on the terra cotta floor where pounds of drying homemade linguine hung from the many horizontal slats. More dried pasta was lying on the table, this cut short for soup. The smell of tomato and olive oil mingled with the garlic. How good to be home!

Carmela curtseyed to the Madonna statue that stood on a stand beside the front door. It was an intimidating one with the Madonna in black, with seven daggers in her breast symbolizing Her Seven Sorrows. It was a copy of the one in the village church.

She shook out her shawl and went to hang it on one of the large pegs by the back door. This door led to the kitchen garden, a tiny postage stamp-sized patio which divided the property from their neighbors. The little patch of land had tomatoes, basil and rosemary planted along the perimeter. The garden was surrounded by other houses and was inaccessible from the road. This was a private oasis in the otherwise humdrum lives of these people.

Carmela crossed the large room to greet the matron of the house, who, as usual, was preparing food. "*Buona sera, Mama!*" she saluted her mother, Marianna. Coming up behind her mother, the daughter rested her hands on her mother's shoulders, bent over the little woman and kissed her cheek, momentarily nuzzling into the older woman's white hair. Marianna wiped away the damp wisps of hair from her forehead, looked up at her daughter and smiled.

"*Buona sera, mia bella*! How was work?" She turned back to the vegetables she was chopping for the minestrone she would serve her family as lunch for the next few days. Carmela cleared the soup pasta off the tablecloth, filling a large deep bowl. She then grabbed nine large shallow bowls off the shelf above her mother and started distributing them around the table.

"I went to Signora Salerno's house," Carmela explained. "She has crocheted several lovely baby blankets for the new grandchild they are expecting. One is white with yellow edging and the other is yellow with white edging. Maybe her daughter is going to have twins, eh?" Carmela laughed. "Well, I squared them for her and she was pleased with my work. And then Signora Pace asked me to do her new tablecloth. It is very intricate. Two colors of threads. One on top of the other, looking like little flowers, all over the top. And she tatted around the edges. It took two hours to square, starch and iron it, because it was so large."

"So, you put in a good day's work, eh?" Marianna said, nodding satisfactorily. "The blacksmith shop is not doing so well this month. And it is not harvest time yet. The money you have earned will come in handy."

"I am glad to help. That's what families are for," commented the daughter. Her father and brother owned the local blacksmith shop and a small olive plantation.

"There are few horses and just as few new construction projects going on in this village. No one seems to have the money for horseshoes or hardware. The only going concern in the village is the charcoal making plant. Back before Garibaldi, the south was doing so well. I remember how it was." Marianna sighed.

The daughter shrugged her shoulders. She did not remember those times.

Carmela put several pounds of the dried linguini into the large pot of boiling water hung on the hook in the fireplace, then turned back to Marianna. "Mama, I need some money for myself this month."

Marianna put down her chopping knife and looked at her daughter, one eyebrow raised. "What is it for? There are no festivals this month."

"I would like to dress myself up a little," said Carmela, with eyes cast down. She was a little embarrassed.

"Oh!" chuckled the mama. She crossed her arms over her ample chest and cocked her head to the side. "Who is the young man?" she asked with a wink.

"Mama!" Carmela blushed. "I have been running into Giuseppe Amato often lately. He said he would be proud to take me out for an evening walk sometime."

"Hmmm! That one, eh?" Marianna looked pensive. "I think you should talk to your papa. I have my doubts about that boy."

"Mama! He is no longer a boy. He is a cobbler and you know he works in his papa's shop. He is a respectable member of the community."

"Except on Saturday evenings when he runs with that rough crowd of young men. We don't know where they go or what they do. But they always have enough money."

"Mama! I am a big girl now. A 26-year-old woman has her own mind and can see past the superficial! He is a good man and a good cobbler. He is restless, that is all. A wife would settle him down, I know."

"We will discuss this later," Marianna said, turning back to the last of the vegetables.

At that moment, a very pregnant Maria waddled in with her two little ones, Nickie and Teresa. She had shooed them outside when Marianna started dinner to get them to exercise some of the toddler energy out of them before they ate.

"*Zia Carmela!*" the two cried and ran to grab their

aunt's skirts. Maria plopped her heavy form onto the nearest chair. She fanned herself with a *mapine* to cool off. She tried to pull some of her sweat-soaked hair away from her face and refasten the runaway tendrils up into her bun. She looked very much like her younger sister with the same heavy eyebrows, but with darker, straighter hair.

"Those *bambini*!" she declared. "Run! Run! Run! And I have to keep up with them so they don't get lost in the alleys!"

Maria struggled to her feet. "Hey, you two! Leave your aunt alone! She worked hard all day. She needs rest and dinner. Come. Let us wash for supper." And she herded the two children out the back door to the miniature garden patio where a pitcher of cool water and a bowl for washing stood on an old bureau.

The women inside, going about their meal preparations, could hear the children laughing happily as their mother washed their hands and faces for dinner.

One by one, the rest of the family came in, washed up and seated themselves at the long table. Each had worked all day. Even the youngest of Marianna's girls, Stella, had been helping a neighbor with her children, in exchange for some vegetables from her garden.

"Look, Mama! How big these eggplants are!" Stella announced as she came through the door. Marianna smiled at her second-to-youngest, now a maturing young lady.

"We will have eggplant parmigiana for dinner tomorrow," the proud mother smiled. "Everyone get to the table. The pasta is almost ready." She heaped the steaming linguini onto a massive serving platter and poured on the sauce, a rich, thick, garlicky tomato sauce filled with mushrooms her husband had picked from the forest floor the day before.

The table was crowded with the immediate family. Maria had tied the *mapini* around the necks of her little ones, and then sat down between them to supervise. Her little brother, Bruno, aged 11, sat next to his nephew, who was only nine years his junior. Stella, Concetta, Giuseppe and Carmela sat opposite. Francescantonio Amato, the patriarch, sat at the head of the table, by the door. He was a short, rather weathered man, having worked outdoors or in a sweaty blacksmith shop all his life. A shock of grey hair sat above the stern expression he always wore. His hands were gnarled from work and he was missing a few teeth, indicating the hard life he had lived. Marianna, his wife of almost 38 years, sat at the opposite end, closest to the stove. Ciro, the oldest son, sat to the right of his father. They said grace quickly and proceeded to attack the pounds of pasta heaped upon the serving platter. Dinner was eaten in relative silence, except for Nickie and Teresa giggling their way through every mouthful.

That is when Carmela decided to announce her intentions. "Giuseppe Amato wants to court me," she blurted out. Her 15-year-old brother's head shot up momentarily, thinking someone was talking about him, until he realized his sister was talking about a distant relative with a similar name. He immediately went back to something more interesting to a growing youth--food.

Concetta stifled a choking cough and Carmela kicked her under the table.

"Why him?" Ciro snarled. "He has too many odd friends." Ciro was a serious young man of thirty. He was slender, with a thick head of dark curls. He would have been considered handsome if it weren't for his severely pockmarked face, remnants of smallpox as a child.

Giuseppe chuckled. He was old enough to have heard

the antics of a certain group of young men in the village. Carmela elbowed her younger brother, who eyed her antagonistically.

"He is much better than most of them, Ciro!" Carmela said, defensively. "He has a job."

"I have trouble with a man who would still want to hang around with his boyhood friends after realizing they are good for nothing," the older brother answered.

"This is coming from a man who spends his entire free time reading books! You have no social skills! And how can you talk about questionable friends? What about the time you helped Giacomo escape from the *carabinieri* in the olive orchards when they were chasing him?"

"He had done nothing wrong…"

"And, besides." Carmela did not wish to be interrupted. "Giuseppe has a good career. He works hard during the week and what is the problem with his enjoying himself with a few old friends on Saturday night?"

"Everyone enjoys a few whiskeys with old friends on Saturday nights," pointed out Francescantonio. "That is not the problem. It is what else the friends do when they are together that worries me."

"What do they do, Papa?" asked Stella, innocently. She had recently realized she was no longer a child and was trying to enter her siblings' world. She was inquisitive and willing to take on responsibility. Her long black braids belied her newfound maturity and her recent growth spurt had outpaced her hemline, making her look several years younger than her age.

Carmela glared at her little sister. This was not meant to be a family discussion. This was supposed to have been an adult discussion. She wanted to hit herself for being so stupid as to bring it up at the dinner table.

"We are not sure, but the *carabinieri* have asked questions on Monday mornings and the same names keep coming up. Those names seem to be associated with thefts in other villages, and threats of damage to the landowners. Not a good recommendation for a future husband," responded the patriarch.

"Well, I am sure Giuseppe is not among the thieves and robbers as you say. He does not need money. He has enough from the cobbler shop. He just likes his old friends."

"Birds of a feather flock together," quoted Concetta, tossing her dark head. Carmela glared at her middle sister. Five years difference in age made Carmela feel superior in judgment to the other.

As the dinner ended, Francescantonio turned to Carmela.

"Come outside with me as soon as you are finished with the table. Concetta, you go get the water."

"But I planned on doing sewing tonight!"

"You don't disrespect my order! Or your mother's! Just do it! There will still be time for you to do your sewing."

Concetta backed off her argument and went to get the pail. Carmela calculated that it would take 20 minutes to get the water at the square and bring it home. There would still be enough sunlight left for Concetta's sewing. Carmela's memory of being punished as a child for some infraction often caused her to obey, more than the respect she had for her father. The Amato siblings could, easily, in a mind's eye, still remember the sting of the shaving strap across their legs.

Stella left her seat and went about cleaning the table. Maria took her children up to their bedroom to prepare them for bed. Marianna went to look for her basket of needlework under her rocker where there were always socks to mend or knitting to be done for her son-in-law overseas in America. Domenico, Maria's husband, had gone over eight months ago. Socks, hats and scarves were sent in care packages to him routinely. If he didn't need them, some other man from Serra San Bruno who lived nearby, in that same American city, could use them. It was time for Marianna to close out the day with some relaxation, so she sat and rocked for a while.

Ciro pulled out his books and put them on the kitchen table to read before the light was too dull. He got his books mostly from the parish priest. Ciro had often told the padre that he would love to design and build large beautiful buildings, something people would admire. So the padre indulged him by begging and borrowing anything related to architecture for his spiritual son. They would then discuss architecture throughout the world and how it influences society. Ciro was a thinker as well as a doer. He was only at the books a minute or two when Maria came down the stairs.

"*Zio Ciro!*" she summoned quietly. Ciro's head came up and he turned to look at her. "The children want a story. Do you mind?"

Ciro chuckled, closed his book and pushed back his chair. "I will be remembered as a story-teller, not an architect, I am afraid!" he responded, smiling. Then he followed his sister up the stairs to paint enchanting word pictures of noblemen, ladies in trouble and dragons to the two little ones.

It only took Carmela a moment to help Stella. Then, Francescantonio took Carmela's elbow and escorted her out to the garden, closing the door behind him. They sat on the low stone fence demarking the property line.

He turned to his most beautiful and most anxiety-causing daughter. "Now, explain to me what it is you see in this man, this Giuseppe Amato. We are related, way back in time. But that does not help me see him in a better light."

He began to cough, a compulsion of late, bending over, coughing long and loud until he could catch his breath. His large *mapine* caught blood-tinged sputum. Carmela caught sight of this and winced. She looked down at him, with anxiety, waiting until he could speak.

She should have just sneaked around behind Papa's back rather than face this questioning. Why did she always give in and do things the proper way? No wonder she was 26 and still unmarried. The padre was happy and pleased to see her control her desires, but she was wondering if she cared, to tell the truth.

She looked into her father's kindly eyes. He was tough and demanding, but gave his children the gift of expressing themselves and explaining their reasoning. That was rare in an area where just surviving was a difficult chore.

"Don't say anything about this to your mother," Francescantonio warned when he could speak again, indicating his coughing spell. Carmela thought that the noise of his coughing could have easily pierced the door and gotten to her mother's ears. But she figured she would not mention that to him at this time.

After he wiped his mouth with his *mapine*, she began in earnest. "Papa, Giuseppe is good and kind. He has a good job. And," she sighed, "he smiles so nicely."

"Eh, *bella*!" Francescantonio chuckled. "That last one is not what makes a good husband. I scowl often. But, I make a good husband. Ask your Mama!"

"*Si*, Papa! But you are older. Beauty means something at my age."

"And it should. But so does responsibility and money.And the ability to hold on to money."

"Papa! Giuseppe has dreams. And dreams cost money. He is saving his money because he wants to go to America, too."

"Like all the others!" said Francescantonio, exasperated. "They go, but many never come home."

"Papa! If he can work and save money, then he will be a good provider."

"*Si, si*! I see that. But his friends! We all know he has friends of ill repute. I cannot let my daughter be exposed to them. I cannot trust a man who would be willing to befriend such people and still be married to you!"

"But, Papa!" Carmela pleaded. "I will take his attentions away from them. He just has nothing better to do than associate with them. If he is committed to me, he will not find need for them, anymore."

"Let us settle this discussion," said the patriarch, slowly getting to his feet. "If he can show himself to be righteous and upstanding, not associating with these men for a few months, I will allow this courtship." He crossed his arms and looked sternly at his daughter. "And you can tell him, for me, that I will watch his movements. I have said what I will say."

"Oh, thank you, Papa!" Carmela jumped from her perch. "I will tell him tonight!"

"No!" barked her father. "At least, not until you have finished helping your sister clean the kitchen." His eyes twinkled.

CHAPTER 4

HARTFORD, 1930

"So, what was so bad about his behavior?" asked Santoro as he scribbled a note for himself on his notepad. "Did he associate with Mafia members over there? Or just common thugs?"

"I do not know, sir," answered the young lady. "I was born here. I hear stories but not always the details. I cannot tell you what I do not know." She took another sip of water from her glass and put it back on the desk.

"So, go on. What else do you know about them in Italy?"

"My real father, Giuseppe Amato, was handsome! I remember that, and his moustache! He had a long one, thick in the middle and thinning as it was pulled out at the ends with a little wax. And curled at the ends. It was the style of the day. Many of the American men wore their moustaches like that. Papa told me he was tall, like Americans. Taller by half a head than most of the other Italian men in the area. He had a twinkle in his eye that we all saw. But, his wild side showed up with certain friends."

Santoro nodded, remembering his own well-admired thick moustache and he scratched his upper lip where there was a small white imitation, now. He also remembered that Giuseppe was just a little taller than his own 5'7".

CHAPTER 5

SERRA SAN BRUNO, 1899

Giuseppe Amato was tall, for a southern Italian. He was dark, but not swarthy, and showed no signs of the Greek ancestry that was so common in the lower peninsula of Italy. His black hair was always combed, with a part down the middle, painstakingly well, and his mustache was always trimmed, with that little twist at the ends. His sense of self-esteem showed in how he wore his rough clothes. It is not that he had time or money to have his shirts and jackets made of well combed linens and wools, like in the big cities, but he put on the air of one who was well-settled, affecting the appearance of a man of means. He reasoned that it could draw people to his father's cobbler shop if he already looked successful. And he was partly right. Except that very few people had the money to purchase the shoes he made. So, his dress for success idea only worked so far.

Amato was leaning against his parents' whitewashed house, less than a mile away from Carmela's house at the other end of the village. He watched the cobbled road, confidant that he would be seeing her before long this evening.

The house was plain with few windows looking on the street. The two windows that showed had deep sills where red geraniums sat in pots, lending color to the otherwise plain stucco walls. He smoked a hand rolled cigarette as he waited for her and glanced at the other houses on the street. Some of them had writing on the walls. Little girls had found pieces of charcoal at the charcoal making facility and used them to write little endearing messages to their love interests in the neighborhood. Giuseppe laughed to himself, remembering little girls writing to him ten years ago. At the time, he had ignored them, thinking only of the fun he would have of an evening with his friends.

Giuseppe mentally reviewed the past weekend's activities. He and friends Salvatore and Vincenzo had gone to a large ranch and taken two sheep from the pasture. They had been told to do this by the *capo* of the village. Sometimes these things just needed to be done. If the *capo* wanted it, it was a necessity. All the young men wished to please the *capo*. It was nothing bad, he reasoned. The owner needed to learn who was the boss of this town.

Since the time Giuseppe turned 20, he helped the *capo*. Sometimes there was money or a chicken in it for him. And with the cobbler shop doing poorly, he needed an extra source of income.

But now, he wanted to take a bride. After all, he was almost twenty-four. It was time to put aside the fun of youth and take on the responsibilities of adulthood. Not that he would abandon the *capo*! One does not walk away from a vow! He remembered when the boss burned the holy card of St Michael the Archangel, binding Giuseppe to his *capo* just two years ago. Moving away to America would be an extenuating circumstance, he was sure.

What more could a man ask for than a brood of children to climb on his lap and kiss him goodnight, or a son to enjoy hunting with? He thought often of America, where he would go, soon, to chase the good life. He could picture the children growing up with all those advantages he had heard about from his friends who had already made the crossing. Schools, electricity, telephones!

Almost losing himself in those thoughts, he spied Carmela rounding the corner, gliding along the road, shawl over her head, like all women, against the mountain's evening breezes. He gazed at her, assessing her attributes. Her wide hips showed good chances of carrying many children to term. Good skin and complexion, and that beautiful hair. Yes, this was a wise move on his part.

Giuseppe threw down the last of his cigarette, ground it with his foot and stepped out of the shadow of his doorway to greet her.

"*Buona serra, cara!*" he said happily. He stopped before her and looked down half a foot below him and melted a little. *Ah, so lovely*, he thought.

"*Buona serra*, Giuseppe!" she said quietly. He took a step closer to her and boldly put his arm around her shoulder.

"May I have the honor of accompanying you on a walk tonight?" he asked playfully.

Carmela's shoulders warmed to his touch. "Of course you may. My father has approved." She smiled. "With contingencies."

"Ah! He wants contingencies!" Giuseppe smirked as he began to guide her along the cobbled street. "Pray tell, what might they be?"

"He says he will watch you. He doesn't like the men you associate with sometimes. He feels they are beneath the dignity he wants of a son-in-law."

"Well, *cara*, I think I will agree with your father. My friends are staying too young for me. They have their little adventures, but I am tiring of that activity. As a matter of fact, I rarely go out with them at all, anymore. I have someone else I would rather be with." And with that he stopped, turned to face her and took her chin. He tilted back her head so that she would have to look up at him. He smiled down. "How about we go up to the old monastery and watch the sun set?"

Carmela nodded her assent and, with his arm brazenly still around her shoulder, Giuseppe accompanied her up the street, out of town, to the old *certosa* of San Bruno.

They walked through the forest, past the oaks, pine and beech, some older than the oldest residents of the village. The smells of the evening, last year's leaves which had molded into mulch, wildflowers in full bloom, the lingering aroma of sauce from the dinner tables throughout the village, all combined to make a very comforting environment. The young couple made their way up the mountain to the ancient monastery, said to have been built by Saint Bruno himself, 900 years before. They skirted the ancient walls, extensively repaired after the earthquake of 1783. The large ancient towers were all that was left standing of the original structure. They stood against the evening sky, guarding against any intrusion of noisy modern life.

Some 100 yards or so away from the monastery walls, Giuseppe chose a place to sit where a large granite rock rose above the soil. He took off his jacket and spread it on the mossy rock for Carmela to sit and helped her down to the seat.

It is said that if you are in the right place on this mountaintop, you can look east and see the Ionian Sea, the part of the Mediterranean separating Italy from Greece. Then, you can look west and see the Tyrrhenian Sea, a bay of the Mediterranean just north of Sicily. That is how narrow the peninsula of Italy is at that point. Giuseppe wanted to share the sunset and seascape with Carmela. So they sat, facing west, he behind her, supporting her back, awaiting the sun sinking into the Tyrrhenian.

"The breezes are picking up," noted Giuseppe. "If I put my arms around you, we will both be warmer." His eyes twinkled with anticipation. "You do not have to tell your mother, *cara!* You do not have to go to confession before Mass next Sunday. It is so old fashioned. Every hug certainly cannot be a sin." He had seen her go to confession several times on a Sunday morning, when he bothered to go to Mass at all.

As if in response, Carmela glanced back and smiled, then nuzzled into his shoulder. "Look at how pretty it is," she murmured, enjoying the view as well as the feel of his arms. She had seen this view a hundred times, but not in the arms of a man. Even Giuseppe thought it took on a sense of magic this way.

"Not as pretty as the little girl in my arms," he murmured back into her ear. Carmela smiled again and Giuseppe felt his decision was the right one.

As the sun was setting, the orange globe sank into the sea, sending rays of pale light out towards the starry black. Carmela looked up at them. She whispered a wish upon those stars and sighed.

"What is that sigh for? Do you not like my company?" quipped Giuseppe. He was hoping that she had asked the Fates for a successful relationship with him. He figured that teasing would out her wishes.

"Oh, I just wished on a star. I am hoping it will come true."

"Tell me what it is," he said, turning her around to face him. "And I will make it come true." There was a slight feeling of insistence in his voice.

"I will not tell," Carmela said, teasingly. "I will wait for the angels to decide." Giuseppe looked up at the stars.

"I don't believe in that stuff. I believe you make your own luck, your own future. And I know I am going to do well." He stood up and put out his hand. "It is getting late. I don't want your father to think ill of me. I should get you home." Carmela took his hand and stepped off the rock. He grabbed his coat and started to put it on. Then, thinking better of it, he pulled it off and put it around Carmela's shoulders for the walk down the mountainside and back into town.

CHAPTER 6

HARTFORD, 1930

"So, it was a marriage of love more than convenience?" asked Santoro, mopping his nose again with the handkerchief.

Miss Amato smiled. "My mother was a romantic, thinking that adventure would be in her future. My father had gotten into some scrapes with his friends and wanted to leave the area permanently. She admired him. He admired her. It was a good fit. In the end, her parents allowed the marriage. Of course, at her age, she would have made up her own mind, anyhow. So, I think that there was both love and convenience in the union."

The desk phone rang and Santoro answered it. He listened for a moment and then barked, "I told her husband he didn't need to stay around! Tell him to go back to his sister's house and we will contact him when I am damn good and ready!" Santoro smacked down the receiver.

He looked up at the young lady across from him. "Sorry, miss!" he added apologetically and turned back to his notes. "So, when did your parents get married? You wouldn't believe all the answers we got the first time around. Were they married when they lived here?"

"My parents married on January 18, 1900," Anna Amato continued. "A new year. A new century. A new life. It is cold in the mountains that time of year. It was the season when the rain falls incessantly and the air temperature, at night, is a little above freezing.

"I try to picture what the wedding would have looked

like, what my mother must have looked like on her wedding day. I have just one picture of her, in her wedding dress, heavy dark brown satin, with the sun glinting off her shimmery dress and her dangling earrings. She had that stern look on her face even then. It was probably from boredom waiting for the flash to go off.

"There is no picture of my father on that day, nor on any other day. All those pictures are gone. I do not know exactly how that happened. I heard that he must have taken them all and destroyed them."

No parent chaperone!!

CHAPTER 7

SERRA SAN BRUNO, JANUARY 18, 1900

"Wake up, sleepyhead!" Stella shook her sister's shoulder. Stella was already sitting up in the bed she shared with her two older sisters. She was looking forward to the day's events. "Wake up! It's Thursday! Finally!"

Carmela opened her eyes slowly and smiled. "Oh! And I was having such a nice dream!" she yawned and stretched her arms.

Concetta, who was already out of the bed, snickered. "And I can imagine what that dream was about! Your wedding night, perhaps?" The younger sisters both knowingly laughed.

"No," insisted the soon-to-be-bride. "No. You should not know about those things. You are not getting married soon!"

Both younger sisters laughed again.

"And, no, you silly girls! I had the most lovely dream about my *bambini*. Two little girls, one red-head and one with dark hair. And two little boys who looked just like their father, tall and dark and handsome!" Carmela put her hands together, as in prayer, and looked out the second story window, as if she could pray that the children would come down the street at her will. The sisters laughed and pushed her off the edge of the bed to get her going. She playfully yelled, grabbed her pillow and threw it at them.

"Well, silly! You aren't going to get *bambini* by daydreaming!"

"Oh, I know! But it was such a joy to see them all!"

Stella joked. "Remember what Mama says. It takes lots of work to raise children. And today you will celebrate the beginning of all that work!" The sisters laughed again.

"Come, wash up! I want to see you in your dress! Mama has been hiding it from all of us. She says no one should see the bride in the dress before the wedding day! Bad luck!" Concetta pulled the dress from the cupboard. "It is very pretty!"

Carmela went to the pitcher. "Ugh! Cold water!"

"Let me get you some warm water to add to the bowl. I won't be a minute!" shouted Stella over her shoulder as she ran down the steps to the main floor. A moment later she was back with a pitcher of warm water.

"You are a good little sister." Carmela smiled as the warm water was poured in the bowl. She kissed her sister lightly as Stella stepped aside after emptying the pitcher.

"I am only doing this because it is your wedding day," the young girl quipped at her. "Any other day and you could have done it yourself."

"Ha! Ha!" Carmela laughed. "After this I will have my own house and I won't have to share a bed with you." She pulled her hair back from her face and proceeded to wash.

"Have to be shiny clean for your world traveler, right, big sister?" Concetta teased. Carmela glared at the two girls as she dried off. She knew he would be going to America before they had been married a year. That was the only thing that was marring this day.

Maria came in without the three children who always seemed underfoot. "Put on your new camisole and petticoats. But do not put on the dress until Rosaria gets here. Let me do your hair."

Carmela sat on the edge of the bed and allowed

herself the luxury of someone else working to whip those curls into a controlled look. By eight, Maria had dressed her sister's hair in soft waves atop her head rather than the braids practically twisted around her crown, as usual.

The small bedroom started to feel closed in as Marianna walked in with Rosaria. "Here we are!" she sang out as she entered the room!

"Now may I put on my dress?" Carmela asked in mock anguish. The dress Marianna had made for her fit well. The brown shimmery satin, with ruffles at the neckline and cuffs, set off her auburn hair and made it look more golden than usual.

"Oh, Carmela! You look so beautiful!"

"The color is just right with her hair!"

"Mama! You did a beautiful job on the dress!" Carmela looked at herself in the long mirror and then twirled around the small room showing off the dress to her sisters. Then she stepped to her mother and threw her arms around the old woman's neck. A lump in her throat prevented the bride from saying a thing. But the tears in her eyes spilled over so that all the young women could witness the emotions she could not express.

"There, there, Carmela!" Marianna pulled her handkerchief out of the pocket of her black satin Sunday dress and dabbed at the corner of her own eyes, then turning the linen to another corner, dabbed the eyes of her number three daughter. "It is bad luck to cry on your wedding day."

The sisters nodded, but each had her own linen handkerchief out.

"Come, child! You should have a little water to drink before we go. It will be ten o'clock before we know it. You haven't broken your fast, have you?"

Carmela stared in horror just at the thought of not

being able to go to Communion on her own wedding day.

Marianna chuckled and patted her arm. "I didn't think so. But, as your mama, I had to ask!"

The ladies all tripped down the stairs, getting into a more festive spirit. Carmela was ready. And nervous. It was going to be a long day.

"What time does the first ceremony begin?" asked Stella, looking out the window at the dark clouds. "I hope it does not rain until we are back here."

"They have to be at the town hall at nine, and the Mass is at ten. Then we will be back here before noon," Maria noted. "But it is still too early to leave!"

"Here is a new mantilla, Carmela," Rosaria offered. "I made it for you specially for your wedding. It is not meant for the cold weather, but you can take your shawl off in the church and the town hall and just use this for your head covering."

"Oh, Rosaria! Thank you!" Carmela hugged her sister. Rosaria was the fragile one in the family. Married six years, she had lost every pregnancy and felt a failure. With no children, she had learned exquisite lace work and often made items for others. Rosaria helped Carmela pin the mantilla in place so they could admire the finished look.

Maria's two bigger children were excited. Nickie and Teresa had been scrubbed and dressed in their Sunday clothes. They did not understand the concept of marriage, yet, but they knew that a party followed. They also knew that they could not go outside to play, their mother not trusting them to stay clean for more than a moment. They amused themselves by playing with Anna, their baby sister.

Carmela sat at the kitchen table, praying for time to go by quickly. Her stomach was in knots. Now she looked forward to the ceremonies being over with.

All dressed and ready, the four sisters and their mother lined up in front of her. She looked at them, wondering why.

"We have decided," said her mother. "We will give you some advice as part of our wedding present to you." Carmela sat up, more attentive. She loved these women and admired their ingenuity.

Maria stepped out of line and smiled. "Dear Carmela, I advise you to remember that the way to a man's heart is through his stomach. And to look at Giuseppe, he needs love!" Then she stepped back amid laughter. Her Domenico had quickly put on some weight after marrying her. But he was always happy and laughing.

Stella was next to step out of line. "Dear Carmela, you should have many children and make Giuseppe very proud of his accomplishments." The ladies all nodded in assent and prayed that the children would all be healthy.

Rosaria then stepped forward with her bit of advice. "Remember to kiss and make up before going to sleep at night." The ladies all nodded and approved of that sage advice.

Concetta had her turn next. "Do not spoil your children. Keep them in their place. And don't let Giuseppe push you around. Stand up for what you want." Marianna's eyebrows went up, listening to her fourth daughter talk like those American women she had heard of. Concetta backed up and looked at her little mother, nudging her forward.

"*Mia cara figlia,* Carmela," she began. "I am giving you important advice, here. You need to be a little more aware of your cleaning duties. A man works hard. He comes home at night and he needs a calm place to come home to. Make your house clean and neat at all times.

Make it a welcome sight for your *marito*."

"*Si*, Mama!" Carmela said, quietly, looking down. She knew she was not a very good housekeeper. She had worked outside the house so long that it had not seemed very necessary. But, as of today, she was a homemaker. The bride got out of her seat and went to each of the women, in turn, and gave them tearful hugs and kisses, thanking them for their advice and good wishes.

A moment later, Ciro and Francescantonio entered the kitchen. "Hey, *bambina*! Are you ready?" Ciro asked. The women all assured him that she was. "Well, I have a surprise for you!" He took his sister's heavy shawl, threw it across her shoulders, and led Carmela out the front door. On the street in front of the house was a donkey, his breath steaming from his nostrils on this chilly morning. Behind him was a cart festooned with white ribbons for the walk to the town center.

Carmela squealed with delight and hugged her big brother. The children squealed, too, and begged to go in the cart.

"No, little ones!" said their *Zio* Ciro. "This is only for *Zia* Carmela! She is the princess of the day!" The children listened to *Zio* Ciro. He spoke with authority. He always was the one who told the children stories of kings and queens, princes and princesses. He knew of what he spoke!

Father and brother both put out their hands to help Carmela into the cart. Ciro waited for her to smooth out her dress before tapping the donkey with the crop and beginning her little parade. Everyone else walked behind, dressed in their Sunday clothes. Marianna and Francescantonio, who proudly had closed the blacksmith shop for the day in honor of his daughter, walked arm in arm. Rosaria walked with her husband, Gennaro, happily recalling her wedding day, also a chilly winter day. Stella and Concetta helped with the children as Maria carried the baby. Sal and Rosaria Timpano and a few other friends, who could take the day off from work, fell in behind as the little troupe walked along the cobbled village streets towards the town hall.

On the steps of the town hall, Giuseppe, his family and their friends waited for his bride. The sun moved out from behind the clouds for a little while, drying the cobblestones and making the remaining raindrops on the bare trees sparkle like thousands of prisms. Carmela stepped out of the donkey cart, with Ciro's aide, admiring how pretty the morning had become. When she stopped to straighten her skirts. Giuseppe walked up to her and smiled, admiringly. He handed his intended ant a small bouquet of flowers. They went inside where a civil celebration took place, per the current Napoleonic laws still in place. By law the witnesses were the town hall guards, Grigorio Politi and Francesco Vavala.

Then they went to Carmela's family church, Chiesa di Maria SS dei Sette Dolore o dell'Addolorata, (Church of Our Lady of the Seven Sorrows) where the padre was waiting for them. The beautiful little Baroque church on Tozzo Place, with its impressive granite façade, was full of statues and paintings.

As she entered the dark church, lit only with candles, Carmela looked at all the familiar statues and felt less nervous, feeling that she was surrounded by these spiritual friends she had visited every Sunday since she could remember. Looking around, Carmela saw St. Bruno, St. Rita and the painting of the death of St. Ann, her mother's patron saint. She looked at the altar, a remnant of the old Carthusian monastery, rescued from the ruins after the earthquake, and said a little prayer to

* by —

St. Bruno, who had lived at that monastery so many years before.

Then she looked at the large statue of the Holy Virgin over the altar. All dressed in black, the Virgin had seven daggers in Her heart, representing the seven major sorrows that She had suffered. Carmela had memorized all seven as a child. *

"Oh, please, Blessed Virgin!" Carmela silently prayed. "Don't let me go through the sorrows You saw. Let me have a happy life with this man I love!"

To get control of her nerves, Carmela adjusted her mantilla. Then, with her hand on Giuseppe's arm, she walked down the center aisle towards the antique altar and God's blessing on their marriage.

After the church wedding, all the friends and both families walked back to the home of Marianna Tozzo and Francescantonio Amato, hailed by well-wishers along the way. There they found a banquet waiting for them. Marianna's friends had spread out a buffet of shrimp and lobster, so plentiful this close to the seacoast, many types of mushrooms picked fresh from the forests and a variety of cookies, made by neighbors and family. Music and wine both flowed for hours as partyers came and went. There was singing by all, accompanied by mandolin and flute, a joyous time in the little house.

Then, someone with an American camera came by and took a few posed pictures of the wedding party, out on the little patio. Carmela stood behind the seated Maria and Concetta, squinting into the winter sun. Giuseppe stood beside his new wife with his hand proudly on her shoulder.

After a few hours, the sun began to set and the chilly winter mountain breezes rose. Final goodbyes were made to the newly married couple and all left. Then it was time

*each chapter spotlights an indiv. sorrow

for Carmela and Giuseppe to go to their own little cottage on the edge of town, which Giuseppe had rented. There they became husband and wife for real.

CHAPTER 8

HARTFORD, 1930

Frank Santoro was getting a little tired of sitting straight up at his desk. He shifted slightly and leaned back to look at his young guest. He knew she had not wanted to be in her present position, but the Chief wanted this old file brought up to date and closed, if possible. And Frank was most anxious to comply, wishing he could find out what had really happened to his old friend.

"So then your parents came to Hartford, right?" he questioned, sitting comfortably with arms crossed over his vest.

"No. It ended up being not so very easy," Miss Amato replied, crossing her ankles the opposite way they had been to get the circulation going again. "It didn't take long for my mother's fear of sorrows to become a reality. First, Rosaria discovered that she was pregnant again. Then Mother found out that she was pregnant. Two months later, in May, Francescantonio, my grandfather, died. Things were going much too fast. Caring for Rosaria, who was bed-ridden most of the time, plus taking care of the mourning Marianna, made the time go by much too quickly.

"Soon, it was July and time for my father to go to America. They must have planned and talked about it for a long time. I cannot believe how difficult it must be for a woman to give up her husband for a dream. I don't think I ever could."

CHAPTER 9

FIRST SORROW: SIMEON'S PROPHECY

SERRA SAN BRUNO, JULY, 1900

"This is not new! You knew when we married that I had plans to go to America," Giuseppe said, exasperated by his wife's whining and pleading.

"I know," she said sobbing. "But it is so hard to have been married for only seven months and then have to return like a child to my mother's house."

"Maria has done it for almost two years," Giuseppe retorted.

"Yes, that is true, but she has three children to remind her that she is a wife."

Giuseppe placed his hand on his wife's abdomen. "And I have left you a reminder, too."

Carmela sniffed, wiped her tears and smiled at her husband. "Well, that is true. But you won't know if it is a boy or a girl until you have been in America for a while."

Giuseppe lifted his little wife and twirled her around. "I think we should keep guessing until I leave! What do you say?"

Carmela giggled and kissed his nose.

He put her down and swatted her back end. "I will miss you, Maria Carmela Amato. Do not fear! I will work hard and get you over there as soon as possible. And little Giuseppe, too." He then sighed and looked pensive. "It is good that you are not coming. Your father's death came as a surprise to your mother. It will not be three months since he died when I leave. Marianna will need the excitement of two *bambini* to ease her sadness. And you never know about Rosaria's health. I do believe both of you sisters will bring Marianna hope again. "

Carmela nodded in acknowledgement, still sniffling, and turned to set out plates for dinner. As she did, she said a little prayer. *Oh dearest blessed Mother, you did not wait long to give me my first sorrow. My dear Papa. Gone! My dear Mama, so sad. Please do not give me more sorrows. Seven this bad would kill me!*

"Well, we have three more days," Giuseppe continued to chide her. "You never know. I may get a smile out of Marianna before I leave!"

Carmela swallowed the last of her tears and got back into homemaker mode. "I will be baking bread tomorrow. You will have ten loaves. That should be enough for the trip. And there will be two small rounds of provolone, dried mushrooms and some sausage in oil. Nothing else?"

"Your mother's *cose dolci*!" Giuseppe smiled.

"Of course!" My mother's *cose dolci* are always wanted." Carmela smiled back. Everyone loved Marianna's cookies and pastries. "For you, I think she is baking!"

Within days, Carmela had packed Giuseppe's small trunk with the cold weather clothes that she and his mother had sewn for him, plenty of knitted wool socks (Domenico had written that it got quite cold in the winter, even to the point of snow!) and enough food for a trip of two weeks.

Too soon, it was time for him to go. "I would have liked to celebrate our one year anniversary together, Carmela," Giuseppe whispered into her ear as they got ready for the night. "But there is time later for more celebrating. This is the last night for a while so, we celebrated, tonight, too!" She had made Giuseppe his favorites, stuffed mushrooms and pasta. Now it was dark and they were in bed, together, for the last time for who knew how long.

"Tell me, again, how you will get there," she said, snuggling into his shoulder.

"In the morning, I will take a hay wagon to Brognatura. There I will meet with your cousin, Bruno Valente and his son, Luigi, and a few others."

"Who are these few others?" Carmela asked uncertainly, pulling away slightly so that she could see his eyes.

"Oh, don't worry! None of the boys I hung out with before we made our pledge. They are dead and gone to me."

Carmela snuggled in a little closer again.

"Anyhow... We will ride down the mountain to Tropea and spend the night. Then, the next morning, we will take the boat to Marseilles. It will take all day. Then, when we dock, we must register with the quartermaster of the SS Burgundia. He will tell us if we need to find a place to sleep for the night, or if we can go on board. I hope to go on board early. It will save me money, and the others, too. We will not have beautiful quarters. We will all sleep together and eat together. It will probably be hot, but I don't care. It will be a dream come true. With the exception of missing you, of course." Giuseppe kissed his wife's forehead and gave her shoulders a hug. Carmela sighed contentedly.

"We will land in New York City in early August," he went on. "I will get to Hartford, Connecticut, a day or two later. Domenico says he will be able to get me a job. Who knows! I may become a barber, like he is."

"But you are a cobbler!" Carmela objected. She raised herself on one elbow to look down at him. She was surprised that he could say such a thing.

"In America, you can change who you are! You can reject the past and build a new future.You can become whatever you want! It is the land of opportunity. For everyone. Even us peons from the mountains of Italy! It is a wonderful place. Just you wait and see!"

"You will not forget me, will you?"

"How can I forget my *bella marita*! You are my heart!" And he pulled her back down to kiss her soundly and longingly.

The next morning, the families gathered to give Giuseppe a sendoff. Giuseppe's parents, Giuseppe Sr. and Teresa Pace seemed so proud of their son going on such an adventure, as had so many young men from the village. His brothers were excited for him. Marianna had told him she was more concerned with her daughter being disappointed that she could not accompany him, but glad that she, Marianna, did not have to give up another member of the family so soon after her husband's death. But what else could Giovanni do, with so little chances for income and advancement in southern Italy?

Gathered outside Giuseppe, Sr.'s house, Nickie and Teresa were trying to understand how *Zio* Giuseppe was going away for a long time, like Papa. They held on to his legs, begging him not to go. Maria handed her brother-in-law a small package.

"This is for Domenico. Please put it somewhere safe. There are letters and drawings from the children. And a little *cose dolci*, too." She gave him a teary smile. "Tell my man I love him and miss him."

"Si, Maria! I will do this as soon as I see him. In less than three weeks. I promise." And he gave her a good-bye hug.

Rosaria, seven months pregnant and safely past the

point where her other children had died, was allowed to leave her bed for an hour to see her new brother-in-law off. Stella and Concetta hugged him good-bye then backed away so that Carmela could get in one more kiss as they watched the hay wagon arrive. Giuseppe's brothers threw his trunk on board for him and shook his hand heartily. Then, Giuseppe hopped on the back as the cart started to move.

As they all waved good-bye, Giuseppe yelled, "When you see me next, I will be able to speak good American!" He was, in fact, rejecting his past and turning his head west towards a new life in a new country with new people!

CHAPTER 10

HARTFORD, 1930

"So, how long before Carmela came to Hartford?" asked Santoro. He was scribbling on the margins of the file pages. He had asked her for everything she knew. He had no idea she knew so much!

Miss Amato again sipped the water in her glass. Then she began again.

"It took three years before Father came back for Mother. Three years of one letter a month and the hopes that he did not forget her. Meanwhile, Rosaria managed to have a baby boy in September. Because of Francescantonio's death in the spring, she named her son Francesco Antonio. And my mother, who had her son in December, named her boy Giuseppe Francescantonio. They must have loved their father very much to go against common tradition which says you name the first boy after the paternal grandfather. In the meantime, Aunt Mary was so lonely for Uncle Dominick. You have met both of them?"

"Your uncle the red-head, eh?" Santora said.

Miss Amato nodded.

Santoro considered. "I knew them slightly. Years back I met them during the investigation. But they were too busy with raising all those children to help much. Your aunt would always start crying when I asked questions. I sat and spoke to your uncle once or twice at his barbershop but I always felt there were things he was leaving out. Maybe private things he did not want to have overheard at his business. Never could meet up with him

In America they name the child after the father.

outside the shop."

"Uncle Dominick was always so busy with the children and work. He felt what was passed was passed." Anna Amato shrugged her shoulders as if to say, what can you do? "My uncle always has a smile for everyone. He was a barber in the old country and he wanted to move to America. After two children, he sailed in 1898 and moved to Hartford. He made a career here as a barber and has lived out his long life in central Connecticut. Apparently, my uncle is not a man who vascillates. He moved, came back once, and that was it. In 1901, he sent for my aunt and three children, Nicky, Teresa and Marianna, or Anna, as we call her. In 1903, both Aunt Mary and Uncle Dominick became naturalized citizens.

"That left my mother with her baby and younger siblings, and a widowed mother. They were not happy, I would imagine."

CHAPTER 11

SECOND SORROW: THE FLIGHT INTO EGYPT

SERRA SAN BRUNO, SUMMER, 1901

The letters to Carmela were always upbeat and positive:

> *Mia cara marita,*
> I am here in Hartford, Connecticut. It is beautiful. So many large buildings, you would not believe. More marble and granite than in all the churches in Calabria, I think. The streets are so wide that they have to make the carriages extra wide just to take up the space. They have electricity all over the place. Even in the apartments. And all the public buildings have telephones. It is amazing to me.
> I found out something about America I did not know. They have what they call ready to wear clothes. That means someone makes the clothes and you buy them already done and no one measured you for them. They come in many sizes so that there is something for everyone. But you go to a store to get them, not to the cobbler or the seamstress. The shoes are made in factories. A factory is no place for me. I would not be happy there. No sunlight all day!!!

So, Domenico got me a job in one of the barbershops. It is not hard work. And I have a talent for this. Someday, when you come, I will have enough money to start my own shop. Then, see how rich we will be! I hope that little Giuseppe is being a good little boy for his mother. We will make many brothers and sisters for him when we are together again.

cute!

I long for you, *cara mia*!

Giuseppe

Carmela kept all of her husband's missives in her dresser and would take them out at night to read. She would look at her baby and sigh, thinking of his papa so far away.

A little more than a year after Giuseppe left, Domenico sent a thick letter to Maria. She was excited but waited until she got home from the post office to read it. Walking into the kitchen, she tore open the envelope and anxiously read through the letter. Immediately, she fell into the nearest chair, burst into tears, covering her face with her apron. Nickie and Teresa, frightened at their mother's response, rushed up to her, trying to uncover her face and understand this sudden change of behavior. Baby Anna, not quite old enough to understand, burst into tears, herself, at the sight of her mother crying and toddled over to grab her mother's skirts. Marianna, on the patio, rushed in to see what had happened.

Carmela came running in from the pantry. She saw the letter where Maria had dropped it on the floor and read it, herself:

Mia cara Maria,

I am so lonely without you. I cannot stand it. I have forgone food and entertainment for months to more quickly raise money for your journey.

I want you and the children to come as quickly as possible. I think that the money in the enclosed check should be sufficient. Write to me and tell me how soon I can see you again. We have been planning for so long! I am so happy the time has finally come.

I do not want you to travel alone. Ciro has been wanting to come for a long time, too. Perhaps he can accompany you over here. The apartment I found is big enough for all of us.

I kiss you and I kiss the bambini. And I love you all. Tell me all the details as soon as possible. I wait anxiously for your news.

Con tanto amore,
Domenico

"*Bambini!*" Carmela pulled the little arms off their mother. "Let your Mama cry. She is happy!"

Nickie looked puzzled. "Why is she crying if she is happy? I don't cry when I am happy!"

Carmela laughed. "Everyone is different. But when your mother stops crying, I think she has a surprise for you." Then she put her arms around her big sister and gave her a hug.

"Good news, eh, Maria? Soon you will be with him again." Maria nodded and wiped her eyes with the edge of her apron.

"Come, *miei piccoli*! We are going to see Papa soon!" The children did not comprehend for a moment.

"Now?" they asked.

"No!" their mother laughed tearfully. "We have to go to him and it takes a while. But first we must pack all our things. We have to take everything with us and leave nothing at *nonna*'s house."

The children looked at her quizzically then began to jump around the kitchen yelling, "We will see Papa! We will see Papa!" Little Anna, still not steady when she walked, tried to keep up with her older siblings but they were too fast for her little pudgy legs.

Nickie, too wise for five, finally slowed down enough to ask, "But where is Papa? He is far away. But where?"

Maria gathered her three on her lap and hugged them all at once. "He is far away in America. You remember *Zio* Ciro telling you stories about America? Well, that is where Papa is. It is a big beautiful country, with lots of big buildings and lots of room to play. You will go to school there and get even smarter than you are. And Papa and I will be so proud of you!"

"Will we see *nonna* when we go?" asked Teresa.

"No. I am afraid, she has to stay here and take care of *Zia* Stella and *Zio* Giuseppe and *Zio* Bruno. We will go by ourselves." The children were quiet for a moment, pondering the situation. Then they wiggled off her lap and began to dance around again, singing "We will see Papa! We will see Papa!"

As the family came in one by one at the end of the work day, the news was shared and the excitement rose. At dinner time, it was hard to eat, with all the discussion flying around the table.

"I will go to Tropea in the morning and check on the ships sailing in the next month," said Ciro. "I have to go soon to buy some iron for an order, anyhow. What is one more chore?"

"Who will you go with, Maria?" asked Marianna. "A woman cannot go with three *bambini*, alone. It is too much for you."

"Can I help you pack?" asked Concetta.

"Do you need more clothes for the bambini? I can ask around for anyone giving away things that are too small for their family," contributed Stella.

"Mama!" began Ciro. They turned towards him. He was sitting at the head of the table, where his father used to sit. "Mama, you know how much I have worked at the shop. You know how we are not making enough money for two families. You know I would like to marry and have children of my own, but I cannot. I have had to stay here helping you." The family nodded in silence. Ciro had given his whole youth trying to make enough money for the family.

"Domenico has suggested that I come to America, too," Ciro continued. "There are so many buildings being built all the time that I would have no trouble getting a good job quickly. So, I propose that I sell the shop and accompany Maria and the *bambini* to America." He downed his glass of wine, quickly, as if he had completed a task he was not sure he wanted to do. "But, Mama, I do not plan to abandon you. With a good job, I can send money to you so you will not have to be afraid of taking care of yourself. Just like Domenico does now."

Marianna cleared her throat. She raised her glass in a toast. "My oldest son, Ciro. You have worked extraordinarily hard for 15 years in the blacksmith shop. It has not paid off for you. You are so busy trying to make the family business stay afloat that you have not thought of your own future. It is time you move on. Just like Domenico did. He is doing well, now. You do likewise. You go with my blessing."

Everyone raised their glasses for the toast. "*A salut!*"

Carmela was soon left without half her family. She talked to the blessed Mother and complained about the number of sorrows that she, Carmela, was expected to bear.

"This is the second in two years! Do You expect me to have to put up with seven sorrows, also?" she whined to the Madonna statue in the house as she folded diapers. "It is all right for You. You are a saint! And Your son is God! How is it that You expect the same out of me?"

Carmela did not share these conversations with her mother or sisters. They would laugh at her relationship with the statue in the church and the one at the house.

CHAPTER 12

HARTFORD, 1930

"So that is how Ciro ended up here!" mused Santoro, still reclining slightly in his large leather chair. His handkerchief seemed used up and he fished through his desk drawer until he found another. The detective remembered the wide-eyed young man who so admired American architecture when he first arrived. The same man was wracked with tears when Santoro saw him again eleven years later. *why?*

"Yes," replied Miss Amato. "In early October, 1901, Maria, Ciro and the three children left for Palermo, Sicily. There they boarded the ship for the trip to New York City. Maria and Domenico were finally reunited in late October. And they have been married over thirty five years now.

"Then, less than a year later, my Uncle Giuseppe, by then 18, moved to Newark, New Jersey with friends. It seemed like all the Amatos were leaving." The young witness stretched out her legs in front of her and stifled a yawn.

"If you think I am going to let you go before we are done, you have another guess coming, lady. I want this done and over with. I am not going to wait another eighteen years to wrap this up. You will go back to New York and I will have a time of it following through. No, you are staying. Right here!" Santoro was smiling as he said that but he was serious. Looking at the grown-up Anna, he decided that she looked very much like her father.

Miss Amato took a deep breath and got as comfortable as she could on the hard wooden chair.

"Eventually, Father came home. But he made it clear that he did not plan on staying. He liked the freedom and money that America afforded him much better than a little backwoods town with no modern amenities. He and Mother planned on moving back to America together. They made their plans and enjoyed their little boy. It was like a six month long holiday."

CHAPTER 13

SERRA SAN BRUNO, 1903

Carmela checked the mail most days on her way back from shopping or taking little Giuseppe for a walk. She was looking forward to a letter from Maria, perhaps, telling how happy she was, how the children were doing in school, how her latest pregnancy was doing, how Ciro was doing with his fiancée, Emilia Capocasale. Perhaps there would be a letter from Ciro or her brother, Giuseppe. Or, perhaps she would get a letter from her husband, telling her when he would come for her.

It had been so long. Almost three years. Had she married or was it just a pleasant dream? It was hard to remember sometimes except for her darling little boy, Giuseppe, who looked just like her husband with the same blue eyes and dark hair.At the post office, she received the letter she most wanted.

It was one of her monthly missives from Giuseppe. Carmela tore it open and read it on the way home.

Cara Carmela,

I have good news. I have finally saved enough money to come home and get you. We will finally have the life I have wanted to give you for three years. It has been so long, but my feelings for you are still the same. I will be home by July 1, God willing. I have so much to tell you and show you.

Tell your Mama that I want lots of her *cosa dolci.* No one in Hartford makes them like she does. Not even your sister!

When we come back here, we will live with Domenico and Maria at their apartment on Asylum Street It is odd. We go 3000 miles away from home and live with the same people. Anyhow, Dom said we may as well not waste our money until I find a new job. Of course, I am quitting my job as a barber to come back for you. We will stay in Serra a few months, then, we will say good-bye to the old country forever and the three of us will move to this fabulous place.

Dom and Maria are becoming American citizens. They might even change their last name to make it sound more American. Maybe Francis.

In a month or so, I will finally have you in my arms again!

Con amore

Carmela had gotten to the door of the family home. She sighed and decided she did not want to go in, yet. She wanted to enjoy this news alone for a little while, so she went back to the square. Sitting on the retaining wall of the fountain she smiled as she watched the clouds waft by.

Concetta came down the cobbled street, to get water from the fountain. She saw her older sister sitting alone seemingly lost in her thoughts, so she placed the bucket down and went over to sit beside her.

"Carm," she began. "Carm, I have to talk to someone before I burst." Her body was not fidgeting like an excited person. She seemed to have perfect control over her voice. She turned to face Carmela directly.

"I have to share something with someone, too," smiled the older.

"You, first," responded her sister.

Carmela waved the letter. "Giuseppe is coming home! In a month!" The two young women squealed with delight and hugged each other. After a moment, Carmela looked into Concetta's eyes and saw the excitement. "Now, your turn."

"You know Raffaele Migale?"

"Sure. He is the one whose wife died last year leaving him with a newborn. They lived out of town a ways. Right?"

"*Si!*" Concetta responded. "Well, he needs a wife. And…"

"You have been seeing him and it hasn't even been a year yet?" Carmela's eyes went wide with surprise. Concetta nodded and looked at her hands to avoid the look in her sister's eyes. "Do you love him, Concetta?"

"Bah! This love stuff is silly," Concetta sniffed. "A woman needs a protector and a provider. When the man protects and provides then the woman loves him."

"And Raffaele needs a mother for his little girl."

"I am not going to raise someone else's child. She can live with her grandparents!"   *Woe!*

Carmela was aghast but kept it to herself. That was an argument she would not be able to win with her very stubborn sister.

"Will you even see her?"

"No. I doubt it. Raffaele has plans to move back to Canada next year. He heard that they are opening many mines in the west. There is good money to be made in mining, you know."

"Well," said Carmela. "You had better get married before Giuseppe takes me to America. I want to see your wedding."

"You will, I promise," Concetta assured her. "But we cannot announce our intentions until the year of mourning is up. It will be soon after Giuseppe comes back."

"I can't wait for the announcement. It has been just too boring around here, lately," Carmela said. "No baptisms, no weddings! If it weren't for little Giuseppe and Frankie and the church festivals we would have no excitement at all. I am glad Giuseppe is coming in the summer. At least he will be here for the Feast of the Assumption. Best festival of the year!"

"Now, Carm," warned Concetta. "You won't tell anyone, right? It's a secret between you and me."

"Are you going to tell Rosaria?"

"No. She talks too much. Besides, she has too many problems of her own, poor thing," responded Concetta. "It is just between you and me, all right?"

"Absolutely, little sister," Carmela chided her. Concetta was almost 25.

The welcome home party for Giuseppe was as lively and full of food as the wedding party three years before. Carmela wore her wedding dress to remind him of that happy day. Giuseppe saw his son for the very first time, admiring the little boy's abilities and charms. Friends and family all came to welcome him home and admire his new American look. He demonstrated his English and bragged about his job. Wine flowed and all the neighbors brought food to pass. It was an event, even though many in the village had seen sons and daughters come and go for years. The Amatos loved parties.

But nighttime finally came, and, once again, Carmela was a bride in the same little cottage where they had spent their first few months. But this time, she was with a virtual stranger who just happened to be the father of her child. "Giuseppe, you are so, so . . . American!" she commented when they were finally alone.

"Do you like it?" He held himself differently, more

self-assured than ever.

"Your clothes are no longer the clothes like you have always worn, like everyone else in the village. You have an American suit!" It was an off-the-rack suit, a gray summer weight wool, with a vest, which did not fit as well as those stylish suits the middle-class Americans wore, but it was certainly nicer than anything she had seen him in before. His white shirt, wrinkled after two weeks on a ship with no laundry facilities, was held in place around the forearms with garters, typical of a barber of the time.

"And your hair!" It was beginning to thin on top and he had started to part his hair on the side so that he could comb over the thin spot. "It is very different. You used to part it in the middle."

He laughed a little and replied, "We are getting older, eh?"

In the meantime, Giuseppe had evaluated Carmela and was uncomfortable with what he found. "You are different, too." He played with her auburn hair, unbraiding the hair she kept tightly wound around her head to control the curls. It seemed so old-fashioned compared to the American styles. Her everyday clothes were of a dull color and her wedding dress, after three years of wearing it every Sunday, was fraying around the cuffs and collar.

"I will teach you how to do your hair like the American women. They put it in a bun. Here," he pointed to the top of her head. "And they do not pull it tight to hide the curl. They do it loosely. Like so." Giuseppe twisted her hair simply into a loose topknot with tendrils in front of her ears and moved her to stand in front of the looking glass, while he stood behind her, hands on her shoulders. Carmella smiled at the effect. And Giuseppe, seeing her relax, smiled back and kissed her neck. He looked at her in the mirror and addressed the reflection.

"It seems that the village is so dull after the lights and sounds of Hartford. I know I would not be happy staying here for the rest of my life. I have grown used to the excitement of the big city, and the opportunities for money that are there. We have discussed this, but I want to know if you understand what this means. I will stay until after the holy holidays and then I plan to return." He looked into his wife's eyes and prayed for her to understand. After just a day, he knew he didn't belong in Serra San Bruno anymore.

"I am married to you," Carmela said. "Where you go, I will go. I still love you." And, with that, they became as husband and wife, again. As the days passed, they became comfortable with each other all over again, and began in earnest to make plans to go back to America together.

By fall, Carmela had great news for her husband. She put the baby to bed and then made another of his favorite dishes, mushroom and *pasta al olio*. "What's this? My favorite?" asked the young husband. "Is it a special occasion?"

Carmela sat beside him at the little table. Her eyes were twinkling. "Yes, it is! Little Giuseppe's brother has made his announcement!"

"Ah! *Mia cara*! Is it true?" He jumped up, grabbed her around the waist and twirled her round and round the kitchen, laughing and kissing her by turn. "This is a day I have waited for!" he declared as he set her gently down. "When is he to come?"

"The best I can figure is early summer," she responded.

They ate dinner smiling at each other in excitement. Then, after dinner, Giuseppe sat with his coffee as he watched his wife clean up, pondering the news.

"This changes our plans, *cara*!" he pointed out. "You do not want to be on a ship while expecting."

Carmela turned towards him, questioning what he was saying. "What does that mean for our plans?" she asked. She put down the *mapine* that she had been wiping the dishes with and turned to face him expectantly.

"We won't be leaving right after the holidays. You cannot travel. We will have to wait."

"Will you wait with me?"

"Without a job, it is not a good idea to do that. I have to go back and start making money again. You cannot travel until you are sure the baby is healthy. You and Giuseppe and he won't be able to travel until probably next fall."

"Oh, no!" cried Carmela, putting her fist up to her mouth. "Not again!" Her face showed her fear at the thought of his leaving her once more and she began to weep.

Giuseppe left his chair, crossed over to her and grabbed her shoulders.

"Please don't start to cry!" he pleaded. "I will stay with you for a while yet. Then I will leave, go back to Hartford, and find another job so that we will have things for him. As soon as he is big enough, you will come. It will only be a few months, this time."

"Are you sure?" Carmela tearfully asked.

"Of course, *cara mia*!" He gently kissed her.

CHAPTER 14

THIRD SORROW: LOSS OF THE CHILD JESUS IN THE TEMPLE

SERRA SAN BRUNO, FALL, 1903

Carmela was not well during this pregnancy. She needed help with both a very rambunctious toddler and household chores.

One day in early October, Carmela took little Giuseppe and a large bundle of dirty clothes over to her mother's. Laundry was tedious and time consuming but the day would be spent gossiping as they washed. It was enjoyable to be with her mother all day and share the joys of her little boy.

The wash water was already being prepared as Carmela ushered the prancing little boy into the house.

"You were up early this morning, Mama!" Carmela commented. "How did you get the wash tub up onto those chairs by yourself?"

"I had help," Marianna smiled. "Stella did it all before she went out."

"What would you do without Stella!" Carmela exclaimed. "She is your right hand!" Marianna nodded as she crossed over to the fireplace to see if the water was steaming yet.

"I will put the baby on the floor and give him some toys." Carmela led him over to the front window. "You sit like a good boy and play with your blocks while Mama and *nonna* wash clothes in the garden. I will leave the door open so you can see us. But don't run around."

The little boy smiled up at her and dumped out his bag of toys.

"Can you help me carry this cauldron over to the wash pot?" asked Marianna. "I already put the cold water in the pot." Carmela hiked up her skirts and tucked them into her waistband. She walked over to the fireplace and got a thick *mapine* to wrap around the handle on her side of the cauldron. Her mother did the same and they slowly staggered across the room to the patio where the wash pot was standing on the chairs. Out of the corner of her eye, Carmela saw her boy run towards them chasing a small ball. Before she could react, he had bumped into her leg.

Carmela lost her balance and dropped her side of the cauldron. The steaming water poured onto her baby!

He immediately began to screech in pain and shock. The child was horribly scalded! Carmela was burned, too, but hardly to the extent of the boy.

"Oh, my God! Oh, mother of God! No! No! No!" Both grandmother and mother began to cry in horror as Carmela instinctively dropped to the floor to pick up her baby.

"My baby! My baby! Get me towels, Mama!" Carmela screamed, but hardly loud enough to be heard over the screams of the baby. "Oh, God! He won't let me touch him!"

Taking off her apron, she attempted to wrap it around the flailing child. "Oh, my God! How red his skin is. It is already starting to blister!!"

The shrieking was so loud that the neighbor ladies came running to the house within a minute. Immediately, the old wives' remedies were applied. "Roll him in towels!" insisted one woman.

Giuseppe was rolled in rugs and towels as he screeched in pain.

"Find the butter!" frantically insisted another woman.

They applied cold butter to his burns, which only made them redder.

Everyone was crying. Carmela screamed at the Madonna statue. "Do something! Santa Maria, do not give me more! You can't do this to me again! Giuseppe! Where is my *marito*?"

One of the ladies sent her son, Luigi, racing to the square, where Guiseppe was in conversation with some of his old friends.

"Giuseppe! Giuseppe!" Luigi interrupted the men, gasping from his run.

"Do you not see that I am talking with my friends, you little squirt?" Giuseppe retorted. He looked at the frightened look on the child's face and said, "Eh? What is the matter? Are you sick?"

"There has been an accident! Your boy is hurt! My mother told me to come get you!"

Giuseppe jumped up from where he was sitting in the shade, almost overturning the table with its glasses of wine. He was just as frightened as the young boy. The two of them raced back to the house.

They found all in chaos. It seemed like the entire neighborhood was in the front room. The ladies were all sobbing at their lack of positive results. Carmela was sitting in her mother's rocker, crying, holding the wrapped baby who was still screaming. He looked awful. The redness covered him. The skin was already beginning to fall away. The distraught father made the Sign of the Cross.

"Carmela!" he yelled at her, grabbing the shoulders of the sobbing woman and shaking her. "You must be brave! I will go get Signor Valente!" Carmela looked up with glazed eyes and did not appear to see him. All she could see was her baby.

Giuseppe set off at a dead run, brushing past his friends in the town square as he raced to the only medical man in town. He reached the house in two minutes and pounded on the door. It was opened by the medical man himself.

"Hey! Giuseppe, my boy!" greeted the physician, ready to smile, until he saw the young father's face. "What is the matter? You look like you have seen a ghost!"

"It's my boy, Valente! He has been burned! The hot laundry water!" Giuseppe was leaning against the door jamb, gasping for breath from running the whole way.

"Wait! Let me grab my bag!" said the older man. He could not run to the house. So the return was slower. Valente got every bit of information he could out of Giuseppe and thought he knew what to do as soon as he arrived at the house.

The child was still hysterical when they got back. He was lying, still wrapped in the blankets, at his mother's feet, his hands clenched, wailing pitifully. Carmela was still sitting on the rocker, her face buried in her hands, sobbing loudly. Other women milled around, bringing cold, damp towels to cool him, some sitting at the kitchen table. Others were holding the crying Marianna and Teresa Pace, Giuseppe's mother, who had been summoned and had arrived in Giuseppe's absence.

"Let me see the burns," ordered the medical man as he walked through the door. "Take the towels off this child! The burns need air! Leave the bottom blanket alone!" The two women who had been applying the towels jumped into action, tearing them off and wiping off some of the butter, taking skin with them. The baby howled in pain!

"*Madre mio!*" the older man gasped. "This is not good!" Carmela burst into screaming, again. At that point, Marianna and Teresa, despite their own grief, ran to her side, pulled Carmela out of the rocker, and got her across the kitchen to the patio door.

BVM "I have to stay! I have to stay with my *bambino*! The WR Virgin! She is expecting me to suffer like She did!" Carmela cried, arms extended towards her boy, as the two older women pulled her away from the scene.

"No, *cara mia*! The Virgin loves you and Giuseppe. It is an accident!" Marianna crooned. "We must look at your legs. They are burned." She was in tears as she pulled her daughter out the door.

"Clear out of here, all you ladies!" Valente yelled. "You can't help anymore!" And he shooed them all out.

Reluctantly, they knew he was right. But they all huddled outside the front door, walking back and forth in front of the house, waiting for word. Then he turned to Giuseppe, who stood aghast, looking down at his little boy.

"The child is not going to make it, Giuseppe, my son. Best you can do is give him as much wine as he can handle and do not touch his skin as much as possible. The pain is going to be bad." Giuseppe nodded without saying a word. "Your wife is pregnant, right?"

"*Si!*" Giuseppe practically whispered. Valente looked down at the younger man and felt great pity for his loss. He opened his bag and pulled out a bottle of chloroform and a thick cotton cloth. He proceeded to dampen the cloth with the liquid as he continued to speak.

"Well, if you don't want her to lose the next one, too, even before it is born, you had better stay with the boy until the end and keep her doing something useless."

"Useless?"

Angie's friend experienced this accident w/her baby. It died to. 72

"Oh, have her bringing in cold cloths every ten minutes if you have to. This shouldn't last too long. He is little. He hasn't the strength to fight this."

For the first time since hearing the news, Giuseppe choked up. "There is nothing you can do, Valente?"

"There is very little we can do but wait for God to take him. But this will help. Pick up the *bambino*. Carefully." Giuseppe stepped over to the rocker that his little wife had recently occupied and, picking up the blanket with the squalling child, eased himself onto the seat. Valente placed the cloth over the child's mouth and nose and within seconds the child went limp and closed his eyes. Giuseppe looked up at the medical man in awe.

"Now, all I can do is pray. And you, too. You will not be able to keep him comfortable without this. But you must do it just like I did. Too much and poof! He is dead. You do not have the right to kill even a suffering child. Dear God that I am even suggesting this! So, the best you can do is keep him unconscious."

The older man had tears in his eyes as he handed the cloth and the small bottle to the distraught father. "I am sorry, Giuseppe," he said with heartfelt sadness. Then he picked up his hat and bag. "See to it that the child receives Extreme Unction soon. I will stop by the church and tell the padre that he does not have much time."

"Thank you, Valente. Thank you for your honesty." Giuseppe looked down at his now still baby. He suddenly didn't have the energy to stand as Signor Valente walked to the door.

"God bless you in your troubles." Valente let himself out the front door. The ladies were outside and surrounded him, attacking him with questions.

A moment later, the two grandmothers reentered the house with Carmela between them. Giuseppe watched as they walked the silent mother up the stairs to the bedrooms. Carmela was too incoherent to be of use. He realized that she was finally stunned into silence, too much in shock to cry any more.

Giuseppe sat and rocked his child, unable to pray. He had never practiced.

"What did Signor Valente say to do?" asked Marianna after she and Teresa returned from putting her poor daughter down on one of the beds. She put on her brave mother's face and faced her son-in-law. "My poor daughter is so sick. You and I will have to do everything the rest of the day. So what shall we do?"

"Keep him comfortable and unconscious until the end."

"Oh, my God!" Teresa exclaimed staring at her grandson's ashen face. Marianna made the Sign of the Cross and ran over to her Madonna statue. She knelt in front of it and cried her eyes out.

CHAPTER 15
HARTFORD, 1930

"So, that was ~~would have been~~ your older brother?" asked the detective.

"Yes," responded the young lady, shifting in her seat. "He died a day later."

"Did your mother lose the other baby?" he came back again.

"No. Life started improving again and Rosaria had another baby who did not die. This one was a girl, Rose, and she was born in March. My father stayed until April. Then he left again for Hartford. My mother's new baby was born in June, but it was not another son; it was a girl. And my mother named her Maria Teresa, after Giuseppe's mother.

"What happened to your aunt who was supposed to get married?"

"The wedding of Aunt Concetta and Rafaelle Migale took place, as scheduled, five weeks after the baby's funeral, just before the Christmas holiday. It was a somber affair, without the party of the other sisters' weddings. But at least they were married, which is what they wanted."

"So, by now, it was 1904. Did your father go back to America alone?"

"No. He went with many friends. He went on the ship the Citta di Genova, with Uncle Raffaele and some acquaintances. There were, let's see . . ." She started numbering them off on her fingers. "Four or five men who were shirt-tail relations of ours. Of course, almost everyone is somehow related to everyone else, through blood or marriage."

"Did they all go to Hartford?" Santoro asked. He was writing furiously trying to keep up with her words.

"No. Only my father was going to Hartford to live. Uncle Raffaele was planning to eventually join his cousin, Bruno Pisano, in Morrisey, British Columbia, in Canada. But he chose to stay in Hartford until Aunt Concetta came. The others were going to join family members along the East Coast. They arrived in April and separated company, thinking they would never see each other again."

"So then your father got the barber shop on Spruce Street?" Santoro asked.

"No, Father moved back into the apartment on Asylum Street with Domenico, Maria and their four children. Uncle Raffaele also moved in with them. He got day jobs to raise enough money to send for Concetta and his baby daughter, also named Concetta. Father found a new barber job and soon sent for my mother and Teresa. They arrived in November. Father was there to greet them and bring them the rest of the way to their new home.

"Aunt Concetta came across the Atlantic eleven months later. Alone. Just like she said she would, Concetta had left Raffaele's baby in the care of the dead wife's parents. Then she, too, moved into the Asylum Street apartment. And she was just in time to celebrate the birth of Carmela's second daughter in November, 1905.

"That was me."

CHAPTER 16

HARTFORD, CT, SUMMER 1906

Asylum Avenue in Hartford, Connecticut, was a long street going all the way from Main Street in center city to west Hartford's suburbs. Downtown, it was a collection of older two and three story wooden and brick structures constantly being replaced by commercial establishments. Architectural firms competed against one another for more beautiful, creative and increasingly tall buildings. As a result, some of the most eye-appealing creations had arisen in recent years along lower Asylum Ave, probably leaving the new immigrants in awe of their new hometown.

Getting a job helping to put up these buildings or servicing those who did was a fairly easy accomplishment.

Upper Asylum was an upper class area housing the likes of Mr. Colt and Mr. Mark Twain. Middle Asylum, from the 300s up to past Bushnell Park, was still part of the new Italian community which grew by several thousands a year. That section of the street was a collection of little shops and apartments for the lower class Italian community. The area abounded with pushcarts and vendors selling their wares, little shops selling foodstuffs and dry goods. Further down, from Main Street to the 200 block, were the most modern buildings housing professional offices, insurance companies and even Wooley's hardware store.

It was a noisy, busy place, full of commotion all day long. The new automobile was contentiously vying with the electric trolley for space on the streets. And they both vied with the pushcart vendors and the public to be able to move along the streets in a timely fashion. The cacophony of vendors selling fruits and vegetables or collecting old clothes to be resold lasted all day long. And it was into this loud, bustling environment that Giuseppe Amato brought his wife and new baby.

Serra San Bruno was in the past, at last.

"Hey, Joe! How's the baby?"

"Hey, Joe! I need a shave! You got your own shop, yet?" Joe Amato, man about town, walked up Asylum Street greeting friends and *paisanos* alike as he headed back to the apartment at Number 518.

"The baby is growing bigger every day! And my Teresa loves having a little sister."

"I will be getting my own place soon. For sure this time."

"Stop me next week, I will have more news!"

Joe answered everyone with a smile and a firm two-handed handshake, as if he was running for office. Which, indeed he was, if there was an office of favorite Italian barber in the booming Yankee town.

With his signature flat-topped straw hat and three-piece suit, Joe did not look like a recent immigrant. Within just a few years of arriving, he had mastered English and spoke with just a little bit of an accent, besting his brother-in-law, Dominick, who had been in the states five years longer. He could tell by the faces of his friends as he walked along the street that they admired his presence. And he walked a little taller and straighter, knowing he had their respect.

What Giuseppe did not tell these men, who seemingly admired him, was that he did not have sufficient money to start his own business. Most of what he made went to feeding and clothing his wife and two daughters as well as his own fine wardrobe.

Walking along the busy street on his way back to the apartment he still shared with his extended family, Giuseppe reviewed the financial stresses which forced him to keep working for another man.

"Hey, Joe!" a male voice yelled from half a block away.

Giuseppe looked up, vaguely recognizing the voice. Startled, he saw an old friend from home, Tony the Mule.

"Hey! Tony!" he exclaimed.

A short dark man with a bandana around his neck and an earring in his left lobe walked towards him.

"What are you doing here? I haven't seen you in years! When did you get here?" Giuseppe was surprised to see his old friend.

Tony greeted his old friend warmly with a big hug. "I got here about three months ago. Serra isn't the same without the old *amici*," he added. "I'm looking for the old gang. One is in Canada and a few in New York and you are here!" Tony grabbed Guiseppe by the shoulders and stepped back to scrutinize him closely. "You look so successful, so American! You are doing well, eh?"

"*Cosi, cosi*," replied Giuseppe. "I have many mouths to feed now. Two *bambini*! I share a place with my in-laws, but soon I will have my own flat."

"Hey! You got the life, *mio amico*!" replied Tony. "A family, a job, a home. You got the life, I say!"

"So, what have you been doing since you got off the boat?" asked Giuseppe.

"Making money. Lots of money. America truly is the eighth wonder! It is so easy to get rich around here."

"What are you doing to get money? I haven't seen you around and you sound like you have been traveling."

Tony smiled and grabbed Giuseppe by the elbow and guided him into a sidewalk café. "Sit!" he offered. "I got to tell you my story!"

They sat and Tony ordered two black coffees and *biscotti*. They spent half an hour chatting about Hartford, Tony's travels, and his freedom from financial worry.

"Look," Tony said as he wound up. "I know you don't have a lot of money, so I am going to offer you a deal. I am a representative of the Italian lottery."

"Tony," Giuseppe snorted. "I cannot afford investing in the lottery."

"You hear me out first!" Tony had a commanding ring to his voice. "I am going to offer a deal to you only because I like you and I have always trusted you."

Giuseppe put down his coffee cup. He knew that this was going to be a long-winded session.

"You listen to what I got to say!" Tony repeated. "The lottery pays out weekly. Twenty-five cents a ticket. Winning ticket can get $50. Every Monday I drop off a stack of tickets. You sell them. I pick the stubs up on Friday. The winner is pulled on Saturday. Every time you have a winner, you get a dollar. And you get five percent of the sales. So, if you sell 100 tickets, you gross 25 dollars and I pay you a buck and a quarter. It's easy to sell a hundred. What with your personality, I wouldn't be the least bit surprised if you sold a few hundred a week. That's two fifty plus an extra buck every time you sell a winner. Not bad for doing nothing!"

Tony stopped and looked at Giuseppe with a *gotcha* look.

Giuseppe glared at Tony. He did not want to get back into the borderline illegal activities he had left behind. "I cannot sell tickets, Tony. I am only a small time barber working for another man. My boss would not appreciate this lottery work."

"Well, then, why don't you work for yourself?" Tony suggested.

"Ha!" Giuseppe laughed. "This all costs money! I don't have that much. It will be another year before I have enough to consider that."

"What if I made it possible for you to have your own place now?"

Giuseppe looked at his friend aghast. "Even with your lottery and all your other money, that is quite an expense. I figure it would take at least 100 dollars!"

"Well, I have some associates who would be willing to invest in you in exchange for your helping us with the lottery." Tony paused for a few seconds, watching his old friend's eyes.

Giuseppe was not sure if he was the fall guy for an illegal operation or had just gotten the American dream dropped into his lap. His head spun with pictures of Carmela smiling, the children with new shoes, an apartment of his own, his name over the door of his very own business.

"So what do you think of this very generous proposition?" Tony asked after letting Giuseppe review it for a few minutes. "I don't think you will ever get an offer this good ever again."

"I should say not!" replied Giuseppe, still reeling from a proposal he had never thought to hear.

"You had better take my offer, my friend," Tony insisted. "Or I will have to find another to take care of the lottery around here."

With that, he offered Giuseppe his hand to solidify the deal. After a moment's consideration, Giuseppe took Tony's hand and stepped into his American dream.

Said ok.

CHAPTER 17

HARTFORD, SUMMER 1906

Two weeks later, appreciating that he had good news for his family, Joe stopped at the stoop of number 518 and turned to admire the view. This high up on Asylum, the stores petered out and the high school was just down the block. Across the street were a few factories on a side street, leading down to the train tracks and, on the far side, in the distance he could see the beautiful gardens of Bushnell Park. Monuments and bridges made the whole place an architectural dream. Attendants kept the colorful flower beds in bloom all season long. It was a beautiful, peaceful place for the citizens of the city. But, the Italian children rarely went there, for it would mean crossing the tracks or running through the station, neither of which seemed safe to the mothers who preferred their children within shouting range. He considered again the pros and cons of the decision he had just made, took a deep breath and climbed the stairs to the apartment.

"Hey, Joe!" shouted a young man who was cleaning his fingernails with a stiletto. "Want in on a game?"

"No, my friend," Joe responded, trying to ease past the kid and his companion who were blocking the way.

"Too bad," came the reply. "I could have taken you for everything you have in the bank!" The two laughed before moving off to the side.

Joe clamped his teeth and decided not to respond. The two had offered the same game over and over for weeks. As he climbed the two flights of stairs, Joe was doubly glad that he had his news. He really did not want

Carmela and the children exposed to this group. It reminded him of his friends back home. One borderline con artist for an investor was all a man could handle.

"Hey, Carmela!" he called as he walked in the door. Two toddlers looked up. One was his Teresa.

"Papa! Papa! You are home!" The child ran up to her father and jumped up into his arms. She was plain except for a beautiful head of red curls, kept out of her face with a length of ribbon. Void of stockings, she ran around barefooted with just her chemise on this hot afternoon. The other child, a boy, looked up and smiled. He was building something with stones that his oldest brother had found for him. Maria came to the door of the bedroom.

"Peter, where are your manners?" she said sharply to her son.

He stood up, bowed, slightly, and said, "Welcome home, *Zio* Giuseppe!"

"Where is Carmela, Maria?" Joe asked. He absently kissed his daughter as she pulled at his hat.

"She ran out to get milk. In this weather, it doesn't keep well, you know." Maria answered looking at her brother-in-law skeptically. "Why are you home so early on a Saturday?"

Joe's eyes twinkled. "I have a surprise for Carmela. And I will not tell you first." He smiled, kissed his daughter and put her down. "Go play," he ordered her and patted her diapered behind.

"She should be back any time now. She had problems getting Anna down to her nap. The poor thing is teething."

Maria walked into the scullery to finish washing the lunch dishes sitting in a pan of water.

"Good," Joe pronounced as he put his jacket on the hall-tree hook and placed his hat over it. "I will sit right here and wait for her to walk in." He pulled the morning's Hartford Courant, dog-eared and wrinkled, out of his jacket pocket then settled at the large kitchen table to read it. He had not even finished the first page when he heard Carmela's footsteps. Jumping up, he opened the door ahead of her.

"What are you doing home so early on a Saturday?" Carmela asked anxiously. "Are you ill?"

Joe laughed as he took the bottle of milk from her hand. "No. I have a surprise for you." He took the milk over to the icebox and placed it inside close to the melting block of ice, then closed the door firmly.

"Maria," Joe turned to the scullery. "Can you spare my wife for half an hour? I need to take her out."

"That's fine. Anna should still sleep for a while and Teresa is no problem. Go!" She nodded to them, arms deep in dishwater.

"What is going on?" Carmela looked from one to the other, suspecting they were sharing a little secret. But Joe quickly put on his hat and jacket and took her arm before she had a chance to take the hatpin out of her hat.

"I need to show you something." Joe smiled and opened the door, sweeping her out into the hall and down the stairs.

"Where are we going?" Carmela asked. This was not like her husband. His smile was curious, like that cat in Lewis Carroll's story that she had heard about. Maria's girls were reading now and had told her about the story.

"It is just a few blocks," Joe responded, his left hand firmly on her right elbow. He steered her through the thinned crowd shopping for Sunday needs. They turned left onto Spruce Street and down to number 9. There they stopped and he turned her to face the tenement house. "Look!" he exclaimed pointing to a freshly painted sign on the first floor door. It said "Salvatore Timpano, Barber."

"You brought me out to see a new sign? Why do I care if Sal moved his shop?" Carmela didn't see the point of this venture.

"That is not the end of my secret!" Joe said, lips twitching with excitement. He took her elbow again and directed her seven buildings down, directly across from the train station. They stopped in front of number 23. Again, he turned her to face this new tenement house and pointed to another fresh sign. Only this time it said "Giuseppe Amato, Barber."

"Oh, *madre mia*, Joe! How did this happen?" Carmela turned to her husband, eyes ablaze with elation. Her eyes kept flitting back and forth from her husband to the sign and her small body nearly wiggled with delight.

"Sal and I have entered an agreement. He wanted an apartment closer to Asylum. His lease was not up so he offered it to me." He grabbed her by the shoulders and squeezed hard. "Carmela, *mia cara!* This means we have started to achieve our goals!" He was beaming! If they were not in public, he would have kissed her soundly.

"When do you open?" the practical-minded wife asked.

"As soon as I can afford the rest of the equipment. Sal gave me his old chair. It is not much. But a little cleaning up and we will be fine for now."

"How much?" She cocked her head to the side and put her hands on her hips, reminiscent of her mother back home.

"How much to clean up and buy the rest of the equipment?" He paused to add in his head. "Oh, 50 or 60 dollars, I figure."

"And the rent?"

"Ten dollars a month."

"And how much do we have in the bank?" Carmela was calculating in her head as well.

They were facing each other in front of the new shop. She was suddenly not so excited, as the reality hit her.

"Almost 100 dollars."

Carmela was startled. She had no idea he had put away that much. And he was not going to tell her about the lottery agreement at this time. "Well, the children do not need new clothes for a while. Your suit is still in good condition. Heat for winter will not be for a few months." Carmela smiled, full of excitement. "You can afford it."

"Carmela, just you wait and see how well I do. I will get you pretty hats and shoes for the children. We will have meat every day! And some day when we are old, we will have a house, like in the old country. Just you wait and see."

"Work hard, my husband. And we shall see." Her eyes blinked back tears of happiness.

"There is just one thing. I told Sal we would take the lease of his apartment, too. It is only ten a month."

"But we have no furniture for a whole apartment, Joe!" Carmela was suddenly worried again.

"That is fine. Sal will leave us some of his old things and we will buy the rest as we can afford it. You will see," he assured her. Happily overwhelmed at the sudden change of life, the two walked back up to #518, hand in hand, and mounted the stairs, discussing the particulars of the move.

A cacophony of voices reached past the door as they came in. The older children were in from play and Dominick was in from work. Baby Anna had just awakened and Maria was taking it all in stride.

"Here, Carm!" Maria handed her sister a sodden,

sobbing baby. "You take care of her and I will start dinner."

Joe kissed his wife and went to join Dominick who was reading the discarded newspaper at the kitchen table. Carmela went into their bedroom to change the baby. Meal preparation whirled around them as the children set the bowls out and the aroma of the olives and cheese and prosciutto filled the room.

"I have good news, Dom!" Joe proudly announced. He pulled out the chair next to Dominick and moved in close. Dom put his paper down and looked at Joe with his deep blue eyes.

"I have made a deal with Sal Timpano," Joe announced. He had discussed the possibility with Dom once, trying to get Dom to join him in a partnership. Dom had refused on the basis that he had five children and another on the way, whereas Joe, with only two children, needed less money to feed his family and could afford less pay at the beginning. Joe had not told Dom either, about the source of his money.

"So, congratulations are in order, eh?" Dom smiled tenuously. "If you think this is right for you, then my blessings on your new undertaking." He turned to his wife. "Maria! We need four glasses!" And to 10 year old Nickie, "Go get the bottle of wine!" The gallon bottle was in the scullery. When the glasses and bottle were all on the table, Dom poured two glasses, one for himself and one for Joe.

"To your health and your new shop!" Dom raised his glass as did Joe. And they drank the glasses down.

"And there is one other thing," Joe said, rather confidently. Dom raised an eyebrow. "I am going to take over the lease on his apartment, too." He lowered his voice so that Maria could not hear above the din of the children.

"And it is at #23, also?" Dom, following suit, lowered his voice.

"Yes."

"So, when will you move out?"

"As soon as I open the shop. Say, a week or two. I have enough money for the extra equipment and a month's rent."

"You got the chair?" Dom was surprised.

"Yes. And the mugs of all the tenants in that building. That alone is worth $3 a month."

"I'll see what I can do about getting you some soap samples and extra towels. My shop has plenty of extras."

"Thanks, Dom!"

"Now, you tell everyone at dinner," Dom ordered. "Maria will need time to get used to being alone."

"Maria needs time to get used to being alone? Why?" Maria was standing behind Dominick with a basket of bread, ready to place on the table. She had overheard the last sentence.

Joe jumped from his chair, took the basket, placed it on the table, and grabbed her hand in both of his. "Sit. I have good news." He moved over one chair so that she would be between the two men. "I have arranged with Sal Timpano to take over his shop at #23 Spruce. He has decided to move down to #9. He is going to leave me his chair and a few things. And Carm and I and the girls will live in the building."

"Oh," was all Maria could muster at first. Then she took a deep breath. "That building cost the same to rent as this one but it has bigger rooms. I have been there to visit the Timpanos. Dom, I want to move there, too! I won't live here alone without my sister!"

"So, they lived happily ever after. For about six years, eh?" Santoro chuckled at his own joke, eyeing the young lady across the desk from him.

Miss Amato looked at him quizzically. "No. They had problems," she responded, treating the comment seriously. "All Italians, you know how it was, had problems adapting. And then there were the Black Hand groups, the protection groups, the extortion groups. And we have always been proud of those who protected us. Why, I remember when I had moved into the apartment in Newark how they would give me gifts . . ."

"Don't jump the gun, Miss," interrupted the detective, blowing his nose into a third clean handkerchief. "Let's stay in chronological order, here." He held the handkerchief in one hand and paswed through a few pages of notes with the other. "So, Giuseppe started his own shop instead of working for another person. And the whole family moved three blocks away from where they had been living. So then what happened?"

The young lady stretched her arms in a rather unladylike manner. She had been sitting still for over an hour.

"Do you need to get up a bit?" asked Santoro with some concern for the witness who had been brought here under, admittedly, some duress. Miss Amato got up and walked around the office to get the circulation back in her legs. Santoro wasn't about to tell her that she could leave at any time. They weren't holding her on anything. There was no warrant. But apparently her husband was a deputy sheriff at home and so they had cooked up a tale that the warrant was on the judge's desk and that he could be arrested for impeding an investigation if he took his young bride off the police station property before she was excused.

"I am ready to begin again," the young lady said as she returned to her chair. She shivered a little and pulled the shoulders of her coat around her own shoulders.

"Would you prefer a cup of coffee?"

"No, thank you," she replied. "Let's keep going."

"Go ahead."

"Father's name was proudly displayed as proprietor of the barber shop at 23 Spruce St," she began again. "It was a little shop, furnished with whatever he could afford, second and third-hand equipment and two chairs which had seen better days, their paint chipped and the leather on the seat and arms dried and cracked, but it was his. He lived in one of the flats on the second floor and Uncle Dominick and Aunt Mary moved up on the third floor, along with a number of other tenants, almost all Italian. Our little family was now growing, with four little girls, and almost always another one on the way. Aunt Mary and Uncle Dominick's family had grown, as well, with three more children added since she had arrived in 1901.

"And, then, in late 1908, the Tassones moved into a third floor flat with their two babies. The Tassones were shirt-tail relations of ours. Cousins from the old country."

CHAPTER 19

HARTFORD, 1908

Giuseppe was sitting on one of his barber chairs reading the newspaper. No clients had yet shown that morning. He looked up as the bell over the door rang and jumped off the chair in surprise.

"It is not Friday, so why are you here?" Giuseppe questioned his silent partner and lottery superior. Tony threw his coat on one barber chair and sat on Giuseppe's other barber chair, crossed his legs, and lit a cigarette. He left Giuseppe to stand, watching this new visitor very carefully. Tony looked around the room as if he was assessing its worth, which, indeed, he was.

"I am also in the protection business, you know," Tony said. "It is like insurance, you understand? For a small weekly fee, I make sure you don't have any problems. You know, like theft, break-ins. Know what I mean? It is a common business at home, remember?"

Giuseppe recognized the routine. He had seen his friends use it enough in the old country. He gritted his teeth, knowing what was coming next.

"So," continued Tony, blowing out a stream of cigarette smoke. "Now that you have reached a level of income high enough to make you vulnerable, I had to come and offer you this insurance. It is only fair, you and I being *paesans* and all." Tony smiled, showing missing teeth, both up and down.

Giuseppe felt uncomfortable. He assumed that Tony had practiced his "insurance" sales on the other side of the ocean as well as here. The lottery was not that lucrative for a go-getter like Tony, although Giuseppe was making a dollar or two every week.

"I don't know, Tony," Giuseppe began, trying to search for the right way of approaching this. "I got four girls and another on the way, for all I know. That is a lot of mouths to feed. I don't know if I could come up with much extra money."

"Nonsense," retorted Tony, pointing his cigarette at his intended customer. "You're making one or two dollars extra a week just from the lottery. The cost is not that much."

"One or two dollars a week equals new shoes for the girls. Teresa starts school this year and will need them." Guiseppe crossed his arms defensively and leaned against the door jamb.

Tony took a puff and blew smoke in Giuseppe's direction as he watched his reactions. "Well, you know, I heard that theft in this neighborhood is going up. And so are break-ins. I think you should seriously consider this proposal of mine before it is too late."

"I tell you, Tony." Giuseppe was uncomfortable with the way Tony was pushing and even more uncomfortable with the whine in his own voice. "That will make my budget just too tight. And I need to make some improvements to the shop. I bought two used chairs and one is in bad shape. I didn't have the money then, and I want to get a new one.".

"You are giving up a deal, I tell you. There is a bad element around here now and you need what I am offering." Tony stood up.

Giuseppe timorously stood his ground. "How about we handle it this way. You will be back every Friday. Let me think about it and we can talk about it in a few weeks."

"Sure, Joe!" Tony handed him a card, which only had his name and "Insurance Sales" written underneath.

"You got a place I can contact you?" Joe asked.

"Sure," said Tony. He took the card back and wrote an out of town address on the back. "But I'll be around again in a few days. Making a lot of calls. I'll stop in to talk about this again the end of next week. How's that?"

"Yah, sure, Tony." They shook hands and the visitor left.

The afternoon business was brisk and Giuseppe took in more than he expected. Eight dollars in the till was a good day! But he closed late, due to the overflow, and did not have time to go to the bank. So he put the money in a drawer, locked the door, and went home to supper.

In the morning, Giuseppe returned to his shop, to find the door unlocked, drawers rifled, and all the money missing. All else had been left alone. That was practically a whole month's rent gone.

Giuseppe was furious. His experience in Italy led him to believe that police do not help the victims and, although he knew many of them well, he did not report the break-in. He assumed it was more than a coincidence that Tony had stopped over, selling his "insurance", and the very same night, he had been broken into. This was a warning. He heard it. He knew, from the old days, that Tony and his people would not stop until he signed up. That was Thursday morning.

Friday morning, bright and early, Tony showed up to collect the lottery money. His "insurance" sales pitch was more easily accepted this time.

CHAPTER 20

HARTFORD, 1930

"So this Tony was in the protection racket, eh? You got a last name?" Santoro had heard the name of "Tony the Mule" over the years, but no one had ever pinned down this man.

Miss Amato sighed. "Please. Do you really think I know such details? I was very little when Tony came around. And we rarely went into the barber shop. My father said it was no place for little girls to play. The only time I ever met this man was a few years later, probably when I was six, and that only briefly. He was only introduced as 'Tony'."

"Well, you have a pretty good memory for detail, anyhow," he said encouragingly.

"Thank you."

CHAPTER 21

HARTFORD, 1910

Giuseppe's business was doing well at last. His little barber shop was always full of men needing a shave or a trim, or maybe just a little pomade to delight the ladies. This business, he hesitantly admitted to himself, seemed to be the result of paying Tony's associates for "protection". The down side was that as his business increased, so did the cost of protection.

What began as a low sum, had doubled in cost over the past two years. So, although his business looked good and profitable, his family's income had not changed. Hiding this from Carmela was a daily chore.

The little bell over the door rang again as Guiseppe was just cleaning up after three haircuts in a row. It was Detective Lieutenant Santoro. Born in this country, Santoro was proud of his Italian heritage, yet accepted by the Yankee officials who ran the town. Despite his being only half-Italian, his mother being Irish, Santoro was fluent in Italian. He liked being able to practice speaking with the new immigrants. Guiseppe liked to practice his English with Santoro.

"Hey! My good friend, the detective!" Guiseppe greeted him. "Have a seat!"

Santoro took off his uniform jacket and hung it on the hall tree.

"You got a new chair, eh?" the detective commented, sitting on the shiny new chair with its soft leather seat. "Nice! You're moving up in the world!"

Guiseppe put a large white cloth over the detective's

front and back, pinning it in place. "Sure! I am making good money, now. I gotta show it. Right?" He pulled Santoro's mug off the shelf. "You want a haircut or just a shave?"

"Do the works, Joe. I want to talk."

"Sure, sure. What do you got on your mind?" Guiseppe set the mug down while he pulled out a clean blade and tested the edge.

"I've seen some new faces in town. I wanted to know if you knew them. They hang out around here, I know. Patrolman Butler has seen them around the train station. That's been his beat for a while, now. He knows faces."

Guiseppe nodded noncommittedly, as he reached for Santoro's mug, wet the soap, and stirred up a lather.

He'd heard rumors about the Sicilians having thrown out the Calabresi in New York. Those people could not do business there anymore. They were likely to scatter afield, perhaps to Hartford. Many of his friends from the old country had moved away from the big city, choosing, instead, to go to Canada or upstate New York. Some, like his friend Rudolfo LoPrete, had decided to go home to Italy to find a good wife.

The Black Hand, as the individuals were collectively called, were all along the East Coast, selling fake lottery tickets or threatening fire bombings if they did not receive monies. Probably 90 percent of Italians faced this menace.

But Giuseppe was wary of the detective. So far, the police either did not know he was selling lottery tickets or chose to turn their backs on the problem. After all, didn't he give them a good price on his services and give them information when he could? He didn't have much to say.

Just as Santoro was putting on his coat, the bell over the door rang its little tinkling sound as another customer came it. But it was only Dominick, Giuseppe's brother-in-law. Dominick was a big man, always smiling, with a shock of red hair indicating his French-Italian heritage. He was a little shorter than Giuseppe, and a little rounder, giving credence to Maria's saying that the way to a man's heart is through his stomach. He didn't need a shave. He worked in another barber shop. Santoro tipped his hat to the newcomer as he was leaving, saying nothing to Dominick.

"Hey, Guiseppe! What are you working so late for?" Dominick asked. He viewed the shop's latest addition. "What's this?" he asked before Giuseppe had time to answer. "A new chair?"

Giuseppe nodded as he cleaned up the counters and the sink in preparation for closing.

"You can afford a nice new chair and leave your wife to live in squalor, eh?" Dominick looked at his brother-in-law in disgust.

"I needed it, Dom," responded Giuseppe. "Now that I am so busy, it looked bad to have that shabby used thing in here."

"Well, it is nice to know you have the money," Dom said sarcastically.

"I don't have the money." Giuseppe looked a little sheepish. "That's the thing. I had to borrow it from the bank. After all, a successful business must look successful."

And that new chair did look good. Chrome-plated, with a thick black leather seat, back and arms, it had a hydraulic pump to go up and down more smoothly than any of his old chairs.

"It will only cost $1.00 per week for two years," Guiseppe ended lamely.

"And in the meantime, your wife and daughters do without. And another one on the way, besides. I was young and stupid once, but I got over it. Not you!"

"Well surely, in two years, when the loan is done, I will buy Carmela a nice sofa. I will be able to afford it, then."

"And let them live like paupers in the meantime, eh? You and your American success story!" Dom spat on the floor. "How about you and the American family story? Or did you forget about family responsibility when you got off the boat?"

"That's only one of my problems. Carmela is getting frustrated. She wants more. And I can't give it to her. And, my God! She gets pregnant every time I look at her, it seems. My wife is like a rabbit! At this rate I will have 20 in that apartment before I have enough money to furnish it! I don't blame her for whining. But it gets to me. She is not happy. She wants a nice apartment. The children need this and that!"

Dominick shook his head slowly thinking how twisted his brother-in-law's thinking was.

"Look, Dom! Can you keep a secret?" Giuseppe looked out the window to assure himself no one was coming in.

"What? You got a secret about how to make money? You had better use it yourself!"

"No, really, Dom!"

"Sure, I'm listening." Dominick sat on the new chair, crossed his legs and looked Giuseppe right in the eyes.

"I can't tell anyone else! You never know if you can trust the police." Giuseppe turned back to his cabinets and started to absent-mindedly rub the glossy wood.

"They aren't like at home, Joe!" Dom interrupted. "They get paid. Good money, too! I hear that the starting salary is a thousand a year! They don't need bribes, if that's what you are getting at."

"But I think the police are just like at home. They believe the one with the money. And who am I? I have no money! I give the neighborhood officers a discount on shaves. Only two bits. They talk. I talk. We get to be friendly. But I still don't trust that they would help me in a problem."

"Maybe you should just tell me what this is all about."

Giuseppe stopped rubbing the wood and threw down his dustcloth. "I used to be associated, at home, with a fellow from near Spadola, named Tony. We called him the Mule. He had some underhanded things he was doing over there. And he always had money in his pocket. When I left, I never thought of him again. Until four years ago. Out of the clear blue sky he walks into my life. He tells me about how he sells lottery tickets. So I started helping him with the lottery sales. That's where I got the money to open the shop."

Dom's eyes opened wide. "So that's how you were able to get that deal with Sal Timpano! I wondered how you had worked such magic!"

"Well, the story gets worse. Two years ago, I had finally paid back Tony for the money he had invested and he said I needed insurance. It's cheap, he says. Everybody got to have insurance in America, he says."

"Sure, every business in America got to have insurance! So, what is the problem?"

"It is not that kind of insurance, I found out. When I said no, the next day, my shop was broken into. Nothing was taken but the money in the drawer. I worked late the night before and never went to the bank. I had to lie to Carmela so she wouldn't worry. I told her I gambled it away, accidentally."

"I remember that!" Dom said. "Carmela cried to

Maria. I told Maria, what can you do? So, you don't gamble, eh?"

"No. An occasional lottery ticket, but not much."

"So, you lost the money trying to save money, eh?"

"That's what happened. But I decided that Tony and his *paesani* were behind it. So, I figured I'd better buy the insurance."

"Have you been broken into again?"

"No. Business has been better, too."

"So, what is the problem?"

"They ask for more money every so often. It is getting expensive. And then I had to buy the new chair. The other one was old when I got it. I got a loan from the bank, but I can barely pay all this money out!"

"Not pay and feed the children, too. Guiseppe, why didn't you just paint the chair and get it recovered?"

"Tony told me I had to have good stuff if I wanted my shop protected. He had a man with a new chair that he was willing to get rid of for a good price. I felt cornered. So, I got it."

"*Madremia*!" Dom swore. "You mouse! Stand up for yourself! Tony is a bad lot. You let him use you!"

"*Si, mi amico*! I am afraid that is true. After the money was taken, I thought I could not take chances. If I don't do what they say, they may threaten me further."

"Talk to the police."

"No. I will handle this myself. I don't want to find out that the police want protection money, too." Giuseppe paused for a minute. "Dom, don't tell Maria what I told you. She would be downstairs in minutes telling Carmela all about it. Poor Carmela has enough to worry about with the children and never enough money."

"I will say nothing to Maria. But, you better straighten this out. You have another baby due in

October. If it's another girl, you gotta start saving for a lot of dowries, eh?"

Dominick laughed and his ruddy features flashed redder for a moment. His face quickly went back to a stern expression. He stood up from the chair and poked a figure onto Giuseppe's chest for accent. "Carmela is a fine woman and I love her like a sister. Do not hurt her further." He walked to the door, put his hand on the knob, then turned back to his brother-in-law. "And don't hurt the girls. They are precious."

Dominick turned his back, walked out the door and around to the gangplank of the tenement that led to his apartment.There he ran into his two nieces, Anna and Teresa, who were on the sidewalk in front of the tenement playing.

"Stay out where your mother can see you from the window," he admonished them as he patted their heads. They smiled and giggled.

When he left Teresa turned to her younger sister with a finger to her lips.

"Don't tell anyone we are being detectives and watching Papa. It's our secret."

Anna nodded gravely and put her finger to her lips in imitation.

Giuseppe finished cleaning up the shop and walked slowly up to the apartment, working on a plan as he did. It was well past six o'clock. Carmela was used to his odd hours and had soup waiting for him on top of the stove. Giuseppe walked into the kitchen and realized all was quiet. The children were all in bed and the apartment seemed better picked up than usual.

"Carmela?" he called quietly, not willing to disturb the silence within. Outside in the hallway, he heard the normal sounds of nighttime preparations throughout the apartment house. He closed the door behind him, to keep the sounds at bay and looked around admiringly. The main room was picked up. There were no curtains at the windows, but an attempt at cleaning the glass had been made. The old sofa had a quilt thrown over it to hide the stains. The kitchen table had been scrubbed and the chairs were all pushed in. All the dishes which normally cluttered the sink were put away. She had worked hard today.

Carmela looked up from her rocker where she had been mending socks. Her face did not look welcoming.

"Soup is on the stove. It should still be hot enough." She turned back to her work.

"Will you sit with me while I eat?" he asked. Looking up reluctantly, Carmela nodded and placed the clothes in the mending basket by her chair. She stood up, pulled down her shirt sleeves and came over to the kitchen table, sitting across from him.

Giuseppe ate in silence, watching his wife's emotionless face. She looked exhausted and her face was drawn. This was her sixth pregnancy. Perhaps it was just too much for her. Perhaps she was just angry about the lack of money.

Finishing the last of the soup and bread, he pushed his bowl away from him and turned his attention to his harried wife.

"You are miserably unhappy. I know we do not have what you want. But you have to understand that the expenses of a business are high."

Carmela started to tear up. "I am just so tired! Four girls underfoot all day long! I just want something of my own. You have your shop. Rafaella Tassone has her pretty little furniture. I just need something!"

Giuseppe moved closer to her and took her hand. "I have an idea for money."

"Like your American Dream of the barber shop? You play your American man role and I stay here and pretend I am my mother all over again. What about my dreams? I came to America to be as poor as before!"

"No! Carmela, listen! I want to explain things to you."

He dried her tears with a corner of his *mapine*, feeling guilty about hiding the lottery tickets and insurance from her all this time. He took a deep breath and proceeded with his story.

After five minutes, Carmela understood what she had not been privy to for the past three and a half years. "But how does this help us make money?" she questioned.

"I have been thinking about this lottery thing," Giuseppe responded, leaning in towards his wife in his excitement. "Tony is now making serious money. I would imagine he is making almost 200 dollars a month. He has me and a number of other people all over the state selling tickets for him. I am worth 40 a month to him, alone! I know he has at least ten others doing what I do. That's 400! The payout is 200 a month in prizes and five percent to the sellers, which is 25 or so. Where does the other money go?" He splayed his hands and shrugged his shoulders.

"To Tony?" Carmela whispered in astonishment.

"Yes!" Giuseppe pounded the table to accent his answer. "And that is just the lottery money! How many shops and stores in Connecticut have protection from Tony and his boys? Many! At a dollar or two a week, there goes the lottery earnings back into Tony's hands! Plus all the other fellows who pay for protection but do not sell tickets, that is at least 50 dollars a month extra,

I'll bet. Even if he has to pay his boys a few dollars every Friday to collect, I can see he is doing well."

"But you must pay him every week," Carmela protested. "His hints at trouble, if you don't, are too certain."

"My dream is going to hell!" Giuseppe admitted. Then he grabbed his wife's hand and looked into her eyes. "I have a plan. But I need your help."

Carmela looked at him cautiously. "What do you want me to do?"

"I think I should get more than five percent. I think I should get ten percent. Plus the dollar for every winning ticket."

"I do not think Tony is a negotiator, Guiseppe." Carmela shook her head. "You going to threaten him somehow if he does not do things your way?"

"No. Listen. I have worked on this idea for a few days. I think we can do this." Giuseppe paused for a moment. With this step, he would become the thief that Tony was. He would be going back to what he had run away from. What would Dom think once it was out? He would call him an idiot but pat him on the back for standing up to those people. Giuseppe took a deep breath and crossed the threshold he had never thought he would.

"I sell 100, maybe 200 tickets a week. I'm pretty good at it. I give the numbers to one of the fellows every Friday morning plus the money. Usually 25, sometimes up to 50 dollars. They count it, make sure the money matches the number of tickets sold. But they do not match the numbers on all the tickets." He looked at her to make sure she was following. "What if I did not give all the ticket numbers back? Then I would have too much money, eh?" He smiled slyly. "I would have to hold on to the money myself, right?"

He watched Carmela's face look at him in surprise. "That is stealing!"

"Carmela, stealing from a crook is not stealing. I am taking back my protection money that I have to spend to keep you safe." He squeezed her hand hard. "Do you understand?"

She nodded but her face reflected her worries. "How do I fit into this, this scheme?"

"Next Friday morning, I will give five percent less than the tickets I sell to the man who comes. And I will pocket five percent more money. At lunch, I will give you that five percent. Somewhere between one and two dollars. You will go to the bank. You will open an account in your name. But not your real name. I do not trust those people.They may eventually look for the money. You use a different name. 'Matta.' How's that? Different but similar enough to remember."

"And what do I do with this bank account?"

"We will save it for an emergency. Or maybe someday we will have enough for a house. But we will not spend it on anything else."

Carmela looked at her husband, made the Sign of the Cross, then quietly said, "May the Virgin Mother not condemn us for what we are about to do."

Giuseppe grinned and leaned over to kiss his wife and co-conspirator.

CHAPTER 22

HARTFORD, 1930

"So, how did you know about that?" Santoro asked.

"My mother had a bank book and I opened it once to read the numbers," Anna replied. "It was in her bureau and I was putting away the laundry. Also, Uncle Dominick told me later that there was money in an account that helped with the funeral and resettling all of us."

He held up a yellowed sheet. "It seems like your mother wasn't much of a housekeeper. Did you ever see the newspaper reports of the place?"

"No. I-I would rather not, please," responded the young lady, visibly cringing.

Santoro nodded and put the paper back on his desk. "Fine. Just offered," he said apologetically. "Do you remember the place at all?"

"I remember my sisters and I all sleeping together on one bed. We were all so little, it was not crowded."

"Yeah. I would assume."

"There were always some dirty diapers around, of course. With so many little ones around . . ." She looked up at him expecting him to go on to the next question. He just gazed expectantly at her.

When she did not continue, he asked, "Is that all you remember?"

"We walked to school, Teresa and I. It was several blocks. And I remember thinking I wish we could have curtains that were lacy like at Mrs. Tassone's."

"So you remember her?"

"Mostly I remember her coming down to visit Mama and crying about things."

"Like what?"

"Mama would send us away. Sometimes we went out to the hallway and played with our dolls or the babies, when Mrs. Tassone came to cry. When she came just to visit, we could stay in the apartment."

Detective Santoro sneezed into his handkerchief then he muttered to himself, flipping through the old paperwork. He shook his head as if answering his own silent question then put down the paper. Splaying his hands over the papers, he looked at the young woman across the desk from him.

"There is nothing in the investigation that shows the relationship between your mother and this Mrs. Tassone. What do you remember? Was there, if you don't mind my being a little crass, was there any jealousy between the men or the women?"

Miss Amato smiled slightly. "I was young, sir. My mother would not have shared anything like that with little children."

"I just thought . . ."

"But I will tell you a few things I do remember. I don't know if what I saw will make any sense to you."

"Anything. Anything at all that we can use to wrap this up."

Anna took a deep breath. "My mother was older than Mrs. Tassone, I am pretty sure," began the young lady. "When the men had all gone to work and the breakfast dishes were done, the ladies in the apartment house would often get together. Mrs. Tassone ...well, they called her Rafaella ... She would come down with her children. There were three, I think. Two boys and a baby. A girl, I think I remember. They were all younger than I. We children would play in the living room and the women would do their knitting or sewing or mending sitting around the kitchen table. That way they could chat, drink their coffee and keep an eye on us. Mrs. Tassone would talk a lot. About when she was still unmarried and about the years before they moved to Hartford."

"She and her husband were from Providence," Santoro prompted.

"Yes. And something bad happened in Providence that made them come to Hartford. She would tell the same stories again and again. Teresa and I listened even when the door was closed."

CHAPTER 23

PROVIDENCE, RI, SUMMER 1901

Giovanni Tassone, a distant cousin of Carmela, was born in Spadola, just a few miles outside Serra San Bruno, in March of 1876. His parents were Francesco and Concetta Tassone.

Apparently much poorer than the cousins in the large village, Francesco procured a godfather, or *padrone*, Domenico Russo, of Providence, RI, to hire and care for his sons in America. It was common for a *padrone* to have younger men living with them who were practically indentured servants. The younger men would work where they were told and charged a high sum for room and board.

One by one the sons of Francesco--Dominico, Giovanni, Giuseppe and Bruno--were sent over to America. Giovanni was 19 on May 15, 1895 when he arrived in America. Some were younger. The brothers were very competitive with one another, not friendly or brotherly, in the common sense of the word.

Giovanni was not a handsome man. He was short, 5'4", and somewhat thick, though not fat, just big-boned. He dressed indifferently and had a roughness about him. His dark coloring and large nose made him look like the prototypical Italian immigrant. His hair was dark and more unruly than truly curly. It was a little too long for the norms of the day, indicating an unwillingness to keep up with his personal maintenance. His eyes were of the same deep brown as his hair.

He had a way of looking at someone that pierced

through to their core and challenged them to try to know him. Most people said that he was an uncomfortable person to be around. Despite the fact that he had been in the States since '95, his grasp of the English language had remained poor. His grasp of dealing with others was equally poor.

After four years of working in Providence, RI, Giovanni had quit his job to go home to visit his family in Brognatura, Calabria. His mother admonished him about still being single. The dutiful son thought much about this on the passage back and determined to rectify the situation. He had been back about a year without success.

So he started hunting in saloons for a good Italian father who had an eligible daughter. It was not long before he found what he was looking for. Alfonso Gentile had been in America on and off for years, working his way into a comfortable position. He frequented one of the neighborhood saloons on a routine basis. And he bragged about his lovely daughter, Raffaela.

Thus, on one early fall Saturday evening, Giovanni knocked on the apartment door of the Gentile family and entered a new world, one in which beauty and education were of some importance.

"Come in, Giovanni!" greeted Alfonso heartily as he opened the door. "You are right on time!" He accompanied his guest into the parlor, a little room, handsomely furnished in the latest heavy velvet and knickknacks. A small, dark, wiry man, Alfonso looked out of place in an obviously feminine-inspired room.

"Sit, sit!" Alfonso indicated a small chair, not designed for one of Giovanni's frame. The potential suitor took off his bowler and set it on his knee, smiling a little stiffly. He looked around the room, taking note of the décor. There was a floral rug on the floor displaying maroons and ivory. A pot of fake palms sat next to a stand, containing small framed photos, situated between the twin bay windows overlooking the street below. The windows were closed to bar some of the sounds. The velvet curtains at the windows were pulled aside, revealing lacy under curtains, casting shadows of floral designs on the planked floors and rug. Very American. There was the typical marble topped end table with an ornate ceramic oil lamp, apparently never used, and a 6" high statue of the Madonna in front of it. Giovanni remembered a similar, though larger, one at his mother's home.

"Some anisette?" Alfonso inquired, indicating a small decanter and two matching shot glasses on a tray.

"*Si, grazie!*" Giovanni replied. Alfonso poured some of the clear licorice-flavored liquid into the two glasses, and handed one to his guest.

"To friendship! *A salute!*" toasted Alfonso and they both downed the burning liquid. Alfonso took Giovanni's glass and poured a second round for himself and his guest. Then he sat on the tufted couch across from his guest, glass in hand.

"So!" he began. "Let me explain a little about the family. Maybe a few things we have not gone over before. Just so you know what you are getting into." He took a sip of his anisette and waited for the liquid to slip down his throat, smiling with pleasure. "After all, you are here for a purpose." He knew exactly what the young man was interested in but, seeing him nervous, set up an opening for the discussion.

"We are from Acri, you know," Alfonso continued. "Even though I spent most of my adulthood here, in America, I had my children grow up there. You ever been there?"

"No, *signor*," Giovanni shook his head. Was he to be grilled?

"It is no matter. But it is a beautiful town. With opera and museums. I had my choice to work in the silk factories. But, this is not what I wanted. As a young man, I wanted adventure. So I came here. I sent money to my Rosa, God rest her soul, and came back every few years. To see her and make another *bambino*, eh?" And he laughed.

"*Si*, Signor Gentile!" Giovanni wondered if he should laugh with the older man.

"So, just as I decided that I wanted to become an American, Rosa died. I had Tomasso with me, but the two youngest were still in Acri. I got me a good wife here and had them move here. It has been five years since they came. They are now very American themselves!" Alfonso poured a little more anisette into his glass and took a sip. "So, now you tell me about you!"

Giovanni stuttered some, trying to say correctly what he wanted to say. "It is time for me to marry and begin a family, and you have a daughter of marriageable age."

Alfonso simply nodded, not wishing to stop his guest's thought process.

Giovanni continued. "I am a hard worker. I have regular habits. I have saved up money, so that my wife would not be wanting for anything. I am strong and can protect my woman from any problem. And I am loyal, very loyal. Of course, I would expect her to also be loyal."

"Of course, of course," agreed Alfonso. "I am sure those are all very good characteristics. You understand that I have to protect my little girl. She is my only daughter and the spitting image of my dearly-departed Rosa." At this, he made the Sign of the Cross, which

Giovanni also imitated. He was not a religious man, but he had respect for his elders' traditions.

"Raffaela is a beautiful young woman, if I do say so myself. She is talented, too. She can sing and cook, and her needlework is very good. I left her in Acri when her mother died to be brought up by her aunts until I could find a good step-mother for her. She was taught by the sisters. They did a good job. She came here when she was thirteen so she speaks good English, too. How is your English?"

"Not so good. I prefer the Italian."

. "It doesn't matter. We all speak *italiano*, anyhow." Alfonso waved his hand in the air, then took another sip of his anisette. "What kind of social life do you have?"

"I am not going to say I do not go out to the saloons. You have seen me there. But I am moderate. I need my money for more important things."

"Ah! A good answer!" Alfonso smiled approvingly then asked, "Where do you live now?" He was trying to assess this man who could take his little girl away from him.

"My brothers and I have lived with our *padrone* Dominick Russo, since I came here in '95. Signor Russo and his wife have been like a second family to us, my three brothers and I. The place is sufficient, but not so nice as this apartment."

Alfonso nodded again. "Do you go to church?"

Giovanni looked down at his hat. "No, *signor*. But I would make sure all the *bambini* are baptized. That I can promise. And I would marry in the Church, of course."

Alfonso seemed pleased with the answers to his questions. And, as a protector of his daughter, he already had questioned him about his occupation and work habits long before he had ever invited this young man over. He got up off the sofa and put his empty glass on the tray. "*Scusi, per favore*! I will be right back." He left the room, closing the door behind him.

Giovanni could hear Alfonso's voice and a female voice behind the door. He shifted in his seat and rebalanced his hat on his knee as he downed the last drop from his glass. The door opened and Alfonso entered, accompanied by a woman who looked too old to be Raffaela but too young to be her mother. She was dressed in a dark skirt and white shirtwaist, with a full apron. Her hair was light, piled on top of her head in a simple chignon, making her two inches taller than her husband.

"Jennie," Alfonso addressed her. "This is Signor Giovanni Tassone. Signor Tassone, this is my wife, Johanna." Giovanni had stood the moment she walked into the room. He took two steps towards her, hesitated about what to do with his glass, then placed it on the tray and shook her hand. He was embarrassed that his social acumen was so minimal. Giovanni wanted this interview to be over with. If they would not let him meet Rafaella, so be it. He was sweating from nerves, by now.

Johanna, always referred to as Jennie by her husband, took his hand in both of hers and eased his embarrassment by warmly greeting him. "It is my pleasure, Signor. My husband has told me of the purpose of your visit. *Per favore*, sit." She sat next to her husband on the sofa and Giovanni returned to his chair.

Alfonso began the conversation again. "My wife, she is a modern lady. She says that in America, the mother and father both talk to a prospective suitor. If she is fine with you, then I am fine with you. Ah! This new way of doing things! Not like home!"

Johanna patted her husband's arm and smiled patronizingly. Then she looked at Giovanni. "How old are you, Signor Tassone?"

"Twenty-four," he replied. "I will still be young when my children come and I can play with them and enjoy them." He thought of his father who had neither played with nor enjoyed his children. They were so poor, all there had been was work. And the senior Tassone had sent his boys to be with the *padrone* at a tender age, for the money.

"My step-daughter is used to a nice place to live. Can you afford to keep her in the style to which she is accustomed?"

"*Si, signora*! I would take care of her and be loyal to her!" He said it with a vehemence, surprising Johanna and Alfonso.

"I think we have asked enough questions," said Alfonso. "Let me go get my daughter." He got up from the sofa, again, and went out the door. Rafaella must have been sitting just outside the door, listening to the whole conversation, for he was only out for seconds and returned almost immediately with her.

In stepped the loveliest dream Giovanni ever saw. She was a tiny girl, for 17-going-on-18. Raffaela had thick brown hair, carefully arranged on top of her head, giving her an additional two inches of height. Her dark green dress accented her small waist and the white cuffs and collar were barely whiter than her neck and hands. Her big brown eyes seemed to take up most of her face and her rosebud lips were slightly pouting in distain about the whole affair. But to please her parents she was trying her best.

Giovanni jumped up at her entrance sending his bowler rolling under the end table. He bent down to retrieve it, but it had landed too far away and he did not care to get down on all fours to get it. So he straightened up, red-faced and turned back to the lovely girl. In his embarrassment, he grabbed her hand and shook it as if she was a man. "I am pleased to make your acquaintance!" he said, not releasing her hand.

She murmured some pleasantry, pulled away from his hand, and walked around the other side of the end table to pick up his hat. She shyly handed it to him then crossed the room to sit between her father and step-mother.

"I am already in love with you," blurted out the potential suitor.

Raffaela blushed.

Giovanni saw himself as a bit of a country bumpkin compared to Raffaela and he realized how foolish that sounded. Giovanni thought of all the American school girls who tittered behind his back and talked about the boys they would like to be with. Of course, he was not that kind of man. Thank goodness, Alfonso was too old-fashioned to allow her to pick her own husband. She could only pick from the ones her father presented to her.

The conversation began, strained, but became easier as it went along. He accented all his best qualities, his money and his loyalty. She stepped out at one point and brought in a tray of cookies she had made, to show her skills. Giovanni raved about being able to have cookies by the dozen. Raffaela was pleased with his compliments and seemed to relax a little. Perhaps he had luck on his side, the young man thought. At least he had money so the girl would be able to live as well as her Papa and Mama Johanna did.

By the end of an hour, all had agreed to a trial courtship starting with dinner the following Sunday.

CHAPTER 24

PROVIDENCE, RI, CHRISTMAS EVE 1901

Raffaela and Johanna were working as a team, trying to get everything ready for 6:00 pm dinner. Since early morning, the two had been cleaning the apartment, preparing presents and cooking the dinner. The Christmas Nativity scene was set on an end table in the parlor and wrapped presents were tied with ribbons and set under that table. A large board was sitting on top of the small kitchen table, extending its length, to handle the extra guests who had been invited.

This was one of the most gastronomically delightful dinners of the year. It was the only holiday meal all year which required serving no meat, thus it consisted of pasta, fish and seafood, and fruit. Having come from southern Italy with its abundance of seafood, to living on a bay, also with a ready supply of seafood, led to an easy transition of the tradition from one continent to the other. The smell of garlic and oregano permeated the little kitchen as the tomato sauce simmered for hours. Rafaella spent two hours chopping and stuffing the three pounds of calamari and tossing them into the sauce.

"Mama Johanna," she began, trying to get some thoughts off her mind. "Are you sure that Giovanni will make a good husband?"

Johanna had been soaking the *baccala* in cold water twice to leech out the salt from the cod before cooking. Her hands were red and raw from the ice cold water. "Giovanni will make a good provider and that is what you want most of all."

"My friends talk about love and excitement. I have no excitement with him."

"Bah! Excitement! What do those little Americano girls know about marriage? You need a steady man. You need protection in a big city. Love is like a cloud. It comes. It goes." Johanna shrugged her shoulders. She had found both love and protection in her husband. She had no children of her own, but her marriage outweighed all that.

"I wonder if I will be happy," Raffaela mused.

"Happy? A girl your age does not know what happy is. It is not candy and flowers," Johanna said as she placed the cod on a cutting board. "It is in knowing that there is someone to protect you, to give you beautiful children and to make sure they are fed. That! That is happy!" She accented her words with the big cleaver as she spoke and then brought it down onto the cod.

Raffaela asked no more questions. She had read some of her friends' romantic novels and felt she was missing something in her relationship with Giovanni. Yet, her father had the decisionmaking power and all he could see was Giovanni's proper behavior and bank account. She bit her lip and finished up the squid, then wiped her hands on her apron and began to set the dinner table for eight. This was the first time Giovanni's brothers would be at her home for dinner. She wanted to impress those uneducated factory workers.

The table was set with her stepmother's best linen, large and snowy-white, with white tatting around the edge, and with matching *mapini*. This was part of Johanna's dowry, sent from her grandmother in the old country. The dishes were the heavy pottery that they used every day. But even they seemed to gleam when placed on the beautiful table cloth. Every candleholder in the apartment was cleaned and set with new candles to sparkle and light up the night.

By 4:30 pm they were tired. "Rafaella, put the water on for the pasta and then take a rest," advised Johanna. "I am going to put my feet up for a few minutes." She left the kitchen and went into her bedroom. Rafaella finished her chores and wiped her hands. The men would be here any time, now.

She hurried into her bedroom and started to freshen up when she heard her father, brothers and guests all trooping in, shaking out their coats and hanging them on the hall tree.

Boisterous as normal, Tomasso and Nico Gentile were loudly discussing the American celebration of Christmas vs. the Italian celebration as they walked into the parlor. Two of the Tassone brothers came lumbering up the stairs to the apartment, obviously not accustomed to such comfortable surroundings. Giovanni came up, proudly, as if he already had rights to the place. They did not participate in the lively conversation that the Gentile brothers were having. The Tassone brothers were workers, not students.

Alfonso, having imbibed in sufficient Christmas cheer earlier in the afternoon, offered further proof of his open-heartedness by breaking open a fresh bottle of anisette. The small maroon tufted Victorian sofa and matching chair provided seating for four, comfortably. So the men dragged in more kitchen chairs, making seating for six. Alfonso got out six glasses.

"Papa!" Tomasso exclaimed. "Nico is only a child. He should not have any more!" he said, noting that the young boy had already had a drink when they went to the saloon.

"Bah! He is fine. He can sleep it off later. I was

drinking when I was fifteen!"

"Yes! I heard that story!" Tomasso retorted. "They had to get you drunk to get you on the ship to America! You were too scared!" The men all burst into laughter. Alfonso chuckled as he finished pouring and passed out the glasses to all.

"*Buon natale!*" he toasted the guests. "It is too bad your brother Domenico could not come."

"Thank you, Alfonso," Giovanni commented. "His new baby is not faring well and he and Teresa decided that staying at home would be the best thing for the little one."

The camaraderie continued for a little while until the two women had readied themselves and came out to greet the men. After a round of holiday greetings, Giovanni and Tomasso moved the kitchen chairs back into the kitchen and all sat down for the annual Christmas Eve feeding frenzy. The traditional meal contained twelve items, one for each of the twelve apostles. And, Christmas Eve being a vigil of a holy day, thus it was a day of abstinence from meat. But also, many of the apostles were fishermen.

"Rafaella cooked most of the meal," Johanna told her guests as she watched them enjoy the food. "She is a good cook, yes?"

"Indeed she is," agreed Giovanni as he helped himself to more linguini and clam sauce. His brothers laughed.

"He would agree with anyone who fed him!" Bruno, the youngest brother, commented. "Look at him! He looks like he loves his food!" he added, pointing to Giovanni's less than slender build.

"Ah, but I know good food when I taste it," Giovanni declared happily. "And when we get married, Rafaella, you will cook like this for me, eh?" The intended blushed, but said nothing.

"So, big brother, when is this wedding to be?" asked Giuseppe Tassone.

"Soon, very soon! Eh, Rafaella? We don't want to wait much longer!" Giovanni gave his brothers a sly look and winked. That provoked another round of laughter. Tomasso looked uncomfortably at his father but Alfonso kept his eyes averted from his eldest.

"Come, Giovanni! You must have a date in mind!" urged the unmarried Giuseppe.

"I think three weeks is good," said Giovanni, almost absent-mindedly. "That should give us enough time to find a place of our own."

"It takes a while to plan and buy the furniture," Rafaella piped up, somewhat shocked that her life was suddenly moving too fast.

"That is already taken care of, *cara mia*," Giovanni looked down at her, sitting next to him. He patted her head. "Don't worry your pretty little head. All you have to do is get ready for the wedding night." The brothers all burst out laughing at that.

Giuseppe Tassone, the middle brother, stood and made a toast. "To my beautiful soon-to-be-sister-in-law! May you live long, have healthy babies, and be able to put up with my dumb ox of a brother for years." Much laughter arose from the table again.

Tomasso watched his step-mother and father. Johanna was smiling. She would soon have Alfonso's affection all for herself. Alfonso was smiling because he had found a happy family and a good provider for his daughter. Nico was smiling because he was drunk.

The marriage took place three weeks later, the second Saturday in January, 1902.

CHAPTER 25

PROVIDENCE, SUMMER 1902

Rafaella was going to enjoy a rare day of shopping on a perfect late spring day. Her basket on her arm, a big picture hat pinned securely in place, she stepped down the stairs and made her way along the steep downhill sidewalk to do her early morning shopping before the fruits and vegetables got quickly picked over. It had been some time since she had been out alone and she felt adventurous. In the shopping district of Federal Hill, the Italian area of Providence, she could pretend she was anyone and switch from English to Italian and back again as she pleased. Those old ladies who thought they could charge extra to the little American housewives who wondered over to their area were surprised when the American-looking girl started haggling with them in perfect Calabrian dialect.

Happily browsing through the stalls, Rafaella almost bumped into her school friend, Minnie LaBella.

"Minnie! How are you?" Rafaella squealed with delight. "I haven't seen you in almost a year! Since you got married last summer."

"Oh, Rafaella!" beamed Minnie. "I am so happy to see an old friend." The two young ladies hugged each other, avoiding bumping their big hats. Minnie took Raffaela's hands in hers and looked into her friend's eyes. "How are you, dear! I heard you married Giovanni Tassone. Is everything all right?"

"Why do you ask a question like that?" Rafaella asked, avoiding Minnie's eyes.

"Rafaella! We were best friends in school. I knew your innermost thoughts. I can tell you are smiling on the outside and scowling on the inside. I know you." They were standing in the middle of an aisle, in the other homemakers' way. So they eased their way to the toothless old lady who handled the money to pay for the goods in their baskets.

"Do you have a few minutes for a little walk, Rafaella?" Minnie asked.

"Yes. I have the whole morning."

"Good. Come with me. Let us go walk along the water. It's not far."

Rafaella started, somewhat, and looked around skittishly. "I suppose I could," she replied. Minnie looked at her inquiringly. This was not the vivacious Rafaella she knew. She was anxious to talk to her friend and put her arm through Raffaela's as they walked down the hill towards the wharves.

"Remember when we used to walk along the wharves after school and your step-mother would get so worried?" Minnie asked.

Rafaella laughed. "I felt so bad for her. She was worried that I would get lost and my father would blame her."

"How are they? I remember your step-mother's steamy coffee after school in the winter. She would give us toast to dunk in our coffee for a treat."

"I remember that," Rafaella smiled. She felt so free walking along with a friend, just chatting. "These packages of groceries are growing heavy," she said. "Let's find a place to sit." They found one overlooking the little branch of the Woonasquatucket River that ran only a block past the Gentile's apartment and sat down on a grassy knoll.

"So how are you doing in your new marriage?" asked Minnie. "Isn't it fun decorating your own little apartment? Just for you and your husband? Even if it is with second- and third-hand things?"

"We are rooming at 152 Spruce. Giovanni arranged all that before I knew what he had picked out."

"Oh, how cavalier of him!" Minnie responded, in awe. "My Dominick would never have thought of doing that!" Rafaella did not seem happy with that statement as she stared out into the bay.

"I am expecting," Rafaella stated plainly.

"That is wonderful!" Minnie exclaimed. Rafaella did not seem impressed with the news she had just uttered. Minnie tried another approach. "Are you happy with the news?"

"I would like a family. But Giovanni is so protective! I hate to think how he will react when I tell him."

"What? You have not told your own husband yet?"

Rafaella began to cry softly.

"Oh, my dear!" Minnie watched her in surprise. "We used to share all the details of our lives. Please. Tell me what is going on."

"It is not at all like I thought it would be," Rafaella said tearfully. "Mama Johanna told me that American girls are not practical and think only of how romantic their lives would be. I guess I think like an American. I know I have protection. And Giovanni is a good provider. But that is all there is!"

Minnie put her arm around her friend's heaving shoulders. "Why don't you go to your parents' apartment more often? And maybe make him meals he likes."

"Giovanni said he has had it with parading around in his good clothes every Sunday afternoon to entertain my parents and my brother. We haven't been there in two months. My papa asked why we don't come. I lied and said we needed to spend time as husband and wife for a while." Rafaella paused. She had said so much that she had never shared with anyone. "He even comes home for lunch every day to check on me and make sure I am home."

"Why are you able to be out today?"

"I told him that I wanted to check out the fruit and vegetables myself because he has bought some rotten ones lately."

"He buys the groceries?"

"Yes. He says he does not think that giving me money to go out when he is already out makes any sense. I was surprised that he agreed to let me shop today, to tell you the truth."

"You do not go out at all?"

"Rarely for very long. I go out for a walk in the mornings for a little while. But I don't tell him that."

"Being married can be very difficult," agreed Minnie. "My Dominick is very kind and lets me have the household money to spend as I see fit." She squeezed Raffaela's shoulders. "I cannot wait until I have a baby. It will be so exciting to have my very own little family."

Rafaella nodded slowly. "I hope I have a girl. Giovanni knows nothing about girls. She will be mine to play with alone. I think he will be afraid to touch a girl. Like she will break, or something." The two laughed at that.

"But, dear, is he good to you? You understand what I mean?"

"It is nothing like the novels we used to read after school. No romance, no comfort. Just, just . . .!" Rafaella looked away, not wanting to have Minnie see her reddening face.

"Just like when the bad man in the novels deflowers the innocent girl?"

Rafaella nodded. Minnie gasped at the realization that her friend was very innocent and probably very hurt.

"Well, you know," Minnie tried to encourage her. "Men sometimes think only of themselves at the beginning of marriage and then grow to understand how things should be after a while."

"You think so?"

"Of course I do. I had to straighten out Dominick about a few things in the winter. He did not know enough about women at first. I think you should go tell Giovanni that some things should change. That you should go to your parents' more and you need to handle the household money yourself."

"Oh! Giovanni would never accept that! He says that if he makes the money, he spends the money! And he does not want to go visit my family anymore. We do not see his brothers, either."

"How sad for you!"

"Well, he is my husband. What can I do?" Rafaella shrugged. "Maybe he will get more friendly with them over time."

The Angelus bells from Holy Ghost Church could be heard in the distance. Minnie stood up. "Look, Rafaella! It is getting late. I promised my mother I would see her for lunch. I have to leave." She felt uncomfortable leaving at this point in the conversation. But she could tell this was one of those situations which would not end with one talk. "Promise me you will try to get out regularly. And you will get hold of me as soon as you can again."

Rafaella got off the bench. "I'll try to send you word when I can see you again. Soon." She smiled up at her friend and took Minnie's hands and gave them a squeeze.

"Thank you for listening. It felt good to share."

Minnie squeezed her hands back. "Are you sure you are all right? Will you tell Giovanni soon about the baby? Will he be fine with it?"

Rafaella laughed. "He will be annoyingly ecstatic! He will want to control everything as it happens! I will be fine. Don't you worry."

The young wives parted with assurances of mutual friendship. Rafaella climbed the steep hill to her rooming house. When she got home, she was tired and, in a way, relieved that someone else knew.

In an attempt to improve the marriage, Rafaella spent her Sundays cooking, trying out different dishes on her husband, hoping to find one which would raise his eyebrows in appreciation. But he accepted everything equally. He ate everything with the same amount of gusto. Giovanni was, simply, a glutton. The only reason he never got any heavier was his extreme work conditions, running the machines at the fabric mill.

But Giovanni was an extremist. He was extremely happy, extremely sad, extremely hungry, thirsty, aroused, impatient, accusing, penny-pinching.

Rafaella knew she could not hide that she was pregnant. But she almost hated to tell her husband. His reactions would be so embarrassing. But it had to be done. And he was absolutely enthralled.

"My wife! She will be having a baby! Right after the first of the year! Just in time for our anniversary! Such a man that I am!" And he would have handed out cigars on that news alone if it had not been for the expense.

Giovanni became the overly-concerned expectant father. He would not let her out of the house, for fear she might slip and fall, especially as it grew colder. Ice could be an enemy! Think of the baby! Rafaella could not go to visit her family, even though they lived only a few blocks away.

CHAPTER 26

PROVIDENCE, JANUARY 1903

The baby was born the day before their first anniversary. Johanna found a competent midwife and stayed beside Rafaella throughout the labor. In the tiny parlor of the boarding house, Giovanni, his brothers, and the Gentile men kept coming and going in anticipation of the good news as Johanna boiled water on the wood stove in the Tassones' room and then sent Nico outside to find ice for Rafaella to suck on. After some hours, as the men were all getting sleepy, a loud slap and a baby's cry broke the silence. Giovanni jumped out of his seat and ran to the stairs.

Alfonso called him back. "Not yet, Papa! Give them some time to clean up!" Giovanni looked up the stairs at the bedroom door and realized his father-in-law was right. He went back to his chair and sat on the edge anxiously watching the stairs. It was 15 minutes before the midwife came out with the swaddled baby.

"It is a girl," she announced simply, gingerly stepping down the steps. Giovanni ran to the staircase to snap up the baby from the midwife's arms as soon as she reached the last step. Cradling the baby, he showed her to all around the little room.

"Ah, my little Concetta! Welcome to your home!" He crooned and fondled the baby, finally passing the baby back to the midwife. "Bring her back to her mother. I must tell my friends, now!" He invited all the men to go out with him as he made the rounds of his most frequented saloons to pass on the expected announcement and cigars to his acquaintances. They threw on their coats and hats and disappeared into the night, merrily trudging through the slush that is Providence's excuse for snow in January.

In August, on the feast of the Assumption of the same year, little Concetta died. Dysentery from the hot weather was to blame.

After the funeral, the family came back to the little room in the boarding house where the baby had given so much joy. Rafaella, dressed in black, slowly climbed the stairs behind her husband and step-mother. She did not pay attention to the six others following behind. The last few days were a haze. After the door opened, she walked over to the new rocker Giovanni had bought for her after Concetta's birth. She sat on it without taking off her hat and veil, and rocked herself, humming a lullaby under her breath.

Johanna added wood to the stove and heated the stew she had brought over earlier. The baby's uncles, grandfather and father poured themselves whiskey and sat around the small table quietly sipping their drinks and speaking in hushed undertones.

Giovanni, who had said little for several days, suddenly pushed back his chair and stood up, shaking his fist to heaven. "I hate You! You are not a good God! You are not a benevolent God! You may as well be the Devil himself, for all the good You are!"

The other men looked up in alarm and Johanna stepped back from the stove to give him more room. But no one else moved, staring in disbelief at this outrageous display of defiance, even for a non-church-goer.

"How dare You take my daughter! I will never pray

again, You God-forsaken excuse for a Father!" Giovanni began to cry hysterically and backed into the wall, sliding down the length of it, banging his head against it again and again as he cried out, taking the name of the Lord in vain as many ways as his inventive mind could come up with. Finally, bruised and bleeding, Giovanni staggered to his feet.

"Here, let me help you," Tomasso said quietly as he reached out to help him up. Giovanni shook him off, punching him hard in the arm, and stumbled over to where Rafaella sat alone. He knelt at her chair, put his head on her lap and they both cried uncontrollably as the others left the apartment.

CHAPTER 27

HARTFORD, 1930

"I have heard only half of this before!" said Santoro in amazement. "Mrs. Tassone told us practically nothing. We got nothing from the neighbors, either."

Anna had warmed up to her interrogator as she had given the story of Rafaella. Santoro assumed that because it was a story not personal to her, she could remember details without emotion. With calmness, a witness could usually recall flashes of details she thought long gone.

"Teresa and I were nosy, I guess. We liked to listen to the ladies talk more than we liked to play with our dolls. Then we would play grown-up and invent stories based on what we heard. The worst part of going to school was not being able to listen to the gossip." She smiled slightly.

Santoro was asking questions that had no pertinence to the case. His personal interest in this case had gotten the better of him. Using the warning of a fake warrant, he was now pumping this young lady for any information that could account for the actions of his friend 18 years ago.

CHAPTER 28

PROVIDENCE, DECEMBER 1905

Rafaella and Giovanni had a loveless marriage. Her loss of another child a year after the loss of baby Concetta did nothing to improve the situation. Giovanni tended to go drown his sorrows at the saloon after work while his wife sat in the rocking chair at night, watching the fading light out the window. They continued occasionally as husband and wife, but for the most part they were strangers living together in their single room.

It was closing in on Christmas. The weather was getting chilly and the population was waking up to freezing temperatures in the mornings. The early darkness before dinner time gave the little candles by the windows a mystical look to the men trudging home from work. These men often stopped by the numerous saloons along the way to toast their best holiday wishes to their friends.

Giovanni stopped by the rooming house briefly, as usual, to wash the cotton fibers from the mill off his face and hands. It was the only fastidious thing he did, before heading out to his favorite places.

"Could you stay home tonight?" Rafaella asked. "I made a pot of *pasta ceci*."

"No," he answered. "I have plans. I just wanted to stop in and see if you need anything."

"I am fine, Giovanni. Thank you."

"Don't wait up for me," he said as he tucked his scarf under his jacket collar. He opened the top drawer of his bureau and pulled out his .38, tucking it into his belt. He never took it to work, but everywhere else.

"Why do you always take that gun everywhere?" Rafaella asked, probably for the hundredth time.

"You never know when a man can get into a bind," was the answer, the same as every other time. With that, he walked out the door, down the stairs and out the apartment house door into the chilly night.

Giovanni turned left after stepping off the porch and walked down the hill towards his destination. The newly-installed electric street lights glowed yellow against the smattering of snow on the sidewalks, casting shadows across them as he walked along. As he got closer to the place, he could hear the faint sounds of Christmas carols being sung by the patrons. Not one to go to church, he couldn't place the tune right away, until he got close enough to be able to distinguish the words. *Adeste fideles.*

He walked into the saloon and ordered a double whiskey from the fellow behind the long walnut bar. He dropped a dime on the napkin in front of the bartender. Then he spotted an acquaintance at the other corner of the bar, so he picked up his drink and walked over.

"Buon natale, DiNitto!" he greeted the taller man dressed in a black ankle-length coat.

"Eh! *Buon natale*, Tassone!" DiNitto reached a hand over to shake Giovanni's. His left hand held a scotch.

DiNitto was a fairly big man, dressed well in a fancy American off the rack black suit under his coat. He had a warm muffler around his neck. He was making money somewhere, apparently, thought Giovanni.

Besides DiNitto, a man Giovanni did not recognize sat at the bar. Taller and of a fairer complexion than most of the others in the bar, this man had a decided air of authority. His clothes had cost serious money, assessed Giovanni. The hat and the leather gloves were not seen in this neighborhood. His camel hair coat was made of the finest wool and looked out of place in this workingman's bar.

"Tassone! Let me introduce you to my acquaintance, Pensara. Mr. Pensara, this is my friend, Giovanni Tassone." The two strangers shook hands.

"Please," offered Pensara. "Let me order you another drink."

Giovanni agreed and another round was ordered.

"So, what do you do, Tassone?" Pensara asked while they were waiting for their drinks.

"I work at one of the fabric mills. And I have a fine wife," Giovanni said proudly.

"A very nice looking woman, too," added DiNitto. "Remember that woman I pointed out to you a few days ago?" he asked, turning towards Pensara. "She had that crocheted muffler you had commented on and you said she looked like a little doll. Well, that's the one."

"Yes, yes!" remembered Pensara. "I said something about how pleasing it would be on a winter's night to cozy up with that one. *Una bella fica*!" He laughed and tossed back his whiskey.

Giovanni stood up from his stool and glared at the two men. "Are you making a joke of me?"

"No, no! Never mind us, Tassone! We have had a few. It is just that there are so few beautiful women around here and you got one of the best looking! Sit down. Have your drink!" DiNitto seemed to be aware of a sudden change in the air.

"I do not let anyone talk about my wife like that!" Giovanni retorted. "She is mine. And mine alone!" He banged his fist on the polished bar.

"Get your head on straight, Tassone!" Pensara shot back. "We are a little loose in the tongue. That is all. I was just saying what I had mentioned a few days ago.

That's all. No harm!"

"I want an apology!" shouted Giovanni.

"Who do you think you are talking to, man? I don't apologize to some small time *asino* who is whining about a woman! *Vaffanculo!*" Pensara, apparently seeing himself as superior and out of his element in that saloon, seemed easily angered by what he perceived to be a lack of respect for his person.

By this time, Giovanni had pulled his jacket back sufficiently to reveal his gun, with his hands on his waist. "I want an apology!" he repeated forcefully.

DiNitto grabbed Giovanni by the left shoulder and tried to push him back. "You do not know this man! He is a man of respect!" he hissed.

Giovanni heard but stared angrily at this man he did not know and held his ground. Pensara stood up, glaring at the shorter man.

"You disrespect me, you *gustafave*! I could have you killed for that!"

Having neither respect nor patience, Giovanni simply pulled out his gun and fired. The other patrons in the saloon dove under the tables. In a moment, Pensara was down. He had not even pulled out his gun.

"Oh, *mio Dio!*" DiNitto screamed. "Tassone! What have you done?"

As others ran to the downed man, DiNitto pushed Giovanni towards the door. "Get out of here! Pack a few things and get the hell out of town! Now!" He shoved Giovanni out into the night. "I will meet you at your place as soon as I can. Get going!"

Giovanni had never shot someone before. He was afraid of himself and of what he had done. He ran. All the way up the quiet hill, he ran like the ghost of Pensara was after him. Which it was, for all he knew.

He was breathless by the time he got to the apartment house. It was only then that he realized that he still held the gun in his hand. So, shaking wildly, he managed to stick it back in his belt before entering the building. Then he climbed the stairs, trying to compose himself, which was not a mean feat.

As he entered the apartment, he saw his beautiful Rafaella quietly dozing on her childless rocking chair. He covered his face and began to weep. The noise woke her.

"Giovanni, what is it? What has happened?"

"Raffaela, I have ruined everything! My damned anger! It has done it this time!" He stood there looking at her with his hands on his head. He felt it might burst.

His wife rose from her rocking chair, looking him over carefully. Then she caught her breath.

"Giovanni! Your gun! It is on the other side of your belt! Oh! *Beata vergine madre*! You shot a man! Is he dead?"

"I don't know," he responded weakly. "But we have to get out of here before the police come." But he just stood there, undecided as to what he should do.

Rafaella took control for the first time in their marriage. "I will get dressed and pack a few things. Then I will get the groceries and wrap them. We will go to Papa's house. There we can think." Giovanni simply nodded as she slipped past the dividing curtain into their sleeping area. He dropped into the closest kitchen chair to sort it all out.

Within a few minutes, Rafaella was dressed and was packing a single carpetbag. Then there was a knock on the door followed by a soft voice calling, "Tassone! I know you are in there! It's me. DiNitto!"

Giovanni got up, noiselessly crossed the room and opened the door just enough to let him in, then shut and bolted the door.

"What do you know?"

"The police are there. He is still breathing. The ambulance should be there any time now. Where are you going?"

"We will go to Raffaela's parents tonight. Then we can decide," Giovanni answered. He sat back down at the kitchen table, pointing to another chair for DiNitto to sit but the man refused. He began to pace the floor, his hands deep into his coat pockets.

"Well, we can hold off the police for a little while by pretending not to know Rafaella. But someone will tell them where to find her parents! You got a day, maybe. And you better get out of the state. You know anyone in Massachusetts or Connecticut?"

"No. I don't know anybody except for my brothers here and a few distant relatives in Hartford."

"You better go somewhere and hide. I won't talk, you know that. But you could be having murder charges filed any time now. You got Pensara good. I don't know if he can live with what you did to him." Then DiNitto looked into Giovanni's eyes and sighed. "Why did you do it? I told you he was a man of respect! Didn't you hear me?"

"I get so angry sometimes. And then, I can't control myself. I don't know!" Giovanni put his hands up to his head again. Surely, his head would blow up before the evening was over.

Rafaella walked out of the bedroom with her carpetbag. She was wrapped well against the cold. "Giovanni. Please. The groceries. I have my arms full." Her coat was buttoned up high, with her muffler about her chin. She was ready. "I have a change of clothes for each of us."

"I would advise you to walk," said DiNitto, looking

at Rafaella. "A taxi driver would surely remember a beautiful woman out at night. He would bring the police right to your parents' door."

"Thank you for your advice, *amico*," replied Giovanni. He picked up the big cotton shopping bag in one hand and his overcoat in the other.

"I could walk with you and help you with all that, but it is best if I am not seen with you," DiNitto suggested.

They went downstairs to the porch, looking both ways before opening the door, to assure themselves that no one was around. Then, the three parted ways at the sidewalk, the two men shaking hands. DiNitto walked back down the hill towards the saloon; and the young couple crossed up the hill to the Gentile's apartment on Atwell Street, several blocks away.

A knock on the door at 9:00 at night bodes ill in a city. Alfonso went to answer. "Who is it?" he asked.

"Papa!" Rafaella whispered. Alarmed, Alfonso pulled the cord on the hall light and opened the door slowly to see the couple standing there. He opened the door wide and ushered them into the narrow vestibule.

"Jennie!" he called. "Make coffee!" Johanna, dressed in her wrapper, came out of the bedroom and into the kitchen where she immediately stoked the stove while Rafaella put the carpetbag on the floor in the kitchen until Alfonso could rouse his son from his sleep. Nico soon came out of his bedroom, yawning and scratching his head, to see what was happening.

"What the hell are you doing trudging around the slush at night?" was the first thing out of his mouth.

Giovanni was about to retort when his wife put her hand on his arm as much to say, *I will take care of this.*

"Nico, honey!" Rafaella said. "We need your help. There's been a problem and we can't go home."

That seemed to satisfy her younger brother momentarily and he went into his bedroom to deposit the carpetbag on a chair. Then he returned to the kitchen as his father put the damp coats over the backs of the kitchen chairs to dry.

Alfonso gave Giovanni a quick shot of anisette to calm his nerves. Johanna brought a tray of mugs to the kitchen table and set it down. The parlor in this apartment was larger and there was more seating in it than in the previous one.Johanna had added another plant to the ensemble and there was an electric ceiling light for nighttime use. But Rafaella and Giovanni were family so they all sat around the kitchen table, looking at the crucifix over the door and praying silently over their coffee.

After a few sips of the hot coffee, Alfonso glared at Giovanni. "What has happened that you should take my daughter out at night?"

"Papa!" Rafaella began.

"No, Rafaella! I can speak now," Giovanni interrupted. He was sufficiently recovered, at this point, to make sense out of the evening. He cleared his throat. "I was defending Raffaela's honor."

The eyebrows of all the listeners went up. "Please explain yourself," said the older man, skeptical of the younger.

Giovanni went through the whole story from beginning to end, including the names.

"This Pensara," Alfonso began. "I have heard his name. He is from Boston. Comes here to Providence fairly often. Business, I believe. But, what kind of business, I do not know. Good dresser. Yes?"

Giovanni nodded.

"He was referred to as a man of respect, eh?" Again,

Giovanni nodded. "Well, then, if he survives, you had best be in another state. It will be harder to find you. I do not envy you, Giovanni. Your life will be difficult for a very long time."

"So, where will you go?" Johanna asked quietly.

"I have nowhere to go," Giovanni said. "Bruno moved to Hartford a few months ago. But we do not talk. So, I do not know anyone except here in Providence."

Alfonso took charge. "Nico, when the shops open in the morning, you will send a telegram to Bruno. Get the address. Keep it general. Sign Giovanni's name. Say, hmmm," he paused. "Say, 'Need a vacation. Get us a room right away. Will contact you later with arrival time.' And have it be in Italian. That should do it. Then, go to the train station and find the next train with connections to Hartford."

"Yes, Papa," Nico answered. "I will be out of the house by 7:00."

"Do you have any money on you?" Alfonso asked Giovanni.

"Yes. I have enough for the trip and a month's rent, I believe." Raffaela's eyes opened wide and she caught her breath, but said nothing. She did not realize how much money he carried.

"Good. Give me a dollar for the telegrams." Giovanni, normally secretive about money, pulled a wad out of his pocket and peeled off a dollar bill, handing it to Alfonso, who handed it to Nico. "Here. This should be enough for all the telegrams we will send tomorrow." Then he turned back to his son-in-law. "I am helping you because you are the father of my dead granddaughters. If you were alone, I would let you burn in hell. You are often a stupid man, Giovanni Tassone. Don't make any more mistakes or I will tell them where you are, myself."

Giovanni gritted his teeth but remained silent and merely nodded.

That night, Giovanni and Rafaella squeezed into Nico's bed, where they slept fitfully. And Nico slept on the floor in the kitchen.

The next morning, the Tassones received a telegram from Bruno, also in Italian: "*Testa di merda*! I have my hands full trying to help myself. Why don't you look to your other brothers!"

The help of the other brothers, Dominick and Giuseppe was minimal.

"Tell you what I'm gonna do for you, *stupido*!" offered Dominick. "I will do this one thing for you. When the directory census people come in the spring, I will tell them that you went back home and took your wife with you. I will lie for you this once. Don't ask for any more favors. I am not going to put my wife and children in danger for a murderer!"

They stayed in Providence. Giovanni and Rafaella settled into Alfonso and Johanna's new apartment that Alfonso had decided to rent on Sutton Street. It was a little roomier for five adults. No one would notice a change in address. The Italian community seemed to change addresses as often as hats. Giovanni worked day jobs when he could to pay the rent and supplement the grocery bills. But he did not dare either get a regular job or get an apartment of his own. Spies or tattlers could be anywhere. Despite the problems of close living, Rafaella was overjoyed to again be with her father, step-mother and brother. They settled into a routine which worked well for everyone.

On the day before the fourth anniversary of little Concetta's death, Rafaella was delivered of a boy, Francesco, named for his paternal grandfather. Giovanni was overjoyed. His co-workers received cigars and saw a Giovanni they had not met before. And to the delight of both parents, little Bruno arrived just over a year later, in October, 1908. They could not celebrate much; they could not even register the births.

The four Tassones were all in hiding.

However, soon after the birth of Bruno, their lives changed.

CHAPTER 29

PROVIDENCE, EARLY DECEMBER, 1908

It was dinner time at the Gentile apartment. A dark winter evening, much like the one four years back that had forced the Tassones into hiding. Nico and Alfonso came home from the mills and sat down to dinner with the family.

"I saw a man today. You know him," began Alfonso. "He asked about you, Giovanni." He glared into his son-in-law's eyes, holding his fork like a weapon, pointed at the younger man. "It is now too dangerous for you to be here. You can leave tomorrow."

Rafaella was eating her dinner, with the six week old Bruno in the crook of her arm. She looked sharply at her father. "You are pushing us out of the house? It is almost Christmas. The boys are too little to move."

"I am not going to let my wife be widowed just for a holiday!" grumbled Alfonso. "That Pensara has friends. Too many friends. And his henchman, DiNitto, told me he is sorry that this is how it is. He said he could get killed for simply having warned me."

"You told him I am still here?" exploded Giovanni.

"Watch your temper, *stupido*!" Alfonso retorted. "And, no. I did not tell him you are here. I told him I did not know where you are. Like always. But I don't think he believed me this time. He said he was sorry, but this one warning that if I know where you are I should tell you to go far away, is all he can give. So, I pass it on to you." He scowled at his son-in-law. "If I had known how much trouble you would be, I would not have let you marry my daughter!" And he spit on the floor next to Giovanni's foot.

The family fell silent as they ate. Johanna had Frankie on her lap, alternately feeding him and herself. He was the only one making any noise. At the end of the meal, the women excused themselves to put the babies down and the men stayed at the table with their coffee.

"So, you worthless piece of crap, what do you have to say for yourself?" Alfonso directed his comment, leaning back in the kitchen chair, arms folded over his chest.

"I have to telegraph my brother in Hartford." Giovanni felt small in front of the men. He did not like these two after living with them for four years. They looked down at him, questioned him constantly. They defended Rafaella against him.

"Don't you go out!" interjected Alfonso. "Nico! You go, like before. To the telegraph office in the morning. You send, like before, in Italian. You got money?" he asked, turning to Giovanni.

A much thinner stack of bills came out of Giovanni's pocket this time and he handed over money to Nico. "A dollar is enough," he murmured.

The next day, at noon, a telegraph messenger came to the door. The message, addressed to Nico, but obviously meant for his brother-in-law, read: "Come along. I will find you an apartment. What an ass you are, Gio!"

CHAPTER 30

HARTFORD, 1930

"It's all very interesting, but of no use to me," observed Santoro. "Do you have any memory of later occurrences? How about what happened when they lived in Hartford?"

"I was about four when they moved into the apartment building. I really don't remember a time without them. At first the boys were too little to play with. But by the time Bruno was walking, they would come down to play with Mary and Dora, my little sisters. That is when Mrs. Tassone started telling the stories.

"I think I listened to her because she had prettier dresses than the others. Or maybe because she had no accent in either Italian or English. I am not sure. But she did stand out to an impressionable little child."

Santoro nodded, remembering Rafaella Tassone in the same way. Especially he remembered her that night, looking frightened, wanting to tell everyone everything, looking fragile. His mind was wandering, wondering just what happened to that striking young woman who had impressed him so much that night and again, months later, at the coroner's inquest. He blinked a few times and smiled at his guest.

"Do you remember anything about the relationship of the Tassones after they moved to your building in Hartford?"

CHAPTER 31

HARTFORD, 1910

"You do not need to go home to visit your father and step mother!" Giovanni shouted. "You can have the baby right here. You have friends here, now, and you have me and the boys. You cannot just up and leave when you want to."

The argument had been going on for a week. Rafaella was due in less than a month and she wanted to go back to Providence to be with family for the birth of this baby.

"But I have not seen them in a year and a half," Rafaella tearfully objected. "I am homesick."

"Bah! You are homesick! I have not seen my parents in ten years!"

"You chose to move," she sobbed. "I did not."

Giovanni looked at her without compassion. All he saw was a spoiled child who wanted things her way. He paced the floor in the little apartment, walking back and forth between the red tufted sofa and the scullery, a little room with a sink and cupboards off the larger kitchen-living room combination. He eyed the closed door behind which slept his two boys. Not that he cared whether they heard, he just did not want the interruption of a cryin baby.

"You always want money! Do you think that I have a treasure box hidden under the bed?" His fear and anger made his neck muscles bulge while his face got red.

In her rocker opposite the sofa, beside the window, Rafaella shrank away from him.

He scowled but to her credit, she had not asked for

anything since moving to Hartford at Christmas time, 1908. She had done everything in her power to appease him at every turn. The boys were always clean and quiet and the house was simple but clean and comfortable. His meals were served as he wished and he would soon proudly announce the birth of another child.

"I am afraid of having the baby without Mama Johanna," Raffaella said. "It would only be for a month."

"A month! What do you think I am going to do with two babies, one in diapers, for a month?" Giovanni spit out the words.

"The Amatos and the DeFrancescos said they would help. Maria's girls are big enough to babysit alone and even Carmela's oldest girl can change diapers, now." She was grabbing at straws, and she knew that he knew it.

"So, now I have to pay people to take care of my children while my own wife goes traipsing off to do God knows what in the town where my name is mud!" He stopped and glared at her. "That trip will be expensive!"

"No, no! Giovanni, the ladies will watch the children for nothing. And they will cook for you, too. They told me." She gripped the arms of the chair. The fabric was a little frayed after years of use but it was her favorite piece of furniture.

"I need the money I would have to pay," Giovanni insisted. He started to pace again. "You have no concept of money. This would set me back." His fear of becoming his father had haunted him, though he had never shared it with her.

"I-I could take in laundry when I come back. The boys are so good and the baby would sleep most of the time. I would work hard!"

"No wife of mine will work!" He stopped in front of her to get in her face. "I will not have it!"

Raffaella could smell the whiskey on his breath and held her breath, waiting for his hand to slap her.

He straightened abruptly, with a sudden smile. "I know what I will do! I will take in a boarder! There is always a new man in the neighborhood looking for a place. I could make two dollars a week, if I throw in meals!" He nodded, pleased with himself.

Giovannie began to pace again, slower this time. "This is a good idea. Fifty cents extra in food every week, for a profit of a dollar and a half a week. That would be six extra dollars a month profit. That is an extra week's income a month!" He looked at his wife and sighed. "Very well, then. I will send you to your parents'. One month after the baby is born, you will be home. There will be extra cooking and cleaning for you to do, with an additional man in the family. I will have found someone by then." He smiled to himself, rubbing his hands together, in anticipation. It apparently had not occurred to him that caring for a boarder was no less a chore for his wife than taking in laundry would have been.

Rafaella slapped her hand over her mouth to repress a squeal of excitement. Her eyes teared further than they had already, this time in appreciation. "Thank you, Giovanni!" she whispered.

He went over to the kitchen table and sat down with a pencil and paper, jotting down names of people he had spoken to recently about this very subject. Meanwhile, Rafaella pulled herself out of the rocker and went to bed, smiling at the thought of finally seeing her parents again.

Two days later, Rafaella left the tenement, kissing her little boys over and over, as if she would never see them again. Nickie De Francesco, now a sprouting thirteen year old young man, carried her bag for her as they crossed the street and walked into Union Station. He passed the bag to the porter and smiled at Rafaella. "I hope you have a good ride, Mrs. Tassone," he said in impeccable English. "Don't worry about Frankie and Bruno. My mother and aunt will take good care of them."

"Thank you, Nickie," Rafaella replied, realizing she now had to look up to the boy. "Give my regards to your father and uncle and tell them I say thank you many times over." The boy nodded, handed her up the steps to the porter and waved.

Hours later, Rafaella saw the gold statue of Hope atop the State Capital in Providence, glinting in the evening sun. She was home! Stepping off the train in the noisy station reminded her of Hartford until she saw her little brother, Nico. Of course, he was a grown man, now, but she thought of him as being the same as Nickie, her neighbor's son.

"Nico!" she called, waving her purse. He heard her call and came running over to give her a big hug.

"You look as beautiful as ever, you little cookie!" he said, using a phrase he had begun as a child. "Papa and Johanna are anxiously waiting to see you. They were surprised to get your cable yesterday, but pleased to have you back for a while." He grabbed Raffaela's bag from the porter and placed her arm through his as he directed her out of the station and towards a hansom he had retained. He handed her up to the seats and placed her bag beside her and got in to sit opposite for the mile ride to the house.

"We won't speak in the cab," he said quietly. "The walls have ears, and so do the public cabs," he added, jerking his thumb back over his shoulder at the driver. Rafaella smiled without understanding. "I will explain later," Nico said. The ride was soon over and Nico stepped out, got her and her bag down and paid the hansom driver, all without exposing her face to his view.

Climbing the two flights of stairs to the Gentiles' latest apartment, this one on Atwells Avenue, tired Rafaella. She was very glad to sit after greeting the older couple.

Johanna, her wrapper tightly tied to show off her still small waist, insisted on them all sitting at the kitchen table so she could feed her step-daughter. She quickly got out olives in brine, prosciutto, a few slices of provolone and a hunk of freshly-baked bread. Alfonso got out a jug of wine and poured four glasses. Rafaella looked around the kitchen, noting the newly blacked stove, freshly painted walls and sparkling white porcelain sink. Her step-mother's attention to detail was still intact.

"So, now that you have had something to eat, tell me why you have come." Alfonso was not mincing words. A woman did not leave her husband for any reason, he believed.

"Papa," Rafaella began, tears immediately welling up. "I do not want to be alone when the baby is born. I have lost two. I am afraid."

"Bah!" her father replied, pouring a second glass of wine for himself. "You have a husband. And neighbors. What is the matter that you have to come home?"

"I only trust Johanna. No one else." She staunchly held her argument. She looked sideways at Johanna, to see if she was at all in agreement. Johanna nodded, pleased that her step-daughter thought so highly of her.

The wine was making Rafaella too warm. She took off her jacket, which she had kept on until now and unbuttoned the sleeves of her blouse, rolling them up as she did so. Then, suddenly, she thought better of it and rolled down the right sleeve.

"What is that?" Alfonso grabbed her right wrist,

tightly, holding it immobile against the table, and pulled the sleeve back up. There was a dark mark, with a yellow tinge around the edges, demarking a bruise of about a week old. "What is that?" he demanded again. Rafaella tried to pull away and hide the arm, but her father was much stronger than she was. Her arm was pinned down. "Who did this to you?"

"It is nothing, Papa," she stammered. Johanna got up from her seat across from Alfonso and stepped to her right to stand behind Rafaella. She looked at the bruise, then reached down to grab her left arm. She tugged at the buttons and pulled the sleeve up, revealing a similar, older bruise.

"*Madre mia!*" Johanna whispered. "Is this Giovanni's doing?"

"Please, Johanna!" Rafaella begged. "He just got upset. It is nothing."

"Nothing?" Nico stood up, shocked to see his dear sister hurt in any way. "This is not good! Maybe I should tell those people where he is!"

"What people?" Raffaela blinked a few times and she pulled her arms away from her parents as their attention moved to Nico. She rolled down her sleeves to hide the bruises. "Are you still talking about that, Nico?"

"Don't you remember who Giovanni shot when you had to move?" asked Alfonso.

"Y-yes. A man in the saloon. He was defending my... my honor." Rafaella was trying to put a good spin on her husband's actions.

"Do you remember I said I thought he was a made man?"

"Yes Papa, I think I remember you mentioned something about that."

"And you know what that means?"

Rafaella nodded.

"That group still wants to meet with Giovanni. It would not be good, I can tell you. An eye for an eye! You know?"

"Have they spoken to you?" Rafaella asked fearfully.

"Sure. Even now, every few months they come up to me in the street. Or Nico. They ask if we have heard from you. And, I say no. I don't know where you are. They look for you still. But the police, they don't look no more. They don't have jurisdiction outside the state. So, you are safe, as long as I keep my mouth shut. And Nico, too."

Raffaela's hands went up to her face, in horror. She realized that her husband's life was on the line and only her father and brother stood between Pensara and Giovanni. "Is that why you did not want me to talk in the hansom, Nico?"

"Yes, and I tried to block his having a good view of you. I could have said you were Christina, or another relative. It was easy in the dusk. I took the hansom because it would throw them off if they were looking. Too expensive for us Italians."

Rafaella glanced at her father but he simply nodded.

"You better not plan on walking the streets of this part of town while you are here. You never know who will talk," added Nico.

Johanna stood up straight, and like a sergeant, announced, "I think the girl has had enough excitement for the night. Too much and the baby will come too fast. Nico will sleep on the floor in the kitchen and Rafaella, you get his bedroom. We cleaned out a drawer in his bureau for you. The men have to be at work at 7:00 am, and, look! It is already 9:00 pm!" She shooed everyone out of her kitchen so she could straighten it out for the night and get the coffee pot ready for the morning.

Rafaella remained sequestered in her parents' house, happily relaxing and being treated with more respect than she could have hoped for. Within a week, she bore a little girl. She had the child baptized Teresa, because she liked the name, not because, in true Italian tradition, it was her mother's name. Then, true to her word, Rafaella returned to Giovanni and the boys when the child was one month old.

CHAPTER 32

HARTFORD, APRIL, 1910

Carmela climbed the stairs to her sister Maria's apartment. She clutched a small printed flyer in her hands. As with most apartments, the door was open and she could see the little ones playing.

"Hello boys!" she crooned as she walked in.

"*Zia* Carmela!" the boys answered eagerly as they stood out of respect.

"Where is your Mama?" Carmela inquired.

"Here I am!" Maria answered as she came out of the scullery wiping her hands. "I was just finishing the dishes. The only bad thing about sending the older ones to school is that I have to do the lunch dishes myself," she laughed. Seeing the letter in her sister's hand, she asked, "What do you have there? A letter from Stella?"

"No," Carmela responded. "It is a letter from the U.S. government that I found on the front door. I don't understand. There is a census taker coming tomorrow. Why? What does he want?"

"Oh! That!" Maria laughed again. "When Dom and I were taking lessons to become citizens, we had to learn about this. Every ten years, all the people in the country have to be counted. Dom got counted ten years ago, but the rest of us did not get here until the following year so we have never been counted."

"Will they ask questions?"

"Sure! They ask your name, if you are married, where you were born. Like that."

"Like in the old country when the national police

could track you, eh?"

"No. Not like that. It is for to get the Congressmen to have the right number of people vote for them."

"That sounds suspicious. Why would they spend all that time to count people just for the Congress?"

"That is how they designed the country. I don't know why!" Maria shrugged her shoulders, unsure as how to answer the question.

"Well, I will have to tell Giuseppe to be home tomorrow night so we can all be counted. I will explain it to him at lunch."

"Do not worry about this," reassured Maria. "They will not forget to count you!"

Carmela nodded and turned to go. "I don't want to leave the children alone too long. You never know what trouble they can get into! Come down later for coffee!" She added turning to go.

At dinner, a small meal of chicken soup, a slab of bread and a slice of mozzarella, Carmela presented the flyer to Giuseppe.

"What do you think?" she asked.

"I think that we could get into trouble. Gambling is not approved in this country," Giuseppe responded as he re-read the letter. He stared into space as he took a bite of the bread. "Here is what I think we will do. It is Giuseppe Amato the barber who sells the lottery tickets. It is Carmela Matta who has the bank account. Who is to say that the barber lives in the same building as the shop. Maybe the barber lives somewhere else. Maybe on Front Street. Maybe some other ward."

Carmela looked at him without a word. He had a wonderful imagination and she could see that he was formulating a plan. Whatever it was, she would agree to it. After all, he was her husband.

"There are so many people living in the city, probably 100,000! There will be more than one counter for each of the nine wards. Nobody will ask where is the barber, Giuseppe Amato, living?" He dunked another piece of bread into his soup bowl. "Just in case this lottery thing gets into trouble, we have money in the bank for an emergency, and no one can find where this Amato lives. Because we will not be Amatos!"

The next evening, the knock on the door indicated the expected visitor.

"I am Mr. Russell, here for the census," he said very perfunctorily. "May I come in?" The blonde man had thick glasses and sheaves of paper on a clip board. Carmela offered him a seat at the kitchen table and placed a cup of coffee within easy reach. Giuseppe was already seated, having already determined his course of action. The four little girls were in their Sunday dresses, all sitting quietly on the sofa. Carmela kept her eye on them, having previously told them to make no noise. She looked around the little apartment. Over the past day, she had done everything in her power to make it look clean, non-Catholic and American, washing windows, cleaning floors and hiding her Madonna statue.

With no further conversation, Russell quickly began his questioning. "Last name?"

"Karmarter."

Russell blinked behind his glasses and raised an eyebrow as he looked at Giuseppe. "First name of the husband?"

"Garsten."

Carmela nodded, not at all sure if it sounded American or not. It sounded strange.

"Wife's name?"

"Mary."

"Children's names?"

"Cecilia, Annie, Nunzie and Dora." Russell wrote in the tiny squares of the census form, rarely looking up except to count the number of children on the sofa. He asked several other questions, ages, places of birth and the like. The couple admitted to being Italian. The accents gave them away, anyhow. Russell seemed unaware of the name discrepancy even though all the others in the apartment house had last names that ended with a vowel. He left within a few minutes.

Giuseppe breathed a sigh of relief.

CHAPTER 33

HARTFORD, DECEMBER 30, 1911

Captain Garrett Farrell was at his accustomed place in his office. He was writing up a report for the chief. It was dark out at 4:30 pm. Another hour and a half and he would go home. He looked forward to two days off, New Year's Eve and New Year's Day. So he was furiously finishing off all the paperwork that Chief Gunn had asked for. Lt. Henry Hart, newly elected chief of the detective bureau was catching a smoke during a rare ten minute break. He sat across from Farrell's desk on a worn brown leather upholstered chair and put his feet up on the matching, equally worn ottoman.

"George Butler," Hart began with a cough, interrupting Farrell's thought process. "Who has the post over by the station, talks to the Italians almost as much as Santoro does."

Farrell's deep voice snapped. "Congratulate him for me," he said sarcastically.

"No! Listen, Garrett!" Hart blew a ring of smoke then pulled his pipe out of his mouth and leaned forward.He took his feet off the ottoman and onto the floor. "Butler is concerned. He heard some talk about a kid from New York who was going to be coming up here and isn't welcome."

Farrell lifted his head and looked at Hart over his glasses. "Really concerned? Or just another story from those Italian gossips?"

"Apparently, he heard the same story three different ways in the past shift."

"He call it in?"

"Yes. When he came on shift today at 4:00 pm."

Farrell groaned. This could kill his day off. "Tell you what, go find him and the other two closest foot patrol. Tell them to check with each other often for the next few nights. No stopping into bars for a warm-up. Get the matron to make a strong coffee and get pots out to those boys. I don't want any of them nodding off."

Hart knocked out his tobacco into the ashtray. He got up from the chair. "Ok, Captain. I'll get to it. You going to stay here so we can report in?"

"Sure, sure," Farrell waved him off. "Looks like it will be several hours before I finish off these reports, anyhow."

Hart left the room and Farrell was left to himself. He phoned his wife to tell her not to hold dinner and turned on more lights to settle in.

At 7:00 pm, the phone rang. "Farrell here!" he answered.

"Captain, this is George Butler. I am at the train station. I saw something strange a few minutes ago. A young kid got off the last train from New Haven and was met by a whole delegation of Italian men. They didn't do anything wrong, but I have a funny feeling."

"Did you see which way they went?"

"Last I saw they were walking down towards the Church Street yards."

"Ok. You stay on your beat and I will contact some others.

Hart get you that coffee?"

"Yes. Thanks. It's cold out tonight."

"Keep your eyes open, kid!" Farrell hung up the phone and called a police box phone located on Asylum Ave. It took several attempts before the phone was answered.

"McGrath here!" the patrolman answered.

"This is Captain Farrell. There is some kid in the company of a bunch of Italians, probably from the neighborhood. Butler thinks something is up. He heard rumors yesterday. Keep your eyes open."

"Sure, Captain! Anything else?"

"No. Got your coffee?"

"Yes, thanks."

"I'll stay in the office until midnight. Contact me if anything happens."

"Sure thing."

Nothing happened for hours. The evening sky was bright with stars but the air was cold, even indoors. Farrell fed himself a pot of coffee and stale sandwiches, waiting. At 10:00 pm the phone had not rung. At 11:00 pm, Farrell called Butler. There was no answer. He tried McGrath. Again no answer. Then, within minutes, Hart called from a police box.

"Captain, we need you up here at the rail yards. There has been a shooting."

"Who is the victim?"

"Some kid. Maybe the one who Butler sighted earlier this afternoon."

"Any perps?"

"No. We stumbled on him alone a few minutes ago."

"I'll be down shortly," Farrell responded and hung up. He called up for a car, then took one more sip of tepid coffee as he donned his galoshes and coat. It did not take more than ten minutes to get to the site.

Farrell had to push his way to the front of the crowd gathered at the rail yards. Most of the men had labels in their hats, identifying them as journalists from the various newspapers. It hadn't taken them long to get to the scene!

Some of the police officers had histories with these men which did not give them a kind characterization.

The kid was Italian, about 20 years old and still was holding on to the loaded revolver when Farrell and his driver got to the front. Blood on the snow was minimal.

"Good looking kid," commented Hart as he gazed at the body with the captain. "We didn't move the body. Figured you would want to see how he went down. But we did search through his pockets while we waited. Found a round trip ticket to New Haven, a storage ticket for a shipping place in New York City and a few letters in two different handwritings."

"Got a name?"

"Looks like Antonio something with a P. Italian. I can't read the Italian. We sent for Santoro. He will meet me back at the station."

"Turn him over," ordered Farrell. Two patrolmen gently turned the corpse over to reveal one bullet hole over the heart. "Well," mused the captain. "There's your cause of death."

"You want me to say anything to the press, Captain?"

Farrell frowned. "Tell them we will have more information at 10:00 am. That will give them time for the afternoon editions. Get him to the morgue. Bring all the evidence to my office by 8:00 am. Make a telephone call to that storage place. Get anything you can on the ticket. I'm going home. It's too damn cold." He hunched his shoulders to warm his neck and turned back to the car without another word. Hart barked orders to his men, shooed the press away with a promise and stuffed the papers he had taken off the body into a bag, along with the victim's gun.

Half an hour later, Hart was back at the station. He recorded the items before giving the letters to Santoro for translation. He sat silently and watched as the detective transferred the writers' thoughts to separate pieces of paper. It did not take long. Santoro looked up.

"These two letters are to the young man who was killed. One was from his father, one from his godfather. Both begged him to stop whatever business he was doing, straighten up his life and be a better man." Santoro looked at the letters with regret. "With your permission, I will send letters to both men with our condolences."

"Farrell wants us here at 8:00 am. Do it in the morning," Hart returned. "Let's go home for a while," he added, grabbing his coat.

In the morning, Farrell, Santoro, and Patrolmen Butler and McGrath were sitting in the detective's room. Butler and McGrath grumbled about the timing. They had gotten off at midnight and were already back in action.

"Get over it," snapped Farrell. "This is my day off! How do you think I feel!"

"Where's Hart?"

"In my office making a phone call he couldn't make last night. A lead on the murder. In New York City."

The matron came in with a hot pot of coffee from her apartment at the back of the station.

"Thank you, Mrs. Farr," the men all rang out. It was just what they needed after walking to work in the cold. They drank in silence, waiting.

"I don't see how a kid from Italy could have set up such a scheme so fast!" Hart burst into the detective room with a pad of paper filled with notes.

Farrell sat up from his upholstered chair and set down his newspaper. "What did you find?"

"Here he gets off the boat, probably with guns and razors already. You know how those Italians are, bringing all makes and models of weapons with them. He gets a mail drop at a steamship agency, Italian, of course, in New York. Then he dresses like a bum and goes all over the East Coast, it looks like, extorting money from fellow Italians."

"Another Black Hand?" asked McGrath.

"Possibly," answered Hart. "And, there is more! It looks like the kid stored his trunk at the steamship agency a while back. Then, last week, he came to get it and they couldn't find it. They had to pay him for the lost goods. A few days later, they find it. Since they already paid for it, they opened it."

"Let me guess!" interrupted Butler. "They found stuff that would be useful in his apparent line of work?"

"You are right! Some chloroform, with a receipt from a pharmacy in Scranton, a textbook on how to use nitroglycerin and a few guns."

"Kid was up to no good, I see," Farrell mused.

"I figured all these Italian villains were going to be in the past when that gang was sentenced in New Haven a year and a half ago," Butler commented.

"I figured that they were part of a bigger New York gang and were sent to New Haven to organize some activities for them. How many were there?"

"Five."

"The leader and the other four were probably just the tip of the iceberg. Who knows how many others were in New Haven with him and didn't get caught. They found the ringleader in New York after he robbed that guy here in Connecticut."

"I have to agree with you," Hart responded. "Five is not that big a gang for organizing a city the size of New Haven. Especially if they were doing all the leg work, themselves. Could be there are more and are staying quiet for a year or two."

"Looks like this kid, Pietrolino, doesn't fit with that group. He appears to be a loner, or at least, not with those boys."

"We still don't have any definite leads, Captain," Hart said, getting more serious. "Best we can do so far is listen to the rumors. And you know how those Italians are. Tight-lipped, every one of them."

"Well, what else have you got so far?"

"From the talk around, seems like Pietrolino may have been to Hartford before. Some people seemed to know him and what he was about. Some of those people may have wanted to defend their property, and saw him as someone who was trying to get hold of their assets."

"Yes, well, we knew that!"

"Apparently, a deputation of several men was sent to meet him. They probably walked to that lot where we found the body. I'd say either the talk didn't go too well or they were told to stop him."

"Most likely those men were Italian, too. Considering what George, here, saw." Ferrell nodded in Butler's direction.

"Most likely," Hart agreed.

"I just hope this Black Hand, or whatever it really is, stops. This dirty murder stuff has the makings of a good detective story but it scares too many, especially the closer to New York that you get. And you wonder why we think these Italians are vicious ignorants. Certain parties excepted," Farrell said, nodding to Santoro.

"Or how about the extortion and bombings that you hear about. Not here, in Hartford, so much, but south of here, surely. Give me a good bigamy case. It is so much easier!" Hart agreed.

"I think we should work some extra angles," the captain pondered. "Santoro, I want you to do some hunting around in the Italian district. Ask questions. Especially ask around the railroad station. That's how this kid got into town. See if anyone knows his mug. Get a photo from the morgue. Spend a few days on it."

"Sure, Captain," the detective sergeant replied. He was the most likely person to be asked to do it, since he spoke both English and Italian fluently.

"I am interested in finding out if this was a job from some crazies in the neighborhood or did they do this as self-defense. We are looking for a motive. I can't blame them if they did it for protection."

"I am willing to bet these poor immigrants have had it with people going after their hard-earned money," responded Santoro, playing with the waxed and twisted ends of his mustache as he analyzed the situation. "I know a few of the businesses around the train station. I'll start there this afternoon."

"Thanks, Santoro," the captain replied.

Frank Santoro walked out to the evidence room to look at what the police department had so far. In one small, labeled box there were a gun, those letters in Italian plus a copy of the translations, several photos of the dead man, including a close up of his face, and a stamped train ticket. Not much to go on. Santoro picked up the close up shot. Not a bad looking kid. Almost innocent-looking, he thought. A sorry thing that he turned into scum when he got off the boat. The train ticket was a round trip ticket from New Haven to Hartford. There were implications, there. The boys in the squad room had been talking about the New Haven gang. Was this boy connected?

"Not going to get any answers from this little collection," Santoro muttered to himself. He took the close up photo and put it in his pocket. Then he put the cover back on the box and put it on the "active" shelf.

Next he read the preliminary reports, written in long-hand by a variety of officers. There was nothing he did not already know in them. So, Santoro went back into the detective squad room and grabbed his coat and boots.

"Got what you need?" asked Hart.

When Santoro answered in the affirmative, Hart wished him luck.

Santoro trudged through the slush over Main Street and over Asylum until he could see the train tracks. It was around here that the murder took place. Someone should have seen or heard something. He spent the early afternoon knocking on business doors and asking questions. No luck.

He decided on another tactic, an indirect one. And he knew where to start.

Amato's Barber Shop was fairly busy in the later part of the afternoon. Men who got off their shifts early, or who were lucky enough to be on an extended New Year's holiday, would be stopping by to read the newspaper or chat. Amato often had the latest copy of *La Verita,* the Italian language newspaper, in the shop along with the day's Courant. Santoro figured that he could ask questions of two or three at a time this way.

Traffic was light and the street lights were already beginning to come on as Santoro headed up the stairs to the small stoop leading to the shop. There was one man in each chair, draped with a big sheet so as not to get any hair on their clothes. They were conversing in Italian.

"Hey, Frank!" Giuseppe greeted the detective, switching to English. "How's it going? Need a shave? Trim?" He had his greeting down pat and could talk without looking up from his scissors and comb.

"Hi, Joe! I need both today. The mustache is getting in my sauce!" Giuseppe knew many of the policemen of the town, especially those of Italian descent. They frequented his shop for the gossip and the discount.

"What's new?" Giuseppe asked. Santoro was normally full of good stories.

"Oh, just walking around today and talking to people." Santoro was typically too serious to go walking on a winter's day to chat with pedestrians. So Giuseppe figured he was around to ask about a certain topic. He had seen too many *polizzia* in Italy try that tactic, looking for suspects. So, he bided his time telling little stories about his five girls and the new baby, whom he hoped, this time, would be a boy! Santoro could not seem to get a word in.

Eventually, the two customers were clean, paid and gone. And Giuseppe could pay attention to his customer who always tipped.

"So, what do you need?" he asked. Santoro got into the new chair.

"I need to know the gossip about that kid from New York who got killed here in town last night." Santoro was blunt.

"And you think I know something, eh?" Giuseppe threw a sheet around the police detective's neck and pinned it at the back.

"You run a barbershop. You know everyone in the neighborhood. He wasn't killed too far from here. I think you should have heard something by now."

Giuseppe laughed. "You make a good detective, you know, Frank? You put two and two together fast." He began to trim Frank's thick, impressive mustache. "Here is what I can tell you. That boy, Pietrolino, he was a pain in the ass! He was, how you say, a bully. He had been to this area once before. Last fall. He tried to muscle in on another's territory."

"Whose?"

"Never you mind who! That is irrelevant! Let us just say that there are some insurance people around here. They protect you so nobody break into you business."

Frank pulled his head to get a good look at his barber. "Did they get you to sign up, Joe?"

Giuseppe tilted Frank's head to the right and started clipping around his ear. "That is none of your business. You want the story or don't you?"

"Fine. Go on."

"So. The insurance people say to him, get out. So, he goes off and nobody sees him for months. They figure he's gone." Giuseppe tilted Frank's head a little in the other direction. "A few days after the Holy Day, the kid he shows up again. He don't learn the lesson too good. The insurance people, again, tell him to get out. This time, he say he can carve out a business for hisself. Stupid boy."

"But who killed him?"

"Best I hear is that some insurance people were supposed to meet with him. I guess he said something they didn't want to hear, eh?" Giuseppe chuckled.

"You aren't going to tell me who the insurance people are?" Frank felt the barber was holding back.

"No. I just tell you what I hear. I don't know for sure." He took the sheet off from around Santoro's neck and shook it. Then he wiped the hairs off his patron's neck with a small whisk broom. "Why do you care about this silly boy? He isn't even from here."

"I don't like anyone getting hurt while I am a police officer. It's an honor thing. And if a person does get hurt on my watch, I want to bring the perpetrator to justice."

"You want to finish, eh?"

"That is a good way of putting it. As a detective, I want to finish the job I start. And that includes finding out all the answers to my questions."

"Well, Frank," Giuseppe said, combing a little pomade into his hair. "I wish I could help you, but I don't know any more than what I said. Somebody does. But not me, I am sorry to say."

"Who would know more?" Santoro asked, straightening his jacket and tie. "I want answers, Joe."

"That is something I do not know, also," Giuseppe replied. He actually did not know where Tony lived, even if he lived in Hartford or not. But he figured Tony had something to do with it. But that would just be a guess on his part. And he was not going to mention names on a hunch, only if he was sure.

Santoro got up, handed Giuseppe two quarters and grabbed his coat.

"Being generous today, eh, Frank?" Giuseppe smiled. "Wait until you have as many kids as I do! Then you will know how much I appreciate it."

"You help me and I help you," was the retort. "And if this is a contest, I will have one more kid than you!" They both laughed.

Santoro Frank left the shop and walked into the growing dusk, dissatisfied with the little he was able to find.

CHAPTER 35

Giovanni and Rafaella appeared to have a smoother relationship with more money coming in. Their boarder, Vincenzo Fiore, was polite, helpful, neat and prompt with his payments every week. Fiore was a little man with thin, greying hair, a pencil-thin mustache and the ability to tell stories, which entertained the two little boys for hours. Rafaella was glad to have him around. Vincenzo also worked second shift at a local factory, which meant that he was around to entertain the children in the mornings while Rafaella cleaned and shopped or visited her friends.

"Signor Fiore, I need to go talk to Carmela Amato for a little while," Rafaella announced mid-morning as her tenant was telling the story of Garibaldi's joining all of Italy to the two very attentive boys.

"Sure, sure, Signora Tassone. I be telling the story for longtime yet," he responded. "You take the little one?"

"*Si!* I will! I won't be gone too long!" Rafaella swept the toddling Teresa up into her arms and carried her downstairs.

The Amato apartment door was open all day until it was time for the children to go to bed. The little ones played in the poorly lit hallways and the older ones ran up and down the gangplank and stairs and as far as the public sidewalk all day long. Mothers took turns supervising the multitude of children who poured out of the tenement on a nice day. Raffaela's boys were too little to go out on their own, so she happily left them with Vincenzo and went downstairs to the Amatos.

"*Buon giorno,* Signora Tassone!" the two oldest called out as she walked in the apartment door. The apartment had the look of perpetual chaos. The furniture was cheap, at best. The kitchen table was sturdy but the paint on the legs had chipped over the years. The chairs did not all match, as was expected in a household that kept growing. The sofa was worn with the children climbing on and off, and it had an aroma which indicated that too many diapers had been changed there. As a matter of fact, there was a small pot beside the sofa with dirty diapers waiting to be washed. The windows needed cleaning and so did the floor.

The one feature that did not fit in was a charcoal drawing of Giuseppe, full length, full size, sitting in a pine pedestal frame in the sitting area, a token of appreciation to himself, one would think. All in all, the home of the Amato family represented a woman who was overwhelmed with her responsibilities and could not prioritize well.

Anna was standing precariously on a chair washing the morning dishes. Teresa was kneeling on a chair beside the kitchen table laboriously stirring bread dough as her mother measured more flour into the bowl. Teresa was a stern-looking little girl with a beautiful head of bright auburn curls, just like her mother's had been at that age. Anna had beautifully chiseled looks even at 6, blue eyes like diamonds and dark hair like her father. They were a big help to their mother. Dora and Maria Annunziata were playing with their dolls on the floor. The babies were napping in their bedroom.

"*Buon giorno, bambini!*" Rafaella cheerfully responded.

"Ah! Rafaella! Help yourself to some coffee!" Carmela said, indicating the pot on the top of the stove that seemed always to be full. "Maria is coming down soon. She has a letter from my brother, Ciro. Nickie stopped by to tell me this morning when he went out to work."

"Nickie is so big, now. I remember he was still a little boy when we moved in. Now he is 15? It does not seem possible."

"Nickie is my big cousin!" Anna commented from the scullery. "He takes us for walks sometimes. And especially on school days. He takes us to school."

"That is very nice of your cousin," commented Rafaella.

"Yes. Ever since last year, Giuseppe insists that the girls be accompanied to school. He says it is too much for them to cross the streets with all the cars on the roads nowadays. Too dangerous."

"That is true. My Frankie will start school in the fall. Perhaps Nickie can walk him to school also?"

"Certainly. I am sure he won't mind one more." Teresa stopped stirring and Carmela turned her attention to her oldest. "It is time to knead the bread. Do you remember how I taught you?" Teresa nodded and proceeded to turn the dough out onto the big wooden board where she showed her mother how well she had learned. "Not too many times. Just until the dough is not sticky." Carmela turned back to her guest.

"Are the boys with Signore Fiore again?"

"Yes. It is wonderful having him around. I am so spoiled. He says he does not have a wife so he will treat me as well as one so he can practice being a husband."

Carmela raised an eyebrow. "I would watch a man who would get so familiar like that. Maybe you should consider getting another boarder. He has been there almost two years, now."

"I thought he was just being a gentleman. I don't think there is any harm. Besides, what other boarder would watch my children so I can go shopping alone?"

"I think you should watch your step, Rafaella." Carmela went back to watching Teresa. "That is good. Now, cut the dough in half and flatten the two halves without letting them touch each other."

"I know, Mama!" Teresa insisted. Carmela smiled and patted her daughter's arm. The little girl smiled back and went back to work.

Anna climbed off her chair, dragged the chair back to the kitchen table and smiled up at her mother. "I did all the dishes, Mama!"

"Good girl," Carmela nodded and patted her shoulder. "Now, go play with the girls so that Signora Tassone and I can talk. Zia Maria will come down with Frankie in a little while." Anna happily went to be with her sisters and started drawing pictures for them.

"It is easy to get too familiar, Rafaella," the older woman began again to warn her friend in quiet tones. "You must always watch yourself."

"But it is comfortable to be able to talk to a man who is caring. And Giovanni is so much calmer and polite with me since Vincenzo has moved in. I feel more comfortable with him."

"*Buon giorno*, Rafaella, Carmela!" Maria announced herself. She had four year old Frankie with her. He pulled away from her and ran over to his little cousins. Maria had grown stouter through the years and her dark hair had gotten grey at the temples. She greeted the little girls who all came over to kiss their aunt.

Teresa had just finished putting the loaves on the counter to rise. She washed off the table to make room for her aunt then went over to the other children to enjoy a few minutes of quiet.

Maria took a cup from the stack on the counter, poured herself some coffee from the pot on the stove and sat down. She pulled a letter out of her pocket and unfolded it. "Let me read the letter to you!" She pushed the paper away from her and adjusted her focus:

My very dear sisters,

I hope that this finds you and all my nieces and nephews well.

Emilia and I have moved into a new apartment on High Street in Newark. Same building as Giuseppe. Emilia is very homesick for her sisters and so, we still go up to Rome every few months. But, my business is developing well and I cannot move away. I find it exciting to realize that in just ten years here, I have succeeded more than all the years I worked with Papa at the blacksmith shop. Now, I am not a blacksmith, but a building designer and builder.And that pleases Mama. I hope Papa looks down from Heaven and smiles when he sees how well I do.

Last time I heard from Stella, she said that in Mama was finally getting around again. Rosaria's early death affected her very much. It has been six years! And with Gennaro and the children having moved away to America, too, Mama only has Stella and Bruno left. I worry about her. But my place is here now.

Emilia is no longer interested in having a family after the baby died. I understand this. She is still in mourning. Please pray for her. And the baby.

Giuseppe, Serafina and the family are doing well. Even though we live in the same apartment building, we see them only occasionally for dinners, mostly on Sundays. His boys and Marianna are getting big and little Stella is starting to crawl. They send greetings.

Let us know how you are doing. We miss you all.

Sempre con tanto amore,
Ciro

Maria wiped her eyes with the edge of her apron. "I miss Ciro! I wish he got to visit us more often."

"I wish my family wrote more," said Rafaella dreamily. "And I wish I could see them more."

"It has been two years since you saw them," commented Carmela. "Why don't you go out to see them?"

"Oh, Giovanni would never allow me to go again."

"That is too bad," Carmela replied. "The children do not see their Uncle Bruno, either. Does Giovanni see his brother?"

"No. They do not agree on anything. They rarely say hello if they pass each other on the streets."

"Perhaps you should talk to Giovanni. He has enough money. The children should see their grandparents when they can. Going to Rhode Island is certainly not like going home to Italy." Maria was looking at her little boy playing dolls with his cousins. "My children are so blessed to have their cousins right downstairs. Family is so important."

"Maybe I could talk to Giovanni. We haven't discussed this in a long time, not since I got back from Providence, when Teresa was born."

"Sure, sure!" encouraged Carmela. "You should talk to him. I know I wish I could speak to my mother again.

Letters are rare when they come. I miss her."

Rafaella pondered the advice as she looked into her empty coffee cup. "I will plan everything and then propose the idea to my husband. Could I depend on you to help with the cooking if I went for two weeks, or so?"

"Certainly," responded Maria. "I am sure Giovanni would be welcome to share dinner with one of us every night. I could do one evening and Carmela could do another. When you are cooking for our families, what is one or two more mouths to feed!"

"I do not think either Dominick or Giuseppe would mind. It is only for a little while, anyhow." Carmela smiled at her young neighbor.

Rafaella happily clapped her hands. "My family has not seen the boys in over three years! It would be so good to show them how big they are getting!" She looked out a window and noticed the shadows were short. "It is getting late. I must make dinner for Vincenzo before he leaves for work." She stood up. "Thank you for your advice, both of you! I will see you later. *Ciao!*" She called for little Teresa, scooped her up and hurried out the door.

Maria cocked an eye brow and looked at Carmela. In a low voice she said, "Did you see the bruise on her neck? And the cut on her forehead that she tried to hide with her curls? Something bad is happening to her."

Carmela nodded in agreement, then thoughtfully picked up the bag of rags she was collecting for the ragman's semi-annual collection. "Do you think we should help her by giving her the five cents a pound we get for these things?"

"I do not think that will help her, poor thing," answered Maria.

CHAPTER 36

HARTFORD, MAY 1912

"Again with the traveling!? Can you never be satisfied to stay put with your children and your husband? Must you always look elsewhere for entertainment?"

Raffaela's proposal to Giovanni had not been received well. They were in their bedroom, where she thought her proposal would be best presented if she could look somewhat enticing. It did not work. Wearing her ivory nightgown with the pink ribbons and her hair brushed out and pulled back with a matching pink ribbon only made her look like a waif trying to dress like one of those Christmas angels the Americans put on top of their Christmas trees.

To Giovanni, she looked like a child too young to make decisions.

"I miss them, Giovanni. I have not seen them in two years!" Rafaella pleaded. "They haven't seen the boys in three years." She sat on the edge of the bed and tried to restrain the tears of disappointment.

"Write them a letter!" was the retort.

"I want to see them!" She had worked herself up to anxiety in the planning of this proposal. She had been so sure that if she could just explain how well she had planned the whole thing that he would listen. He was not doing any such thing. He was undressing for bed and not listening to her needs.

"You are acting like a spoiled child again, Rafaella. And what did I tell you would happen the next time you behaved like that?" He unbuckled his belt and yanked it through the pant loops. Without a second's hesitation, he stepped towards his wife and swatted her bare legs with the leather.

"No!" she cried, trying to tuck her legs under the nightgown. He hit her again, this time on her shoulder. "Giovanni! Don't!"

Intuitively, she turned away from him, exposing her other shoulder to his belt and again it came down. Rafaella had gone through this enough times to know how to bite her lip and utter very little sound. She did not want to wake up the children in the room next door. She curled up in a fetal position and let the rain of blows come.

Giovanni finally dropped the belt and grabbed her hair with his right hand and her neck with his left hand, hauling her up further on the bed. "You need a lesson on how to obey your husband. Your problem is that you need another baby. And I will make sure that happens tonight."

He squeezed her neck so hard that she could barely breathe. The pain in her shoulders was so great she could not push him away. She looked at his contorted, red face with fear.

He laughed. "Ah, I see I am making you understand, at last!" And, with that, he fulfilled his promise of another baby that night.

In the morning, Rafaella had difficulty moving her arms. She could not put her hair up so braided it as best she could and left it as is.

Giovanni had laughed after he was finished with her the night before. "That was a good one!" he had sneered. "Bet you will be sore in the morning. I bet even that dull Vincenzo will notice you won't be walking as well. And then he will know what he is missing, not having a wife of his own!"

As predicted, Vincenzo noticed her awkwardness

after Giovanni left for work. "*Scusi, signora!*" he began. "But are you well?"

"I . . . I will be well in a while. Just a little sore from all the cleaning I did yesterday," she lied.

"Please, *signora*! You do not seem well. And, when I came back from work, I heard . . . things. I am worried for you."

"Please, Vincenzo. Really, I am f . . . fine." She reached to open a cabinet door and pulled back with a squeal of pain. He ran over and opened the door for her.

"*Signora*! You are in pain. I can see." In a very uncustomary fashion, Vincenzo took her hand and walked her over to the kitchen table. The children were all playing quietly in their bedroom, Frankie reading a primer to his younger siblings. Rafaella sat, gingerly, looking down at the table, somewhat embarrassed about the attention she was getting. Vincenzo sat opposite, with a concerned look on his face.

"Giovanni maybe is a good man, but he gets angry too quickly. I see it all the time. And I have suspected for some time that he hurts you." Rafaella opened her mouth to object and he raised a hand to silence her. "I do not have a wife. But I know how to treat a lady. And he does not. Some day he may kill you if you do not leave him."

Rafaella looked up at him in surprise. She had thought that the treatment she got was sad and uncomfortable, but she did not think it a precursor to murder. "I . . . I do not think of it that way."

"I think, and excuse my boldness, *signora*, I think that you need to leave."

"Please, Vincenzo. I cannot leave Giovanni. I have no . . . no money of my own."

"Then, please, Rafaella! Come with me and I will take care of you." Rafaella had shrunk back at his calling her by her first name. She stared at him as the second half of what he said penetrated her mind.

"I thought about it this morning," continued Vincenzo. "I have savings. We can go to Philadelphia, where I have family. You would be safe with them. And I could get a job there, easily."

Rafaella teared up, for the first time in a long time. She actually had someone who knew what was happening and could help her.

"Th...thank you, Vincenzo. You are very kind. But I would rather go home to my parents. I am very homesick and the children should know their grandparents. I am . . . I am going to figure out a way to go."

"Well," said Vincenzo, slowly. "I can give you some money to help you on your trip. Let us call this a "goodby present." I was planning on moving on to Philadelphia soon, anyhow."

Rafaella gulped back her tears and looked at him.

"You are very kind, Vincenzo. I will remember you fondly. When . . . when will you leave?"

"I will leave as soon as I know you will be well."

"Thank you. If you . . . you will excuse me, please. I . . . I need to go talk to Carmela Amato." She stood, painfully slowly. "Would you be so kind as to watch the children? I will only be gone half an hour."

"Certainly, *signora*." He reverted to a formal address. "I would be glad to spend some time with them."

Rafaella left her apartment and went down to Carmela's. As usual, the door was open. The little ones were in the hallway, playing with their cousin Frankie. Carmela was changing diapers on baby Giuseppe, with little Julia holding onto her skirts and sucking her thumb. Anna and Teresa were at school.

One look at Rafaella and Carmela gasped. "Sit right

there, Rafaella. I will be right with you." Carmela pointed out a kitchen chair for her friend. She put a rug next to the old sofa, placed two month old Giuseppe on his back on it, gave a doll to 18 month old Julia, and laid two kitchen chairs on their sides to keep Julia from wandering. Then she went to the hall door and called to her number three daughter. "Nunziata, I am going to close this door for a few minutes. You knock if you want to come in, but you and Dora and Frankie stay in the hall and be good. No questions."

"*Si*, Mama," responded the five year old, who went back to playing.

Then Carmela turned to Rafaella. "Let me get you a cup of coffee, my dear." She grabbed a cup from the counter and went to the stove to pour out the already-made coffee.

All this time, Rafaella sat, like a wilted flower, exhausted. Knowing that she had friends who could help her with shouldering her burden was suddenly very important to her. Until now, she had always hidden the problem or denied what others suspected. Except, of course, when her father saw the bruises two years ago. He was not around now, however, to do anything for her.

Carmela handed her friend the cup and sat knee to knee with her, watching her sip the steamy black drink, holding it with two hands. "What happened last night?" She did not mince words. She saw the stiffness in her walk, how she had sat down slowly and the tragic, pained look in her eyes. Last night was not a normal evening at the Tassone household. That was evident.

"I asked . . . I asked Giovanni to . . . to let me go see my . . . my parents." The tears started to run down her cheeks. "He got angry." She shuddered. "He was so very angry!" She closed her eyes and watched the scene in the bedroom all over again.

"Did he beat you?" Carmela asked.

Rafaella nodded. She could not admit to what else had happened.

"Do the wounds need treating?"

Rafaella looked at her blankly.

"Let me see, dear."

Rafaella pulled up her skirts. She had no stockings on. It hurt too much to bend over that morning. There were several welts raised by the belt. But the skin was not broken. Then she proceeded to unbutton her shirtwaist and expose her shoulders. Here the skin was swollen, black and blue, and crusted over with blood. The effect was shocking.

"*Mio Dio!*" Carmela jumped off her chair, ran to the sink and filled a pan with cold water. She got a towel and brought it over to the table. There she carefully touched the shoulders with the wet towel, cleaning the wounds and trying to reduce the swelling a little. Rafaella winced from time to time but made no further conversation. After doing the best she could, Carmela took the pan away and emptied it. Then she refilled the coffee cup from the pot still simmering on the stove and handed it to Rafaella.

"How long has this been going on, Rafaella?" Carmela's face was stern. Her imagination was going in a hundred directions.

"The whole marriage. But it was never this bad before." Rafaella took a sip of the coffee to warm up after that cold water treatment. "Vincenzo says Giovanni could kill me."

"Signor Fiore knows?"

"I didn't know he was aware until this morning. He asked me to go away with him."

"OH!" Carmela squealed in surprise. "What did you

say?"

"I thanked him. But I want to go home to my parents. He said he would give me some money to go." She kept her hands around the cup and stared into the warm liquid, avoiding eye contact.

"Signor Fiore is a better man than I would expect," Carmela commented, nodding. "I am sure Giuseppe will help with the rest. Maybe Dominick can help."

Rafaella looked up from her coffee cup with a surprised look. "You think they would?"

"Once they find out what happened, how could they not help? I will talk to my husband when he gets home. He should be here soon for lunch."

Rafaella set her cup down and rose slowly from her chair. "I do not want to have Giuseppe see me today. I had better leave. The children need their lunches and Teresa needs her nap soon."

Carmela stood with her. She took Rafaella's two hands in hers and looked at her, very concerned. "You are a good friend, Rafaella. I should have seen this a long time ago. Thank you for sharing. We will help."

Rafaella left, leaving the door to the hallway opened for the children.

Nunziata knew she had something important to tell her big sisters when they got home from school. She was not sure but she thought Frank and Bruno's mother was going to run away.

Giuseppe had an hour for lunch every day. He would lock his door to the shop after putting up a sign in the window, "Back in One Hour!" Then he would walk down the few steps to the sidewalk, around to the gangway to the apartment house door and up one flight of stairs. Rare was the day when he did not have to pick his way through a dozen children, just out of toddlerhood, playing on the floors with their balls and sticks and dolls, in the dim light of a single naked bulb. Most of the apartment doors were open this time of day and the aroma of sauce, soup and garlic mingled with the less pleasant aroma of lye and dirty diapers. He noticed these things with disdain as he walked to his own apartment.

Carmela was waiting expectantly. Giuseppe took off his signature straw hat and his suit jacket and tossed them on an empty chair. His place at the table was set and the minestrone soup was simmering on the stove, waiting to be ladled out. A loaf of bread was on the table. His two middle girls were standing on chairs at the sink washing their hands in preparation for lunch. The babies were asleep. As soon as Giuseppe sat down, Carmela served him his soup. The little girls were given their bowls and spoons and told to go out and sit in the hall, which they happily did.

Carmela sat to his left, but without any soup. She turned to him, with a serious expression. "Giuseppe. I need some money."

The soup spoon, halfway to his mouth, stood in suspended animation as he gazed at her. "I am not a bank, *cara*," he said. "Why do you need money all of a sudden? We have been having a rough time of it for a long time. We have managed through. Now, you need money?"

"It is not for me, *mio marito*!" Carmela wanted to explain. She placed her hand on his free one and looked at him pleadingly.

Giuseppe slurped the soup from the spoon and then set it down. "What is this about? Maria needs shoes for Peter and does not want to tell Dominick?" He tried to make a joke because he was concerned about this unusual request. His wife was taking this too seriously.

"Rafaella needs to leave Giuseppe. Immediately. She has to go home to Providence."

"Why? I thought everything was fine since the last time she came back."

"Everything is not well. He beats her."

"What is that to me? Most men slap their wives when they step out of line."

"Listen to me! He beats her! She can hardly move today. If you could see the wounds, you would not say that."

"Are you sure she did not trip and just say he beat her for the sympathy? She is a child, sometimes."

"No, Giuseppe! I saw with my own eyes! If he does it again, he will probably kill her! Her whole body is swollen and bruised. And I think he was even more cruel than that. But I do not think she would tell me anything more." She raised an eyebrow knowingly.

Giuseppe looked at her and was silent for a moment. She would have him pull a five dollar bill out of his hat! Was he a magician? At the same time, Rafaella was a distant cousin. And family is family! "I do not have much. Maybe two dollars. That should help get her to Providence."

Carmela's tense face relaxed. "That, and the money Signor Fiore will give her, should be sufficient."

"What? Vincenzo knows?"

"He talked to her this morning. He had figured out the whole situation. He offered to help."

"Probably wanted her for himself. She is still a beautiful woman." Giuseppe snorted and turned back to his soup. Carmela knew enough not to tell Giuseppe all that Vincenzo Fiore had said. She simply responded, "She wants to go back to her parents."

"It is probably best," Giuseppe agreed and pulled a

large chunk off the loaf of bread and dunked it in the soup.

"When can you do this?" Carmela urged him back on to the subject.

"I will see how much I make today. If I have to go to the bank, it will be tomorrow. We do not touch the emergency money, right?" He looked at her, expecting acknowledgement.

Carmela stood up and stepped behind her seated husband to throw her arms around him. "You will be blessed here on earth and also in Heaven for your good deed!" she murmured in his ear.

"I should be so lucky!" he said, pulling her arms away so he could finish his food. He smiled, glad to bring a little joy to his overworked wife. He popped the last of the bread into his mouth, wiped his hands with a *mapine* and stood up. "Best get to the shop early. If I am going to spend such money, even for a good cause, I had better catch any extra quarters that I can." He slipped on his suit jacket, placed his straw hat on at a jaunty angle.

Just before he walked out the door, he turned to his wife and said, "If anyone asks, I know nothing. If Giovanni is doing as you say, he must be led away from her and I will probably have to do it!"

He left, being careful not to step on either of his daughters still sitting on the floor with their empty bowls.

CHAPTER 37

HARTFORD, 1930

"So, the neighbors were right? Your parents did help Mrs. Tassone leave!" Santoro proclaimed triumphantly.

"I suppose," said the young lady quietly. "I don't think they would have pushed her to do it. I think the poor woman just needed some assistance."

Santoro nodded absentmindedly as he flipped to a hand-written yellowed page. "According to the hospital reports, Mrs. Tassone had a variety of healing bruises. So, I guess your story goes with the evidence."

Watching Anna Amato's face, he again noticed how much she looked like Giuseppe.

CHAPTER 38

PROVIDENCE, MAY, 1912

Carmela shared Rafaella's news with Maria, and Maria it shared with Dominick. Despite the severe money difficulties the families had, Dominick gave Maria two dollars for Rafaella's trip. In all, including the help of Vincenzo, by the end of two days, there were ten dollars. It was enough for a train ride and more. Rafaella rapidly made plans to go home.

"Ten dollars will pay for you and the baby to go to Providence. Plus some living expenses for a while," assured Carmela. "We will watch the boys for you and we will make sure Giovanni has food for a while. As soon as you get a place, we will arrange for Frankie and Bruno to join you."

"I wish I could take them with me. But Papa would not be happy with three little ones underfoot all of a sudden. Giovanni has never shown that he would hurt them. I know they will be fine with you. Please make sure that they do not forget their mama when I am gone. It will be a while before I see them again." Rafaella choked back a sob, then asked, in a worried voice, "Do you think Giovanni will take out his anger on the boys?"

"My Dominick will not let that happen!" assured Maria. "When you begin to pack, I will have them come over to my place to play with Peter and my Frankie. They should not see their mother prepare to leave them."

Rafaella tearfully packed for two that Friday morning. She still could barely move her arms, but the swelling was down and her clothes fit better in the arms.

She had to pack fast. Giovanni left for work at 7:00 am and she wanted to take the 8:35 am train. Vincenzo was taking another train later, to leave town permanently. He offered to carry her bags.

She had kissed her little boys over and over until they pulled away, then she had sent them across the hall to the DeFrancescos. God only knew the next time she would see them, she thought later as she took little Teresa's hand.

She slowly walked out of the building, wearing her good summer dress, grey with lace at the neckline. Her hat was big enough to shade her face, but not big enough to hide it.

The neighbors saw her and Vincenzo together. He was carrying two bags. The gossipy women immediately chatted about the relationship and concluded that the two of them were running away together. That was good in the grand scheme of things. Giuseppe and Dominick could play that sentiment and mislead Giuseppe for days. Perhaps permanently. Food for days of speculation!

Rafaella did not care. She never wanted to be back in that building again!

They crossed the street and walked into Union Station. The train would be there any moment. Vincenzo bought her the ticket and waited with her, helping her onto the train steps and lifting the baby onto the platform. He shook her hand goodbye and walked away only when the train started to roll. The gossips did not see that part.

The train got into Providence just before noon. Vincenzo had sent a telegram the night before, notifying the Gentiles that Rafaella was coming. At such short notice, neither Alfonso nor Nico could get off work, but Johanna and Christina, Tomasso's wife, walked down to the station to greet the traveler and her daughter.

The two women excitedly walked through the crowded station looking for Rafaella and the baby and spotted her slowly getting down the train steps. She was very stiff and seemed to be having difficulty negotiating the few steps. The conductor was behind her, holding Teresa and one bag. Another gentleman was holding the second bag and Raffaela's arm, helping her off.

"What is wrong with Rafaella?" Johanna asked, squinting to see better in the sunlight. "She has always jumped down stairs easily."

Christina, younger, with better eyesight and a broader brimmed hat to keep out the sun, commented, "She seems unwell. Look! She is making Teresa walk, even though it is obvious the child wants to be carried."

As they got closer, Rafaella saw them. Instead of greeting them with a hug, she nodded and smiled, keeping her arms down at her sides, holding Teresa's hand.

"Come, my sweet baby!" crooned Johanna, picking up the child. "Give your *nonna* a kiss!"

Teresa looked at Johanna and then at Rafaella. The baby burst into tears and reached for her mother. Rafaella could not take her from Johanna. Nor could she pick up either of the bags.

"Never mind the bags!" said Christina. She quickly realized the nature of the problem and that Rafaella was not capable of lifting. "I will get a porter to find us a cab."

Johanna's mouth opened in protest at the cost, but Christina responded, "I have some dimes. It will do. It is not far." She summoned a porter and explained what she needed.

He picked up the bags and led the way to the front of the station where taxis were waiting for passengers. They all climbed into the taxi. Rafaella had trouble negotiating the running board, but finally got herself settled in, with her daughter on her lap for the one mile, uphill ride. The other two women asked no questions but just watched her face, trying to imagine the story she would tell.

Johanna called the family into dinner. It was 6:00 pm. Alfonso and Nico got out of work at 5:00 pm. They had just enough time to walk home and wash up before sitting down at the kitchen table. In honor of Raffaela's coming to visit, Tomasso and Christina squeezed an extra two chairs into the kitchen. Being Friday, the meatless dinner was *pasta ceci*, a garlicky and filling soup with pasta, garbanzo beans, and red sauce. Johanna served it with loaves of freshly baked bread and a bowl of black olives covered with spicy red pepper seeds. And, of course, the dry chianti that was present at most dinners was in all the glasses.

"So," began Alfonso. "We got your telegram last night that said you were coming. What is this all about? Your husband shoot someone else?" He was scowling in a most inhospitable way. "It is not that I am not happy to see you and the baby, God bless her. But why are you coming here alone? You should be with Giovanni. He is your husband."

"For God sakes, Pa! Look at her!" said Nico, concerned about his sister. She was sitting next to him and he was watching her expression at every move.

"What you talking about?"

"Pa! Ask her why she is not moving right. Look at her. She's in pain! It's obvious." He deliberately poked her in the shoulder and she yelped, then looked down, embarrassed.

Alfonso reached over and grabbed Raffaela's hand, forcing the spoon out from between her fingers and dumping soup on the tablecloth.

"Look at me!" he barked. Her head came up and she looked into his eyes. Alfonso squinted at her for a moment, going over in his head all the causes of this situation. He knew his daughter. There was probably only one. "Did Giovanni do this?" he asked. She nodded. "Did he leave marks?" She nodded again. At this point, all were listening, spoons suspended in air. He pulled his *mapine* off, and pushed back his chair. "God damn it!" he swore.

"Alfonso! Do not take the name of the Lord in vain!" Johanna reprimanded.

He ignored her statement. "Johanna! Right now. Take her into the bedroom. I want her to show you the marks!"

Johanna rarely saw her husband riled. She stood immediately and asked, "Do you want to see?"

"No! I don't want to see. I only want to know!"

Rafaella, who hadn't said a word, left the kitchen with Johanna. The others resumed their dinner, silently, each entertaining different thoughts about this revelation.

After five minutes, Johanna came back into the kitchen and sat down. She did not begin eating again and there was a thin stream of tears running down both cheeks.

"And so?" asked her husband. Johanna nodded but said nothing.

Rafaella came in a minute later and sat back down. She seemed to have gotten an appetite and began to eat.

Alfonso slammed his hand down on the table, making all the dishes jump, clank together and spill the soup.. Rafaella kept eating and the others stopped and looked at the head of the household. "I will kill him with my bare hands!" the older man announced.

"Pa! You are over 60! What are you talking about?" said Tomasso.

"Giovanni is not going to get away with it this time!" Alfonso did not want to argue with his son. "Jennie! Will she heal? My beautiful daughter!"

"She will heal on the outside in weeks," Johanna said quietly. "It is what has happened on the inside which will take time."

This was not a concept that an old Italian man was going to readily comprehend. He was interested in revenge.

Tomasso felt the need to direct the conversation. "Pa! Let's you, Nico and I go into the parlor. We'll have a shot or two and talk. How does that sound?"

His father got up, leaving his dinner unfinished, and left the room with his sons. The three ladies were left to clean up.

"Is it really bad?" asked Christina, cringing from the truth at the same time that she wanted to know all the gory details.

Johanna got teary again from the question and turned away, hand over mouth to stifle a sob.

Rafaella nodded as she finished her bread. She chewed the last of her dinner thoughtfully, and when finished said, "Giovanni has a bad temper. I don't want to go back."

"What about the boys?" asked Johanna.

"I was hoping someone could help me. I can't do it alone."

"You must heal before you can decide. Please, this is our home, but you should stay here for a while before you make up your mind." Johanna dabbed at her eyes with her napkin.

Christina said, "You need lots of rest to heal. How about I take Teresa sometimes so you can have a little time for yourself? Tomasso and I have no children, yet.

He would love to have a little one around to see."

"Thank you, Christina," said Rafaella. "In a few days, maybe. When she is more familiar with everyone."

Johanna cleaned up quickly as the sisters-in-law spoke. Then she insisted, "Time for you to go to sleep. Only rest will heal. Go. I will tell the men good night for you."

Rafaella left after bidding the two women good night.

Johanna turned to her daughter-in-law. "Go listen at the parlor door. I want to know what those three are up to.

Christina dutifully stood by the door listening until the men drifted off into different subjects. Then she went back to her mother-in-law to report.

"They were talking about a man named Pensara. They said they would contact him."

"Ah! Good!" commented Johanna.

Christina looked at the older woman quizzically.

"It is a long story,' Johanna said. "From years ago. Tomasso can tell you."

CHAPTER 39

FOURTH SORROW: THE MEETING OF JESUS AND MARY ON THE WAY OF THE CROSS

HARTFORD, MAY 1912

"What do you mean 'my wife isn't here'? My boys are here! Where is she?" Giovanni stood at the door, still dirty with sweat and smelling like sausage from work at the Armour Meat Packing plant. He had gone up to his apartment and right back down to the Amatos.

"Giovanni! I told you! Rafaella asked me to watch the boys for a while. That's all I know."

"When did she ask you?"

"Oh, sometime this afternoon," Carmela lied. "Sometime after I put the babies down for their naps," she added when he looked at her in a questioning way.

"Our boarder is also missing. His bag and all his belongings are gone. So are the baby's things." Giovanni stood by the door, arms crossed, not permitting passage to the hallway. "You know something. She is always down here talking to you. I know you know something." His voice was becoming louder.

"Well, Giovanni, why don't you come in and have a seat? Have a cup of coffee. Giuseppe should be home soon. Then you two can talk."

"He probably knows nothing. Wives don't tell their husbands any secrets! I want you to tell me where she is!" Giovanni was beginning to sound menacing even though he had not stepped into the apartment any further.

"Please, Giovanni! The children! Don't raise your

voice so. You will frighten them." Carmela's two oldest glanced at each other as they were setting the table for dinner. Nunziata looked up from where she was drawing pictures on the floor with Frank and Bruno, Giovanni's boys. They had barely noticed when their father showed up. They knew not to get underfoot before dinner time. Julia was sucking her thumb and holding onto her mother's skirts, a little frightened at Giovanni's barking voice. As if on cue, baby Giuseppe began to cry. Carmela went over to him as he lay on a blanket on the floor, and picked him up. She put him against her shoulder and went back to speak to her neighbor.

Giovanni was angry. He stepped into the kitchen and got in Carmela's face. "You tell me where she is or I will go to the police. I will tell them you talked her into some scheme and made her leave me! And if she ran off with Vincenzo, that's adultery! Which is against the law! I will tell them that you encouraged them. I should have known better than to let her talk to you people! Always putting ideas in her head! Bah!"

With that, he turned and walked down the hallway to the gangway to the first floor.

On the public sidewalk, Giovanni turned right and continued down to Asylum Street Not sure of what to do next, but boiling with rage, he turned left onto Asylum and just kept walking. By the end of a block, he heard someone calling him.

"Giovanni! Stop! Wait!" Giuseppe came running up behind his friend. The taller man stopped beside Giovanni to catch his breath. "Where are you going?"

"I am going to the police! My wife, she is gone! Her bag, the baby's things, even my boarder!" Giovanni looked accusingly at his friend.

"Yes, I know. My wife just told me."

"Your wife just told you!" Giovanni mimicked. "I'll bet you two planned the whole thing! She is too stupid to have done it herself without help."

Giuseppe was taken aback by the viciousness in Giovanni's voice but fell into step. They began to walk towards downtown together. "Look, *mio amico*, let me go with you to the police station. We can explain that you think she ran away with Vincenzo and you need their help getting her back."

"I am going to have you help me? You, who cannot control your own wife and let her gossip her way into other people's lives? Maybe if you would put the belt to her every once in a while, my wife would still be with me!" Giovanni walked ahead of Giuseppe but his shorter legs could not outpace his friend's stride.

"I do not think that my belt would have done anything to make your wife stay or go," Giuseppe defended himself. "Besides, I am too American to beat my wife. That is old-fashioned."

"Well, my wife knew who the boss was! And it was fine until we moved here to Hartford. Too many modern ideas!" Giovanni then began to panic. "What will I do without her? She even left me the two boys. How can I take care of them? Who will cook and clean for me? And," he added, turning to Giuseppe, "Who will warm my bed at night? I am used to it after ten years!"

"Don't worry about the boys," reassured Giuseppe. "Carmela and Maria always help when they can. The boys and you will be fed every day. You just help with the groceries."

"Ah, I see! This is all about money! Take away my boarder, reduce my income and then ask me for money! You are just like the rest of them! Money, money! All the time!" Giovanni's outburst was getting louder and people they passed on the street were watching the men argue. They shook their heads and moved to the other side of the sidewalk.

Within a few minutes, the two were on Main Street in front of the large, formidable police station. They climbed the steps to the main entrance and entered the marble-floored foyer. Both looked around in amazement at the well-appointed main hall with its columns and wainscoting. A moment's hesitation and they located the portly desk sergeant behind his overly-large oak structure across the wide room from the entrance. The desk top was not well organized, with papers of various shapes and sizes covering the L shaped writing surface. This was a man Giuseppe did not know.

Crossing the room in a rush, Giovanni arrived first at the desk and began in Italian, "Please, you have to find my wife for me! She ran away with our boarder! I need her back!"

The Yankee sergeant clenched his well-chewed cigar between his teeth, looked at Giovanni's wild-eyed appearance and took a sniff. His nose wrinkled. "Look, pal. I don't speak any I-talian. You speak English?"

Giuseppe spoke to Giovanni in Italian, "Giovanni, you have to speak English." Suddenly, going downtown with Giovanni seemed like a bad idea.

Giovanni was too overwrought to remember the little English he knew. "Tell him what is going on, Joe!" They argued for a moment in Italian, gesticulating animatedly, as to what Giuseppe should say.

Again the sergeant said, "Look, you wops! I don't speak I-talian and you don't speak English, I guess. So, get out of here and go bother someone else!" And he dismissed them with his hand, turning his attention back to his papers.

"Please, sir," Giuseppe began in English.

"No. Don't bother me." The sergeant barked. "You wops are all alike. Jabber, jabber! Not enough English! Go bother someone else!" the sergeant reiterated.

So, the two men, realizing that they were not going to be assisted by this representative of the police, walked out of the police department headquarters, down the staircase and onto the public sidewalk, again.

"I know who can help you," said Giuseppe. "Joe D'Esopo!" D'Esopo was a business owner and a leader in the Italian community, a friend to all. Giuseppe grabbed the other man's arm and walked him around the corner to Temple Street. They walked a block and turned into an alley. Two hundred feet down was a house with a sign over the front door reading "D'Esopo Mortuary Home". Giuseppe banged on the door. When there was no answer, he turned the handle, found it unlocked, and entered. He walked through the small, but tastefully decorated reception area and found the steps to the upstairs apartment. He climbed the stairs and knocked on the door. Giovanni was right behind him.

In a moment the door was answered by Joe D'Esopo, dressed in his dark work suit, still holding the *mapine* he had just removed from his lap. The smell of pasta and sauce came through the open door. It was dinner time and the door opened right into their dining room. Joe's wife, Mary, and two children were already seated at the table. D'Esopo was not happy being disturbed at his meal, but his quiet demeanor belied that.

"Can I help you?" he asked.

"Please, my wife! She has gone away with my boarder! I need to find her!" Giovanni jumped right in.

Joe nodded, then turned to his wife. "*Scusi, cara mia!*

Business, I'm afraid." He went back to the table, kissed the children and his wife and returned to the door. "Downstairs in my office, *per favore, amici.*" And he led the way down, walking with an obvious limp. A work-related accident, years before, when he was in the building business had partly disabled him, forcing him into this new line of work. They went to the back of the building, where he had a small office.

The room was done in maroon, with walnut wainscoting. It was a comforting look, a bit dark, but the lace curtains let in the early summer evening sun and sent patterns dancing on the maroon carpet. There was a large walnut and brass crucifix on the wall above D'Esopo's desk and two leather covered arm chairs in front of it. D'Esopo invited the men to sit on those chairs. Then he went around to the other side of his desk and sat in his larger chair. He placed his hands on the desk and regarded the men.

"Please, start the story from the beginning so I can understand," he said. With that, Giovanni and Giuseppe painted the picture of a young woman, not too smart, who ran away with the boarder and took the baby, but left the little boys motherless. Giovanni, agitated and animated, stumbled over his words and occasionally turned to Giuseppe for help. Giuseppe, on his part, supported the story.

After a few minutes, D'Esopo leaned back in his chair, put his hands together and rested his chin on the fingertips and closed his eyes. He remained quiet for a moment and then looked up. "Gentlemen," he addressed the two. "You need a private detective to look for her." He paused to watch their expressions. "The man I am thinking of charges two dollars a day plus expenses. But he is good and worth all the money. It may take a week or two, but he only charges for the days he does legwork."

He waited to see if there were any objections. Giovanni nodded in agreement.

"I do not think the police will help. She is probably out of the jurisdiction at this point, anyhow," D'Esopo said, anticipating that question. "Do you have any questions?"

The men said no.

"Good. I will get hold of him tomorrow. You come by tomorrow evening, after dinner. Say, about seven? I will have further information for you by then." He stood up, implying an end to the strange meeting interrupting his meal.

"Is that all?" asked Giovanni. "She must be found! She is my wife! She belongs to me! You don't understand!"

Giuseppe patted his shoulder. "Don't worry. D'Esopo, here, knows what he is doing." He stood up and reached his hand across the desk. "*Grazie!*" he said and shook hands with his host. Giovanni did likewise. Then they left for the walk back to Spruce Street in the evening light.

When Joe D'Esopo walked back upstairs to finish his dinner, he and Mary looked at each other. He sat down heavily on his chair and said, with a sorrowful expression, "I can understand why she would chose to leave him!"

CHAPTER 40

PROVIDENCE, JUNE, 1912

Rafaella was finally feeling better and taking short walks around Federal Hill, the Little Italy of Providence. Her father had insisted that it was fine for her to now do this. She enjoyed being home and not having to answer to her husband's questioning. She enjoyed being with Teresa and not having the rambunctious boys always underfoot. Not that she didn't love and cherish them; it was just nice to have a break. The busy food stalls and tiny grocery shops of her old neighborhood were a source of joy, also for Teresa. The old ladies were always giving her a piece of stick candy or a piece of fruit, in exchange for a moment of hugs and kisses from the adorable little toddler. So, on the second week of the visit, the two occupied themselves happily each morning, getting out of Johanna's hair for a little while so that she could have her house to herself.

Almost two weeks after her arrival, Rafaella, feeling up to staying awake past dinner, cornered her father in the parlor where he was playing cards with Nico. It was too hot to go to bed and the windows were all open in an attempt to catch a cross breeze.

"Papa! Are you going to keep your threat about Giovanni?"

"You don't need to know this," was the gruff reply.

"Papa! You are talking about my future!" she insisted.

"Look! I am the head of this household! When I decide you need to know, you will know!" He remained close-mouthed afterwards and resumed his game. Rafaella left the room and waited for her father to go to bed.

Then she decided to question Nico who was sitting on the sofa, reading a book. She peeked in and saw that he was alone, knocked once, like when they were children, and entered. "When did you start reading for fun?" she queried.

"When it stopped being forced on me," he answered. Nico put down his book. It was Jack London's *White Fang*. His sister sat beside him on the sofa and picked up the book.

"You have become a real American, reading books like these."

"Don't let Pa know I am reading adventure books. He would scoff at me, saying I am living in a dream world. I suppose I am. I know I will always work in the mills. But reading is my escape."

"I used to read all my friends' romance novels when I was in school. It is good to have dreams. Something to live up to." She sighed. "What's to become of me?"

Nico, her best friend from early childhood, as well as her brother, put his arm around her. "Well, sweets, it looks like Pa and Tomasso have arranged everything. So, don't you go worrying. No matter what happens in the next few weeks, remember that." He held her at arm's length and looked her in the eyes. "*Capisce?*"

She sighed and nodded. "*Si!* I understand." It was not what she wanted. But it was sufficient.

Rafaella kissed her brother's forehead. "I won't ask more. Good night, Nico!"

"Good night, sweets! Find a good book somewhere! Get lost in dreams, again."

She smiled and left.

Several days later, Rafaella woke to the smell of

coffee. She crawled out of bed easily so as not to disturb Teresa. Putting on her wrapper, she pulled open the drapes to look out the window. The sun had just risen and it promised to be a bright day. Still groggy with sleep, she walked out to the kitchen, the last of the adults to awaken. She slumped into a chair and Johanna pushed a fresh cup of coffee towards her. Picking up the mug, Rafaella took a sip and sighed.

"So, sleepyhead, are you finally feeling human again?" chided Nico.

Rafaella took a second sip of coffee and smiled. "I feel like the old days. Only I sleep with someone who still wets the bed occasionally." They all laughed at that and bantered back and forth for a few minutes until Johanna pulled the bread and cheese out and placed them on the table with some dishes. A moment of thankful prayer, and then they all chose their portions. Soon enough the men got up from the table to throw on their shirts and pull up their braces in preparation for work.

But before that was completed, there was a knock on the door. Johanna looked up from her plate.

"Who would be knocking on the door at 6:30 in the morning?" she asked, not expecting an answer. Nico was in the little vestibule and he opened the door.

Standing outside the door were two tall, burly Italian men and a smaller man between them. The smaller man held out official paperwork with a court seal. But one of the taller Italians did the talking. "Is this the home of Alfonso Gentile?"

"Yes," said Nico. "Can I help you?"

"Yes. We have reason to believe that Rafaella Tassone is on the premises. We have reason to believe that she is not here of her own free will, having been cajoled and duped into coming here. Her husband has hired us to find her and return her to his loving arms and those of her children."

Rafaella, still in the kitchen, gasped and began to rise off her chair,when Johanna pulled her down.

"I'm sorry, but I can't help you," Nico replied, pushing the door closed. But the bigger man put his foot in the way to prevent the door's closing and pushed back. Nico was no match. The door burst open and the three men walked into the vestibule. Alfonso, hearing the commotion, walked out of his bedroom still pulling up his suspenders.

"What is this? Why are you in my house early in the morning?" he demanded.

"We represent Giovanni Tassone and we are here to rescue his wife. We have court papers to prove it."

Alfonso was taken aback by the three. He looked at Nico, then at his wife, who had come out of the kitchen. "We cannot help you," he said staunchly.

"We have reason to believe she is here. We have questioned neighbors and we have credible witnesses. You can either cooperate or we can get the police to arrest you for kidnapping. Take your pick." Johanna blanched and grabbed her husband's arm. Alfonso shook her off then turned and whispered in her ear. She went back into the kitchen.

"You have no proof that we have kidnapped Rafaella," Nico challenged.

"We don't need proof. All we need is the fact that the husband did not give her permission to leave. So, if you are harboring her, you have essentially kidnapped her. Now, where is she?"

Nico opened his mouth to retort but, at that moment, Rafaella walked out of the kitchen. "I am here," she announced. "What do you want of me?"

"Mrs. Tassone, you are to come with us, now."

"As you can see, I am not correctly dressed. Can you give me an hour?" She held her head up and did not seem upset. The men looked at each other. They had expected a stupid, meek, childish thing, not this mature woman. The men nodded their acknowledgement. Johanna shooed them into the parlor and shut the door, promising them coffee in a few minutes.

It was only then that Rafaella let down her guard for a moment. She fell into Nico's arms. "Is it to start all over again?" she sobbed.

He pushed her away at arm's length, like he did the night that they talked. "Remember what I said. No matter what happens . . ."

"Yes, Nico, I will remember," she responded, wiping the tears from her face. Then she turned to her father. "Nico told me not to worry. Is this true?"

The old man felt very old at the moment. He, too, felt like crying. But, as a man, he had to do better. "I swear on your dead mother!" And he made the Sign of the Cross and the others followed suit. "Just do as they say for right now. It will be fine in a few weeks."

Rafaella kissed her brother and father goodbye. They had to leave for work. She went into the bedroom and returned half an hour later with her packed bags, her best grey dress and hat on, with the baby in tow.

She hugged Johanna tightly. "You will be back," Johanna promised. Then the step-mother opened the door to the parlor and invited the men out.

Walking very straight, Rafaella held her head high, tightly gripping little Teresa's hand and stepped out of the door and back into the life she thought she had fled. The men followed behind with her bags.

CHAPTER 41

HARTFORD, 1930

"How do you know all this?" asked Santoro suspiciously.

"I just don't forget much. I've always been like that. Mrs. Tassone came down to my mother once after returning. She cried her eyes out and told her every detail. Teresa and I listened at the door."

"Did she maintain her story?"

"I wouldn't know. Mr. Tassone never let her come down to the apartment again. I did hear my parents argue about these things one night. That's how I knew about Mr. D'Esopo."

"So, your father killed Mr. Tassone because he beat Mrs. Tassone and felt bad for her?" Santoro looked at her quizzically. "That doesn't make sense. We know that his escape was too well planned for a man who has never done anything like that before."

"I wouldn't know about that."

"Were there money problems?"

"I do remember that there were money problems. Not that they spoke about it." The young lady did not seem so reluctant to speak anymore. She apparently had come to terms with the subject and her excellent memory was retrieving minutiae from the past. "I mean, everyone has problems making ends meet. That is just the nature of life. But there seemed to be a mysterious underlying fear that was associated with money."

"Maybe the murder had something to do with the money fears," pondered Santoro. "That could make sense. What do you remember about that?"

CHAPTER 42

FIFTH SORROW: THE CRUCIFIXION

HARTFORD, LATE JUNE, 1912

Back in Hartford, Giuseppe was feeling a financial squeeze like never before. His loan with the bank, more than half paid off, was falling behind. His payments to Tony and his cohorts, although current, were getting harder and harder to come by. Rent, after five years, had gone up a dollar a month for both the shop and the apartment. And, with the new baby, finally a boy, eight mouths to feed is never an easy feat. He simply had to do something. And bringing more money into the shop just did not seem like a reality. The two dollars he gave to Carmela for Raffaela's escape would have really helped.

As Giuseppe sat in his new chair pondering the situation, Tony walked in, making the little bell jingle. Giuseppe jumped off the chair and stepped towards his visitor. "It is not your day! Why are you here?" he immediately blurted out.

"Relax, *mio amico*," Tony responded. "I have good news for you!" he smiled as he took off his bowler and wiped his forehead. "It is very hot out there today. You are lucky to have that fan." He pointed to the rotating ceiling fan.

"Yes, I am," responded Giuseppe nervously. "Why are you here?" he repeated.

"I have a little business that could make you a very lucky guy. Do you mind if I invite a few friends in?"

Giuseppe felt that he was not in a position to say no,

so he nodded. Tony went out onto the stoop and spoke to two men, briefly. Then they followed him back in. One was a man slightly taller than Giuseppe, but of a broader build. He was sporting one of the fashionable windowpane check suits, which were so popular with the actors in the moving pictures, and a well fit bowler. The other, somewhat smaller, wore a plain, grey wool which had seen better days. He had a summer straw hat with a black ribbon. Giuseppe did not remember ever seeing these men before, and he had an eye for faces. So, he assumed they were from out of town. He offered the men a seat.

"No. If you don't mind, I'll stand," said the taller of the two men. "We have been on the train for a few hours and I feel cramped." This affirmed Giuseppe's assumption that they were from out of town. The other also refused and took up a stand by the door.

"May I present my associates. This is DiNitto," Tony said, pointing to the taller man. "And this is Moreno." The men nodded to Giuseppe and he nodded back, unsure of his position. "Like I said before," continued Tony. "These men have a business proposition they want you to hear. You may find that it solves your problems." He winked knowingly.

DiNitto leaned up against the counter, his back to the long mirror, and crossed his arms. He looked at Giuseppe. "Why don't you take a chair. You are the one who has been working all day."

Afraid to antagonize, Giuseppe sat in his new chair.

"We are in America. We speak American, eh?" Giuseppe nodded. "I understand that you have been living in Hartford for 12 years, now," DiNitto began. "And you have this nice business. And a family."

"Yes," Giuseppe responded. "Six children. And

finally, I have a boy!" He felt less tense, talking about the family.

"Congratulations!" DiNitto smiled. "And you have other family and *paesani*, living near you, in the same building, eh?"

"That is true," Giuseppe responded.

"Do you know a Giovanni Tassone?"

"Sure, I do. He lives in my building. He is married to a distant cousin of mine. As a matter of fact, he is a distant cousin of my---"

"Do you know his past?"

"No. He doesn't talk much. They have been here almost four years. His brother lives in town, too. But they both lived in Providence---"

"Do you know why they moved?"

"I heard something about a row and he had to move. They don't talk about it."

"Well, sir," said DiNitto. "I have a little story to tell you." He pulled out a silver cigarette case and matches from an inside jacket pocket. He pulled one out for himself and offered one to Giuseppe. It was refused. So he put the case back and lit the cigarette. He took a few drags, blew out a smoke ring, smiled at his accomplishment and turned back to Giuseppe, who was watching his every move.

"This is how it is. My job takes me between Boston and Providence pretty regularly. I have a friend in Boston, good businessman. Has some money and does a lot of traveling himself. Name's Pensara. Well, a few years ago, just before Christmas, I invited him to Providence for a week or so. He decided to see what he could do about setting up some business contacts. I told him he could stay at my sister's. You know. Good Italian cooking, good company. He's not married and his Mama is gone. So he doesn't get such good food as my sister can make. Understand?"

Giuseppe hesitantly smiled. He thought of how nice an invitation would be if he was in the same boat and he didn't have Carmela's soup or sauce.

"So, anyhow. Me and Pensara stop by a saloon after a day of talking to people. He had been in town a while and, since he is good with people and faces, he and I could talk about who he met and what he liked. And we're sitting at the bar and in comes a friend. The friend has a fine wife. Pretty little thing. And Pensara recognizes who the wife is from how we are talking, this friend and me. So, he makes a few comments about the girl. You know, a warm bed on a cold night." DiNitto laughed. "Well, this friend gets insulted and shows his gun. Pensara is insulted that the guy would stand up to him. Pensara has some money. He's a man of respect. You know what I mean?"

Again Giuseppe, following the story, nodded, with a serious expression on his face. He didn't know where this was going.

"So, Pensara says he won't apologize for such a small remark. My friend demands an apology. Pensara stands up to him and blam!! Two shots right off the bat!" DiNitto watched Giuseppe's eyes to see the reaction. "So, I tell my friend, 'Get out of here. The police will be here soon!' I told him to leave town. He didn't right away, but eventually he did." DiNitto dashed out his cigarette and crossed his arms. "And do you know who my friend was?"

"Tassone?"

DiNitto roared in laughter. "Hey, Tony! You got a smart one here! I didn't even have to give him a hint. He is a smart one!" Looking back at Giuseppe he said, "You'll do all right, I think!" He playfully punched his host in the shoulder. Giuseppe looked at him quizzically. "Don't worry, Amato! I'll fill you in."

Tony, standing behind Giuseppe watched his friend's reactions in the mirror. He smirked at DiNitto's masterful show. Moreno, in the hallway, by the door, chuckled to himself, uncrossed his arms and looked out the door to make sure no one was on their way in. Then he lit a cigar and watched DiNitto's presentation.

"So, now," said DiNitto. "We are going to talk about you." He stopped, again, to watch Giuseppe's reaction, which was minimal.

Giuseppe was still totally unsure about why these men were even talking to him.

"You are in trouble, financially. You owe $50 on this chair. You owe Tony here $5 a month insurance. You owe $11 a month on this shop and another $11 a month on the flat upstairs where your family lives. Business supplies are probably $5 a month, what with soap, hair pomade, aftershave. You have six children and a wife. I heard you lend money to people sometimes when they are in worse trouble than you. You average $40-45 per month, $50 on a real good month. You don't make enough money. You probably have very little time left before the bank clerks start coming by to collect. Then, you will try to stop the insurance coverage you have with Tony. And, then, you will have problems with the gangs around here who break into businesses and rob the shops blind." He watched a silent Giuseppe cringe and sink into the chair.

"You will have to get your wife to take in laundry. Although I doubt she will be able to handle it with six children underfoot all day long. You could take in a boarder, but I doubt it will work, for the same reason. I suppose you can dress one of the older girls as a boy, make her drop out of school and sell papers. But, I take it you are not that type of man. And the little girls are too young to let out as servants.

"I think you are stuck." DiNitto smiled at Giuseppe and paused to take another cigarette out. He smoked for a few minutes in silence as he watched Giuseppe mull over his words and watch his face sink. DiNitto watched until he was sure Giuseppe was ready for the next part. He crushed out his cigarette and walked over to the empty chair. He sat down and turned the chair to face Giuseppe.

"We can fix this," he said, changing tactics to show a concerned friend. "My friend Pensara did not die. He was in the hospital for ten months. Ten damn months! Do you know what a man thinks about when he lays on his back for ten damn months?"

Giuseppe was catching on. "Revenge?" he asked in a small voice.

"Hey, Tony! This guy is all right! He's got a good head on his shoulders. I should hire him and kick out a few of my stupid boys." Tony laughed out loud and nodded. Moreno took the cigar out of his mouth and tipped his hat.

"You are a good guy, Joe!" DiNitto exclaimed. "I am going to offer you the opportunity of a lifetime. You will be out of debt. And all you have to do is a favor for Pensara."

Giuseppe looked up at him, surprised. "I will if I can!"

"So, you will, huh?"

"Will what?"

"Why, kill Tassone, of course! As a favor to Pensara."

Giuseppe looked at DiNitto in stunned silence. It took a moment to grasp the full meaning of what had just been said. He shrank back in his chair.

"I can't do that!"

"You also can't afford your life. I am giving you a way out. Unless you want the embarrassment of losing everything you have to the courts."

"I-I would need time to think about such a thing. I don't know how to do something like that. I wouldn't have the first clue."

"Tell you what. I will meet with you again tomorrow and we will talk further. That will give you a day to decide. We don't want to wait. This needs to be done, soon. Now that we found him." DiNitto got up off his chair, found his hat and stuck out his hand to shake Giuseppe's. "Nice doing business with you. Until tomorrow." They shook hands and the three men walked out the door.

Giuseppe was left to face his greatest fears and hopes simultaneously. Kill Tassone? Okay, so the guy was an *idiota* with his wife. And he had a sharp temper that was easily fused. But to kill him? What was it the padre used to say in his sermons? Thou shalt not kill! It is a mortal sin! Whatever that meant. Something about the worst thing you could do. You could go to hell for that. Not only would he lose a friend and possibly go to hell when he, Giuseppe, died, but everything in his life would change, too. What if he got caught by the police? He could be hung! Or, at best, spend many years in jail! That was not something he would like to have happen!

And what about the Tassone children? They would be fatherless. Well, Rafaella was beautiful. She would easily find another man.

But, then, again, a gift had been handed to him! He told himself. He could escape this life. He could start all over again somewhere else! He could get out of debt with this one action of his. No more bank breathing down his neck. No more Tony coming for his weekly collections. No more rental agent on the first of the month. What a relief that would be.

But, wait! He reminded himself of Carmela and the children? To be honest, being free would be a relief. Every time he had his way with her, she got pregnant! This was getting very annoying and very expensive. This was not what he was anticipating when he married her. A few children, one every two, three years. Sure. But not this constant barrage of more and more! If he could just go somewhere for a while. Get a breath of independence for a while. Then he could send for her and the children. Find a new place to live. Start again. Yes. That would be a good choice. They had enough emergency money. It would be fine. Maybe she would understand. Funny, he'd moved to Hartford to get away from the people in Serra; now he was moving from those same people again!

As he sat pondering his future, his daughter, Teresa, came into his shop. "Papa! Mama sent me down to give you a message."

"Yes, Teresa. What is it?" He took her hand and looked at his child who was the image of his wife.

"Mama says that you should know that Signora Tassone came down to visit. And Mama is crying."

CHAPTER 43

HARTFORD, JULY, 1912

Tony came alone the next afternoon, about an hour before the late afternoon crowd started coming in. "Hey, Joe! How's it going?" he greeted Guiseppe as he walked in. "DiNitto wanted me to stop by and see if he could meet with you tonight."

Giuseppe, still undecided, was wary. The re-appearance and subsequent confining of Rafaella Tassone had pointed out the direction he should take, somewhat, but he had his family to think about. He knew he was between the proverbial rock and the hard place. There was little he could do but listen to the rest of DiNitto's presentation. "Sure, Tony. I can meet with him. Does he want to come here?"

"No. Tonight, he wants to take you out to a little place I found where the pasta is cheap and the vino is plentiful." Tony smiled. "I will pick you up at 7:00 pm. How's that?"

Giuseppe nodded. "Sure. That will give me time to go upstairs and say good night to the *bambini* and tell my Carmela not to wait up."

"Sure. Sure. I will wait on the stoop of the shop for you, then." Tony turned to go, then turned back. "You aren't giving me the dodge, are you?"

"No, Tony, I'm not. I will be here. Seven o'clock."

So, Tony came back, this time with Moreno, the silent one with the frayed grey suit. The three men walked down to Front Street to a little café that Giuseppe had passed before, but never had gone in. It wasn't a big place, holding enough tables to seat 40, and just about every table was filled at this hour. They entered and walked to the back of the room where there were booths. DiNitto was already sitting at one. On the red and white checkered tablecloth there sat a bottle of chianti and four glasses. DiNitto's was already poured and tasted. He stood to welcome his guests.

"Thank you for coming, Amato," he greeted. "I am glad you could join us tonight. Please, sit." Giuseppe sat to his right and Moreno and Tony flanked the two. "I took it upon myself to order for you. I hope you don't mind. It's simple. Cavatelli and gnocchi, meatballs and sausage. They serve on a big platter here. You take what you want. Like at home, eh?"

DiNitto elbowed Giuseppe, who jumped a little. DiNitto laughed raucously. "Eh, Tony! You made him get a little jumpy on the way over?"

Tony laughed at Giuseppe's discomfort. "Don't worry, Joe! You are making new friends. Good friends. We watch out for our own." Tony nodded and watched Giuseppe's eyes.

The bread and cheese was served by a man in a white shirt and black pants. He smiled and asked if they needed another bottle of chianti. DiNitto said yes and the man left.

"Now, let us review what we have discussed before. Tassone. Pensara. Your finances." DiNitto sipped his wine. "Not bad. Almost too sweet, but not quite." He set it down and broke off a hunk of bread. "So, now, we talk about what you can do for us and what we can do for you. Si?" He sprinkled parmesan cheese over his warm bread and took a bite. Then he put it down on his plate, wiped his hands on a napkin and resumed.

"We will come to an agreement about the time and

date. You take care of Tassone that day. We give you a few hours leeway. You know, just in case you get the jitters or you can't get hold of him. You done this before?"

"No, never."

"Well, there's a first time for everything." DiNitto empathized. "So then you got to plan it out. Now you know that you can't stay here, so what are you going to do?"

"I have a brother-in-law in Canada. British Columbia. I could go there. But what about my wife and children?"

"I never moved a whole family before. It don't work. You could take off and then send for her and the bambini. Say, in six months. But I wouldn't tell her what you are planning. She could talk. You know how women are."

"*Si*, I know," said Giuseppe, warming up from the chianti. "She has been accused of being a gossip."

"So. That is set. You will leave immediately afterwards for your brother-in-law in British Columbia. What town?"

"Fernie."

"Mining, right?"

"*Si*. How did you know?"

"We are everywhere. My associates, I mean." DiNitto seemed rather complex to Giuseppe. "So then what you going to do with you shop?"

"I could sell it?" asked Giuseppe hesitantly. He thought they were maybe quizzing him.

"Good. Tony happens to know a man who is looking to buy a shop. You could get, maybe, a hundred dollars. His name is Clementino Mondi." DiNitto looked past Giuseppe at Tony. "Bring him around to Joe in a day or two. Make a deal."

"Sure thing," Tony responded. The waiter returned

with a bottle of wine and uncorked it in front of the men. He refilled the glasses and went off again.

"You know, Joe," said DiNitto. "The police will look for you. This is the dangerous part. We will have to plan this carefully. You can not leave any pictures of youself around. The last thing you want to see is a picture of you in the Hartford Courant."

He took a sip from his glass and continued. "You can't leave much money in the bank. Your wife will need money for the six months or so. You have to leave it somewhere so she can find it. You can't give it to her. What would she think if you handed her fifty or a hundred dollars? She would be asking you plenty of questions. Leave her out from your plans."

Giuseppe's head was spinning by this time. He remembered the growing "emergency fund" that Carmela was adding to every week. She would be fine. His leaving town would amount to an emergency. But all these bits of advice were getting mixed up in his head. Too much to swallow at one sitting. By this time, the food arrived. DiNitto, host of the evening, served the other three men, making comments about the smells and presentation of the food on the plate as he did so. He never seemed to tire of speaking.

"Now, Joe," he went on. "You can take care of the gun?" Giuseppe nodded. "You better practice with it a few times first. You don't want innocent people to get it, eh? We can't help you further if you get the wrong one, you know?" He laughed. "Pensara pays for Tassone, not Smith!" He laughed at what he thought was a good joke.

Moreno and Tony also laughed, but Giuseppe's stomach was in knots and he could not laugh or eat much. He thought the *cavatelli* wasn't as good as Carmela's and the sauce was Sicilian, not Calabrese.

"I want you to have small photos of yourself taken. We will have to make a few identity cards for you. You get them taken and give them to Tony. He will come by your place every day to see how you are doing. You understand?"

Giuseppe nodded, playing with his food. The meatballs tasted wrong.

"You listening to what I am saying, Joe? This is not a game, here!" Suddenly, DiNitto's face was not the jovial host's face. He was deadly serious.

Giuseppe looked up from his plate. "I am hearing you, DiNitto. It's just that my stomach, it's not so good tonight." The food wouldn't go down past his throat.

DiNitto's dark face relaxed and became the host, again. He burst out laughing and clapped Giuseppe on the back. "Ha! Ha! The boy becomes a man and his stomach gives out! That's good! Here, Joe! You just need more vino!" And he poured Joe another glass of wine. "Come on! Drink! *Mangia*! We are helping you with a financial problem and you are helping us with a personal problem. See? Friends!" He lifted his glass and toasted Giuseppe. "To friends!"

Tony and Moreno lifted their glasses for the toast, also. Giuseppe was obligated to follow suit.

The rest of the evening was spent arranging details. What was the likely day? Who would Joe meet first after the deed? What route out of town would they take? Nothing was taken for granted. He was not to pack, as that would raise suspicion. They would get him new clothes. Just leave some money for Carmela and send her money every so often until it was safe to have her come to the new place he would choose for settlement. At least his family would be taken care of . . .

It was Tuesday evening. Giuseppe closed the barber shop an hour early. He was expecting a visitor and he had no intention of anyone overhearing the conversation. At precisely 5:30 pm, a young man walked into the shop.

"Mr. DiNitto told me to stop by," the young man began. He was about thirty, with a dark complexion. With his completely shaven face, he looked like he was trying to imitate the latest silent movie actors. He was an immigrant but had been in the States for a while, judging by his accent.

Giuseppe dropped his cleaning cloth and walked over to the young man. He thought he knew every Italian in this town of over 100,000, but he did not recognize this one. "How do you do?" he said, extending his hand. "I am Giuseppe Amato. Tony told me to expect you."

"Amato, I am Clementino Mondi. I live about a mile from here. I never spent much time this close to the railroad station. It seems like a busy place. Is it?"

"It is busy and growing all the time," Giuseppe responded. "I understand that you are looking for a barber shop to buy."

"Yes, I am. And my friend, Tony, told me you were going to be moving and wanted to make a deal." He looked around appreciatively. "New chair?" he asked as he assessed the shiny chrome of Giuseppe's pride and joy which he had placed closer to the window as an attraction to passers-by.

Giuseppe nodded.

Mondi walked around the small shop, opening drawers and cabinets, assessing the amount of shampoo, shaving soaps and blades, counting the number of shaving mugs on the shelves, which indicated the number of regulars the barber shop had. Either he had experience buying businesses, which seemed unlikely, or he had been coached in how to approach the purchase. Giuseppe stood with his arms folded across his chest, leaning against the door jamb, watching Mondi's every move, not able to read the man's impressions.

"I will take it," Mondi announced decidedly, looking around at the sparse but clean quarters. "I will give you 40 dollars now and another 70 when we sign the papers. How does that sound to you?"

Giuseppe was surprised at the ease with which the transfer was made. Ten minutes before he was not sure how he was going to get out from underneath the barber shop and here he was looking at two month's income, free and clear!

"I accept your terms," he replied with only a moment's hesitation. "When would you like to complete the paperwork?"

"Let us say next Monday?" Mondi suggested.

"Very well, then," Giuseppe nodded in agreement.

Mondi pulled a sealed envelope out of his inner jacket pocket, which he handed to Giuseppe without counting the contents. Giuseppe immediately opened the envelope and counted the bills, nodding contentedly. There were eight five-dollar bills in it.

"I expect you will be ready to move out right afterwards?" Mondi asked.

"It would be within a few days of our doing the paperwork, if you can accept that?"

"That will be fine. I will see you on Monday. The same time as today?"

"That will do," Giuseppe nodded, again, anxious to make sure he was not dreaming. It was all too easy.

Giuseppe left the apartment early the next morning. He walked down Spruce Street and turned left onto

Asylum Street He proceeded towards downtown, past the new and recent construction that was prevalent all up and down the broad street. It was only a fifteen minute walk to 44 Asylum Street

At 8:00 am the store, Wooly Hardware, was already teaming with customers. It was a big, cavernous place. Various departments showed off their wares. Flower and vegetable seeds were sorted on large tables. Vine plants, the few that were left, had discount signs on them. There was a variety of gardening tools, boots and various workmen's outfits lining the aisles as Giuseppe walked to the back of the store. Along the back wall was a display of firearms under glass. He browsed for a few minutes until a tall thin blonde youth came to help him.

"I am looking for a small gun, something that can fit into a pocket. Not too expensive."

"Certainly, sir," said the young man. He took a few items out and placed them on the display stand for Giuseppe to handle, explaining each one in turn. Giuseppe looked over the guns and chose a Colt 32 caliber semi-automatic.

"This one will do. How do you use it?"

The gangly youth showed him how to fill the magazine, aim and shoot. He wrote up the purchase order for the gun, a box of cartridges and a few targets to practice with. "And your name, sir?"

"Why?"

"It is a new law. Every buyer must be registered."

"Oh, fine. The name is . . . Monde. Carmine Monde. 66 Grove Street, in the city," Giuseppe dictated.

"Thank you, Mr. Monde. That is a total of 15 dollars."

Giuseppe paid out of the money Clementino Mondi had paid him the night before. The package was wrapped, tied and handed to Giuseppe, who walked out of the store and turned back up Asylum Street

The second part of the preparation he was responsible for was now complete.

Giuseppe sauntered back up to Spruce Street and to his house. But, instead of going to his apartment or to his shop, he walked downstairs to the basement.

The place had low ceilings with heating ducts and water pipes racing along the rafters. There were a few old chairs scattered around. Giuseppe pulled a few chairs up to beneath the only window. He set up one of the paper targets on the back of a chair. Then he took the gun out of the box, took seven cartridges out of the ammunition box and loaded the clip. Standing back from the chair, he took aim and shot at the target, emptying the clip. He found it difficult to shoot. The trigger was stiffer than he imagined. And the first few times he shot, the flash coming out alarmed him. But, he supposed that a few more times practicing would settle that. Packing the gun back up, he hid it up in the rafters and went upstairs to begin his workday at the shop.

During the rest of the week, Giuseppe tried to avoid his family, and the Tassones, as much as possible. Every time he saw Giovanni, the same argument ensued, so he steered clear of the man. He had too much on his mind, he told Carmela. Or, he said there was so much extra business at the shop. With the heat, everyone was getting haircuts and mustaches trimmed back, he told her.

She complained about his business. It seemed like she complained more often, lately. Didn't she know that he had too much on his mind? Couldn't she just make the children more quiet so he could think more clearly?

Friday evening, Giuseppe ran into Giovanni coming home from work. He passed him on the sidewalk and nodded a greeting, then sped up his pace, as if he had somewhere to go. Giovanni turned around and chased after him and grabbed his shoulder from behind.

"Joe," he sneered. "Aren't you going to congratulate me for having gotten my wife back?"

Giuseppe said nothing, not sure of what could be said on this occasion.

Giovanni choked back what seemed to be a sob. "You thought you could get her to stay away from me? I spent good money! I got her back! You and your wife couldn't keep her away! I cannot live without my Rafaella! I could kill you for what you did to me!" He blinked back his tears then walked back to the apartment house.

Giuseppe broke into a greater sweat than the day's heat could account for. His decision to accept DiNitto's proposition came to mind and he began to understand that it had been the right one, at least for him. He decided that a walk in the park was what he needed to get hold of himself. He walked across the street, around the train station to Union Place and on into Bushnell Park. There, the acres and acres of gardens were in full bloom. Roses of red, yellow and pink climbed over trellises. Annuals of various types filled in spots around trees and along sidewalks. The memorial bridge over the Park River stood high and proud in the late afternoon sun. Here and there, Giuseppe saw young couples strolling the paths, arm in arm, and he remembered a time when he and Carmela would go for walks after work and talk about the future. How innocent they were, at the time, to think that luck would always be with them.

He sought refuge from the sun and found a park bench tucked into a group of trees. It looked inviting and he needed a place to ponder his future. Giuseppe sat, lounging on the bench, and tipped his straw hat over his eyes and crossed his arms.

Ten minutes later, Giuseppe was aroused from his daydreaming by a large dog who came over to pick up a ball that his master had thrown into the grove of trees. The young boy chased after his dog and when he saw Giuseppe with the hat over his head, the boy apologized for the intrusion.

It was getting dusk and the street lights were beginning to turn on. It was late. Giuseppe got up, brushed off his suit, placed his straw hat on at that slightly jaunty angle he always used and proceeded to retrace his steps to the apartment. Crossing Union Place, Giuseppe ran into Police Officer George Butler. Union Place, at night, was his beat.

"Hey, Joe! How are you?" Butler greeted his friend.

"Hi, George! I'm doing fine. But you look like you could use a trim!"

"Yes," Butler laughed. "I've got to get over to your shop. It's been busy lately. We've heard talk about someone from out of town may be looking for trouble around here. If you hear of anything suspicious, let me know."

"So what do you hear?" Giuseppe's hair on the back of his neck stood up. He had gotten a sudden chill.

"Nothing solid. Just a rumor that something in the Italian district might be happening."

Giuseppe tried to laugh. "Rumors. Most time, that is all they are."

"All the same, Joe, if you hear something, you will let me know. Remember that shooting last New Year's?"

"Sure, sure. But I got to go. It's late. Carmela, she's gonna be worried."

"Okay. Good night, Joe."

CHAPTER 44

HARTFORD, MONDAY JULY 22, 1912

Tuesday was the night set by DiNitto and friends for "the deed." Giuseppe had much to do on the day before. He was up earlier than the children and sat at the kitchen table with Carmela having their first cup of coffee of the day, alone. This was a rare occasion.

"Giuseppe, are you well?" Carmela asked, speaking in the Italian they used at home. "You have not been yourself for a long time and it is getting worse."

"I'm sorry, *cara*," Giuseppe responded. "Business is taking all my time and energy lately. I have so many things on my mind. But, soon, you will see, we will reap the fruits of my labor." He put his hand on hers and stared into her eyes as if trying to telepathically say what he could not, verbally. "Things will be crazy for a while, then, you watch, it will all turn around and we will have the life I promised you. Just be patient another year. Please."

"A strange request from you. Have I not been patient all these years? When you wanted to go to America and left me in Serra for three years, did I not wait for you? When you insisted on having the shop and not working for another, despite having the *bambini* to feed, did I not bite my tongue and support you?" Her eyes welled up with emotions she did not usually allow herself. "We have lived on minestrone soup and spaghetti so long, what is one more year? It is still more hopeful here than in Serra!"

Giuseppe remembered how he had loved her when

229

they married. How he had hoped for the ideal life for he had hoped for the ideal life for her and their *bambini*. He wished he could share what was going to happen next with her. But DiNitto's warnings sounded in his head. What could go wrong if he quit? If he couldn't go through with it? He had already taken money from DiNitto. Fifty dollars. He was going to put it in Carmela's drawer before the evening was done. Just before the deed.

Yes, but what would happen if he changed his mind? He had already taken the money from Clementino Mondi. The man may not want to give up the deal. He would have to give back the fifty from DiNitto! But he already spent some of the money Mondi gave him! Would he have enough to pay back DiNitto and support the family while he looked for a job? He could not find another job so quickly as to pay all his expenses. How would he explain to Carmela why he no longer had his shop? *Oh, I was going to kill your cousin, but I changed my mind And, by the way, I am in debt to the bank, too.* No, he could not face her with that story!

"Giuseppe?" Carmela's voice brought him back to the present. "Would you like more coffee? Some bread and jam?"

"No, Carmela. My stomach is bad. I cannot eat this morning. Besides, I have to go to the bank before I open the shop, so I must leave early." He rose from the table and lightly kissed his wife's forehead. "We will talk tonight."

"Is there anything I can do to help you?"

"Maybe some cheese and bread at noon. Maybe by then, I will be able to eat." He pulled his suspenders up over his shirt and tucked in his shirttails better. He grabbed his jacket and straw hat and a list of things he had to do and walked to the door.

Then, he spotted the one thing he had forgotten. There was the full length, full-sized crayon drawing he had ordered, maybe foolishly, made of himself some years back. It was in a pine frame, not very good quality wood, with no glass. He returned to the sitting area and looked at it, sighing.

"What is it, Giuseppe?"

"I can do one thing for you, now," he said. "I will get you a better frame for this picture." He was lying. He knew it. The other small pictures had been dealt with, but he had not yet done anything with the drawing and it had to be out of the apartment and out of anyone's reach. He grabbed the frame and tore it apart, a little too hastily, perhaps. He pulled the canvas out, rolling it up as he did so.

"Giuseppe! This is impractical. You are not going to spend money on such a frivolous thing now, are you?"

"I must do something for you. That is little enough forright now." He tucked the rolled canvas under his arm, kissed her forehead again, patted his hat and strode out the door and into the day.

His first stop was the basement of the building. Giuseppe walked down the stairs, looking along the rafters until he spotted the box. With the box was a paper bag. He pulled the box and bag down and opened the bag. Inside were photographs. All the pictures he could find of himself, even the wedding photo, were in there. He added the rolled picture to the contents and stuffed the bag up into the rafters with the box. He would take care of that in a few hours.

His second stop was the bank. Giuseppe walked down Asylum Street and into the large granite building just as it opened at 8:00 am. He did not stop to admire the innovative use of marble and mahogany as he usually did.

Instead, he walked right up to the first teller he saw opened and greeted him.

"Good morning, Mr. Taylor," Giuseppe said to the bespectacled man on the other side of the grill-work.

"Good morning, Mr. Amato," the young man replied. "How can I help you this morning?"

"I need to make a withdrawal," Giuseppe said. He presented his passbook, opened to the right page.

Mr. Taylor looked at it, then crossed the room behind the tellers' windows to a set of mahogany index card-sized file cabinets. He pulled open a drawer and pulled out a card. Carrying the card, he came back to the window. "Sir, you are a payment behind on your loan. Would you like to pay for that today?"

Giuseppe swallowed hard. "No. I will pay for that on Wednesday. All I want to do today is withdraw some of my money. *Per favore.*"

Taylor looked at him strangely. He wasn't sure what *per favore* meant. All the I-talians used that word. Maybe it was thank you or something like that. He picked up the passbook and looked at it. "You have 62 dollars in the account. How much would you like to withdraw?"

"Fifty," Giuseppe stated simply. The teller counted out the money and handed it to Giuseppe, who carefully pocketed all of it and nodded a goodbye to the young man.

Back outside the bank, Giuseppe walked back up Asylum in time to open his shop at 9:00 am. The clientele was steady all morning and he pocketed another dollar and a half.

By noon, he was truly hungry and kept hoping Carmela would send one of the girls down with the cheese and bread he was looking forward to. He did not dare go up for fear of missing Mondi who was to arrive a little after noon with the rest of the money they had agreed to, which amounted to 70 dollars. He would then have more money on his person than he had ever had at one time. Thinking of all the things he could do with that much money, and the fact that he had a chance at starting over, Giuseppe began to long for the new freedom this "deed" was going to give him.

Just after noon, Mondi walked in. "Hey, Joe! I am here, as promised," he announced.

"I will be with you in a *minuto*. Just cleaning up from the morning work," Giuseppe said as an explanation for why he was sweeping.

"I did not realize last time what a good chair is this one," Mondi commented as he sat in the new chair. "This must have set you back a little."

"Almost as much as what I am selling you the whole shop for," responded Giuseppe. Then he thought to himself, if that chair cost me so much, I really should have asked for $125 or so, not just accepted the $110 for the shop. Well, it is a finished deal, now. "You got yourself a good deal, here!" he added to the younger man,

Giuseppe put the broom and dust shovel away in the closet and came over to Mondi. "I want to finish this quickly. My daughter, she may be coming with my lunch any time and I do not want her to see you. This will be a surprise for my wife and I do not want any hints laying around for her or my girls."

"I understand," said Mondi. "Well, here is the other 70 dollars. I want a receipt." Giuseppe took a piece of paper and wrote "Paid to the order of Clementino Mondi. Receipt of 70 dollars. Paid in full." He handed it to Mondi.

"Will this do?"

Mondi read it. "Sure, Joe. This will do good. So,

when you will you be out?"

"I will have the barbershop ready for you at the end of the week. You will have to deal with the landlord yourself about the rent. But there will be no problem, I am sure. Rent is paid til the end of the month." They shook hands, wished each other good luck and Mondi was off.

Within two minutes, Teresa came with a small basket containing half a loaf of bread, a slab of mozzarella and a few black spiced olives. "Mama says you must eat. She does not want you to get sick. And she says she hopes you are feeling better." Giuseppe smiled down at his oldest and patted her red curls.

"Tell you Mama that my stomach it's better this afternoon and that I thank her for the food."

"*Si*, Papa!" Teresa smiled back.

"Oh, Teresa!" Giuseppe interrupted her before she could leave. "Have you seen Signora Tassone this week?"

"No, Papa. She stays in her apartment. The boys are with her, too. They don't come downstairs to play with Dora and Nunziata anymore. *Zia* Maria says that they keep their door shut. They don't even play with Frankie." Her face looked sad.

"*Grazie*, Teresa," Giuseppe said as he dismissed her. "Go back to you mother, now. I will see you tonight."

The little girl left and Giuseppe sat on his new chair to eat his bread and cheese. He pondered her news and felt sorry for the young neighbor who seemed to have such a lonely life. He thought about how she would be free after he did the deed. He wouldn't be able to stay around long enough for her to thank him, but he could see her, in his mind's eye, smiling and kissing his hands in appreciation for what he had just done for her.

Before he could go much further in his thoughts, Tony came up to the stoop and knocked on the door before coming in. He looked around the shop briefly before greeting Giuseppe. "You got anyone here? I just saw you daughter leave," he asked.

Giuseppe shook his head, his mouth full of bread. "Good," Tony commented.

Tony looked into the food basket, still on Giuseppe's lap and licked his lips. He pulled a 6 inch stiletto knife out of his calf-high boot and stabbed a few olives. Easing into the older barber chair, he bit off each of the olives in turn and chewed them happily.

When he swallowed he asked, "So, you are ready for the big night?" Tony spoke as if they might be going to the circus, almost like an excited child. Then he reached over, stabbed a piece of mozzarella with the point of his stiletto, and stuck it into his mouth.

"You should not be so excited about taking someone's life," Giuseppe commented, squinting up at his friend. He took the last of the cheese before Tony could get at it.

"The man, he's a bag of shit! He would kill my friend. And you know what they say, 'the enemy of my friend is my enemy, too'. So, he is you enemy" Tony spread out his hands and shrugged his shoulders.

Looking at Giuseppe, Tony saw no relief in his eyes. So, he changed tactics. "I hear he don't let his wife or kids out no more. What kind of a life is that, eh? Say, you talk to him again since he threatened you?"

"Just the once. He said he had a gun and will kill me if I ever even look at his wife, or talk to her. And my wife can no talk to her. Poor Carmela. Poor Rafaella."

"When was that?"

"Day before yesterday. He says the same thing every time he sees me. I will be glad to have this done."

"Only a day away, now. You got that big picture out

of the apartment?"

"Yes."

"Did she fight you 'bout it?"

"A little. I told her I do not like the frame and that the least I could do for her was to get a better frame. She could not come up with an objection."

"You know, you are made for this kind of work. You come up with the answers pretty fast." Tony grinned broadly. "I'm proud of you, *mio amico*!" He reviewed questions he needed to ask.

"You been practicing with that gun?"

"Yes. Again yesterday. It sticks a little. Hard to control how fast it shoots."

"That's ok. It is how those semi-automatics work. You practice some more. A little lighter on the finger pressure. You will get it."

"I hope so."

"So. We got ever-thing else taken care of. You hide out after and we come get you at 11:00 pm. The train yards are the place to hide, so long as you don't give the police more than an hour to search it. Watch for the signal on the west side of the yards." Tony stopped to give Giuseppe a chance to digest it all. "You need for me to come tomorrow?"

"No. I'll be all right."

"You gonna be here at the shop tomorrow?"

"In the morning. I will be too nervous in the afternoon. I'm gonna give myself a half day holiday."

"That's good! That's real good!" nodded Tony.

"I may need a little liquid courage before I do it."

"Well, I'll be watching, just in case you get cold feet!" Tony got up off the chair and stopped to look closely at his partner in crime. "See you tomorrow night. *Ciao*!"

He let himself out as Giuseppe considered whether those words constituted a threat.

CHAPTER 45

HARTFORD, 1930

"Oh, that's right!" Miss Amato looked up at Santoro's eyes. "I remember something else!"

The old detective contemplated the little lady and waited for her.

"Teresa and I were worried about Mrs. Tassone and we were playing detective. We didn't really understand the whole situation but we would listen in when we were not supposed to. So, Teresa overheard parts of the conversation. She had seen this Tony come to the shop and had returned to the front door to listen through the screen. My father had a screen door on the front. For the heat. So it was easy to stand nearby and listen."

"We never heard any of this before," wondered the detective. Then he chuckled. "Playing detective, eh?"

CHAPTER 46

SIXTH SORROW: JESUS IS TAKEN DOWN
FROM THE CROSS

HARTFORD, TUESDAY, JULY 23, 1912

Tuesday morning, Giuseppe opened his shop at 8:00 am. He now had $123 in cash. Another good day like yesterday and he could have an easy $125, $126 in his pocket. Even after storing away the $50 DiNitto gave him for Carmela, he still had over two month's earnings in his possession. He was almost jovial with his customers that morning, looking forward to the adventure he would have after the deed was finished.

Some of the men noticed the change from the brooding man of the past couple of months and commented on it. "Hey, Joe! What's with the smile?" a few asked.

"Oh, I'm having a good day," he replied. "It is a beautiful sunny, summer day and I feel young," he added. It sounded plausible, anyhow. And he did have a fruitful morning, pocketing almost $2.50.

At noon, Giuseppe closed up. He swept and polished all the woodwork, dusted the light fixtures and cleaned out the sink. After all, for a 110 dollars, Mondi ought to get a clean place.

Instead of going up to the apartment for lunch, Giuseppe went down the street to James Freney's saloon for a beer and crackers. He chatted with the patrons, trying to relax and spend the last hours before the deed as a normal citizen.

About 2:00 pm, Giuseppe went back to the tenement house and down into the basement. He pulled the box out from over the rafters and set up his target again. He filled the clip and snapped it up into the gun. Taking aim, he fired several times, finally catching on to the pressure needed to release one bullet at a time, quickly. Satisfied, he sat on the chair and cleaned the gun well, refilled the magazine, pulled back the slide and released it, loading a bullet into the chamber. He then put the gun into his pants pocket where the bulge would be covered by his jacket.

Finally, he pulled the bag of pictures out of the rafters and looked at them all one last time. Suddenly, he could not destroy the wedding picture. So he folded it in half, carefully, from top to bottom and tore it. The half with his face on it went back into the bag and the half with Carmela's face went into his coat pocket. Rolling up the bag loosely, he went to the back of the basement to the big coal octopus furnace. He opened the coal chute and held the bag over it. Scraping a matchstick against the metal furnace, he lit the bag and held it, watching it burn for a moment, then dropped it into the chute.

Finally he climbed the stairs to spend a few hours with his family for the last time in a long time. Some of the girls were in the hallway and were delighted to see their father this time of day. They followed him into the apartment, dancing.

Carmela was glad to see her husband so early in the afternoon. "You closed early on a Tuesday? Are you ill?"

"No, I am fine, *cara!*" he insisted, sitting on the old sofa. "I just thought that, since I had no appointments late today, I would come up and have supper with the children."

The little girls wanted to climb on his lap and give him kisses, which he allowed them to do. Teresa and

Anna went to get the two little ones so he could hold them and give everyone a little attention. Giuseppe was proud of his youngest, his only surviving boy, and already had dreams for the child. *Someday,* he thought. *Some day we will be together, again. And, then, I will teach you what I know.*

He rode the two babies on his knees and spoke to the girls. They showed him pictures they had drawn and stories they had written.

Carmela was quietly pleased that her husband would come and be part of the family for a while. It had been so difficult lately with the problems the Tassones were having, Carmela virtually losing her friend, Rafaella, and keeping the six children in line. And, she had just found out that she was pregnant, again. She had seen her husband so little that she had not had time to tell him. Maybe tonight, after a nice supper. When the children were all asleep. Then she could tell him. Maybe another boy for him. That would be his dream!

Even though it was only Tuesday, Carmela cooked some sausage to go with the spaghetti. Sausage and peppers was usually the Wednesday meal. Spaghetti was Tuesdays and Thursdays. Meat was only twice a week. Who had money to buy meat for every day? But, she was so happy that they would eat like a family, all together, that she decided to celebrate.

Giuseppe and Teresa both noticed the sausage smell at the same time. "What's this? Meat on Tuesday?" Giuseppe asked.

"I thought, since you were home early, like a holiday, I would cook like it is a holiday," responded Carmela with a grin. The children were thrilled.

After a few more minutes of attention, Giuseppe pulled the children off his lap and told them to go play. "I have to talk to Mama," he explained.

They scattered and he turned to his wife. "I have to go talk to Giovanni tonight. We have to solve this vendetta he has going on."

Carmela stopped in the middle of her preparations and looked at him solemnly. "Are you sure that's wise?"

"*Cara*! It has been two weeks that he has kept her upstairs and away from everyone while he threatens to kill me every time he sees me. It is not my fault she didn't want any more beatings. It is not my fault she ran away. He should look to himself!"

"You cannot say that to his face!"

"I will be more diplomatic. But, yes, I should say exactly that to his face!" He grimaced at the thought. "However, I think I should invite him to Feeney's for a few beers and sit and talk man to man with him. I do not think he will threaten to kill me in front of so many others."

"Be careful, Giuseppe! Giovanni is a violent man at times. He shot a man in a saloon once!"

"How do you know this?" Giuseppe was startled by this revelation.

"Rafaella told me when she was trying to decide if she should leave him. That is why they moved to Hartford."

"I will be careful not to push him tonight," Giuseppe promised. He didn't want to let on that he knew the story, too.

Carmela nodded and turned back to the meal preparations. Giuseppe sat at the table and quietly pulled the torn wedding picture from his pocket. He looked at it once more and then reached for one of the children's books. He put it between two pages and put the book back. Then he took the newspaper which he always bought for the shop in the morning and tried to read.

He wondered if Giovanni would carry his gun to the saloon. Then Giuseppe thought about the discussion they would have when they got there. He thought through the plans for the evening, egging Giovanni on until he, Giuseppe, would not be shooting an innocent man, but a man on the verge of attacking him. As he considered the conversation, he decided that one beer would not give him the courage to do what he needed to do. Several whiskeys would be more appropriate.

Just after five o'clock, Giuseppe excused himself from the family and walked up to the Tassone apartment and knocked on the door. Little Frankie answered the door.

"Is your papa at home, yet?" Giuseppe asked.

"He is in his bedroom. He said he had a headache and he went to lay down for a few minutes before dinner."

"Can your mama come to the door?"

"No. She is in the bathroom down the hall. She is throwing up."

"Is she sick?"

"No. She says that new babies make mamas do that. My papa don't want me to talk to you. I have to go." Frankie started to shut the door when Giovanni came out of his bedroom in his undershirt, suspenders dangling from his waistband.

"Hey, Amato! What do you want?" he asked in a gruff voice.

"I thought you wouldn't mind coming out with me tonight over to Feeney's. My treat. I thought we could talk."

"Your treat, eh? So, you are not *un avaro*, tonight! You can spare a nickel for a beer, eh?"

"Sure. For a friend. Say 7:30?"

"As long as my lazy wife finishes giving me dinner. She says she doesn't feel well. So, right now, she is hiding in the bathroom. No dinner ready yet."

Giuseppe decided not to comment. "So, I will see you after dinner!" he responded and turned away from the door. He walked down the dark hall to the stairs, stepping around the last of the children who had yet to be called to supper.

At 7:30 pm, Giovanni came downstairs to the second floor of the tenement house and greeted the Amatos cordially, but stood outside the open door.

"How is Rafaella?" Carmela asked, anxious for news of her friend.

"I told her to make my dinner. After all, I work all day! What does she do? Play with children! Hide in the toilet! You know, you have to be hard with these women! Or they will take you for all you're worth! I made her make my dinner," he finished proudly, directing his argumentative statements to Giuseppe. Carmela cringed and backed up against the scullery counter. Giuseppe, noting his wife's discomfort, grabbed his hat and quickly walked to the doorway.

"Let's go! There is a beer with your name on it!" Giovanni was all too happy to oblige.

The walk was down the street to 47 Spruce Street. Freney's saloon was a pleasant one in the sultry July evening and the two men made small talk. They entered Freney's, a dark little place with a long bar and a handful of tables. Giuseppe ordered two beers, for starters. He laid down a dime, and they picked up their glasses and took them to a small table in the back. Dominick DeFrancesco was there with a friend, having a quick one after a long day of work and he greeted them pleasantly. But most of the other neighborhood men had been avoiding Giovanni recently and said nothing as he passed their tables.

They sat down and immediately Giovanni began to ask questions, speaking Italian, as was his norm. "We are not so good friends that we go drinking together. What do you want?"

"I thought we could discuss what is going on between the two families. I realize you are angry and I would like to clear up any misunderstandings between us."

"Yeah! Sure. You tried to ruin my marriage. You and your gossipy wife talked my wife into running off. It took $50 to find her. That was a large part of my savings. So, not only did you ruin my marriage, you ruined my money situation. So, what do you want to discuss?" Giovanni downed the glass of beer and signaled the bartender to bring him another.

Giuseppe sighed. This was not going as planned. He needed that liquid fortification. When the bartender asked if he needed a refill, he asked for a shot of whiskey, instead.

"Giovanni, I did not try to ruin your marriage. You are responsible for your wife's action. My wife was just lending an ear. That's all." The bartender returned with the two new glasses. Both men had downed theirs before Feeney got back behind the bar.

"You damned piece of crap! You let your wife loose to gossip and have a dirty home and you blame me for controlling my wife too much? Maybe if you had smacked yours more often, she would keep her trap shut better!"

Giuseppe was taken aback by the words. He had to admit, as long as he had known Carmela, she wasn't much of a housekeeper. But she had other virtues he admired. So he had not made her housekeeping a big priority. Still, that was not the purpose of the discussion.

He tried again.

"Look, Giovanni! I am sorry that your wife took off. I even helped you look for her, remember? She is back and all is normal, again. I just want to let bygones be bygones and think we should go on as before."

"No. I think I should make you see how I feel. How would you like a slug between your eyes?" Giovanni was red in the face. His anger was out of line, Giuseppe thought as he listened to the tirade. Maybe Bruno Tassone was right when he said that his brother was a little sick in the head. "Then your little wife will know how I felt with my wife gone God only knows where," Giovanni was continuing. "I got a gun. I could use it. Maybe just kill Carmela. There. Then you would know how I felt. Maybe I should shoot one of the girls so you would know how I felt when my little Concetta died!" Then Giovanni laid down his head on the table and wept.

Giuseppe was alarmed. He signaled over to Feeney for another round. He needed it. "Look," he said, trying to soften the conversation. "There is no need to threaten my family!"

Giovanni's head came up and his tense face was red. "Oh, I see! You can only threaten my family. I cannot do it back!"

"I did not threaten your family. Your wife did what she wanted to do!"

"My little woman is too stupid to plan something like that. You and your wife did it!" Giovanni's voice was getting louder.

Freney came with two full glasses on his tray. Giuseppe gave him a quarter. He downed this second glass, wiped the corners of his mouth with his fingertips and looked Giovanni in the eyes. "I say we talk to Rafaella, all four of us together in a room, and have her explain herself."

"Fine," Giovanni said. "How about as soon as I finish my beer?" He sipped it, smiling slyly over the edge of the glass.

"I'll do you one better. I will buy another round, first." Giuseppe felt another whiskey would settle his nerves better.

There were two more rounds before the two men got up from their chairs and started moving, none too steadily, towards the door. It was almost dark, after nine o'clock on that July night. When they hit the hot humid air outside the door, the alcohol took over and they both became bitter towards one another.

Their voices became loud as they walked up the street towards the *apartment* where they were going to confront Rafaella.

"My Rafaella will tell you she made a mistake listening to you Amatos. She knows her place now. She cannot live without me!"

"Gio! She is not a stupid child. She made her own decisions! She will tell us that!"

"Bah! You *stupido!* My wife is loyal! Just like I am loyal! She wants me and I can take care of her! Not her father!"

"Shut up you two drunks!" came yells from one of the open windows that they passed.

"Go screw yourselves!" Giovanni yelled back.

They parted at the second floor landing, Giovanni promising to bring Rafaella down in a few minutes to prove his point. Giuseppe walked slowly to his apartment, stopping at the door to move the gun from his pants pocket to his jacket pocket.

Carmela was dozing on the couch, still dressed, waiting for her husband to return, hoping he had settled the weeks old argument. It was close to 10:00 pm when he entered the dim kitchen. He closed the door softly behind him and walked a few steps before she looked up.

"What happened?" she asked.

"He is going to bring Rafaella down so she can tell her side of the story which, according to him, will prove that she was talked into running away, against her better judgment."

"What? Oh no, she won't!" Carmela exclaimed, coming quickly off the sofa to face her husband. "If she says something like that it is because he forced her to say it. He is not a nice man! That's why she left him!" Her voice was raising enough to penetrate the thin plaster walls.

"Hush, Carmela! I don't want the whole house to know our business."

"They all know, anyhow!" she said as loud as before. She walked up to him and sniffed his breath. "And you have had quite a bit to drink, eh? Some talk that must have been!"

"I needed the strength to face him!"

"How is it you can afford the strength and I cannot afford the diapers? My God, man! He is not a monster who is going to strike you! He is just a big bully! Preying on the little girl who is his wife!"

"Carmela, please! They will be here soon!"

"What? You are afraid of facing the truth? I saw her wounds! I did nothing to make her leave him! She left of her own accord! If I helped, so what?"

The knock on the door interrupted them and Carmela took a deep breath and answered the door. Giovanni walked in first, rolling a little with each step. "Have a seat at the table," Carmela offered, scowling at him. She stopped Rafaella, momentarily, to give her a hug hello.

"Can I get you some water? It is very hot tonight." She turned towards the table.

"No. No water for me!" Giovanni answered too loudly. He walked over to the table. "You people think that I don't know what you have done. Well, I have brought down my wife to prove to you . . ." He stopped and looked quizzically at Giuseppe. "Hey, Joe! What's that you got in your pocket?"

Carmela looked at her husband questioningly.

Without seeming to think, Giuseppe pulled out his little semi-automatic Colt. Carmela screamed in surprise.

Giovanni looked dumb-founded. "What….?"

Giuseppe's little gun went off. The first round hit Giovanni in the thigh. The victim yelped and grabbed his leg, looking startled.

"Joe, what are you doing?" Carmela screamed as she moved quickly towards her neighbor. Giuseppe was not listening and he shot again. In the next instant, Carmela felt a sharp pain in her breast. Shocked, she fell back and looked down at her bodice, turning a bright red. Stunned, she watched Giuseppe shoot Giovanni again, aiming higher but only in the abdomen. Giovanni's hand went to his left side and he went down on one knee. Grabbing a chair he tried to hoist himself up.

Carmela glanced up at Raffaela's frightened face as she ran towards her husband but Giuseppe, determined to kill his neighbor, shot again. This time, Rafaella was hit just below the waistline. She stopped in her tracks, as a final bullet went into Giovanni's head above his left ear, exploding on impact and Giovanni's broken body crumpled to the floor within a second. The two women screamed in horror as suddenly there was blood and sticky debris all over the floor and walls and on the kitchen table cloth.

The smell of ammonia made Carmela nauseous. The warm blood streaming down her front scared her. And she continued to scream along with Rafaella, shocked at what awful gore was left of her friend's husband.

Giuseppe backed away from them, still holding the little gun. "Shut up! Shut up, you two!" he screamed. He was shocked at what had just happened. His sense of timing wasn't working. He remembered pulling the gun out but wasn't sure how his neighbor died so suddenly. Why wouldn't the gun just stop?

Carmela felt that warm stinging sensation once more, this time below the waistband. She almost passed out and grabbed at the table to steady herself. Her apron had sprouted a dreadful scarlet stain. Before she could look up another shot rang out, going wide and making a hole in the children's bedroom door. Giuseppe spent only a split second more in the kitchen before he dashed out the door and headed for the stairs. The ladies, dazed but conscious, followed, screaming for help, holding their already wet aprons over their wounds. The bedroom door with the bullet hole opened a crack and two pairs of eyes stared out.

The screams and shots had awakened neighbors. Carmela saw people opening their doors just in time to see her husband running past.

Giuseppe ran like the wind, screaming, "Get out of my way or I'll shoot!" and waving his gun in the air.

The women continued to chase him. Carmela got to the bottom of the gangway on the first floor before collapsing and watched as Rafaella managed to get to the front of the next building, before she, too, crumpled to the sidewalk.

CHAPTER 47

HARTFORD, 1930

Miss Amato teared up at this point. She reached for her handkerchief, tucked up into her left sleeve, and dabbed at her eyes. "I'm sorry. All these years. We never really spoke about it. Ma wouldn't allow me. Teresa and I talked about it once or twice after we moved to Newark, but we didn't live together anymore, so it was difficult."

"What did you see?" asked Santoro coaxingly. The young lady took a sip of water and blew her nose. Composing herself, but holding on to the handkerchief, she continued.

"It was night. We were all asleep. Then I woke up, hearing the arguing. I woke up Teresa. We were going to look through the keyhole and spy on them. You know, playing detective again. But then we heard the bangs and the screams. We thought we heard Mrs. Tassone's voice. The bangs scared us. We didn't dare move for a moment. Then, the screams faded away. We got brave and decided to go look. Our bedroom door opened onto the kitchen. It was very hot and we only had on our chemises but the fear made us shudder, like we were cold. There was a really nasty smell in the kitchen. Like ammonia. When we looked out, the light was still on. There was a funny thing on the floor. With man's clothes on. But ripped up. Like how the ragmen dress. You know . . . the old men who come around with their pushcarts and buy old clothes."

The old detective nodded but said nothing. He knew when to keep quiet and when to coax. This was a time to wait silently. The young lady dabbed at her eyes and gulped hard. She sighed and continued.

"Teresa and I were shocked. We had never seen anything like that before. We just stared and stared. We were both pretty sure that it was a man. But his hair was gone and you could . . .you could see . . ." She shuddered and started to sob.

Santoro pressed the intercom on his desk. "Bring me a clean glass," he barked into the microphone. A moment later, Charlie brought in a glass and handed it to the detective as the witness continued to sob. Not being excused, Charlie stood there watching. Santoro pulled open his bottom right drawer, pulled out a bottle of Irish whiskey and poured two fingers worth into the glass. He handed it to Charlie and nodded to the weeping woman.

"Here, Miss," Charlie closed her hand around the glass, then stood protectively beside her chair while she had a sip. "That's a girl," he crooned. "Warm up your insides and the world looks better." He looked askance at the detective. "What are you doing, making this young lady cry like that?"

Miss Amato began to hiccup as her weeping ended. "It's all right, honestly," she said between the hiccups . "I just was overwhelmed with memories. Mr. Santoro did nothing wrong."

"All right, then, Miss. I'll go. I have typing to do." Charlie nodded to his boss and left.

Santoro looked down on the woman and, again, was saddened that such memories could come from such a becoming young thing. "Are you okay to continue?"

She nodded.

"I have the police reports and the newspaper articles which gave great detail about the investigation. Have you ever seen them?"

She shook her head. He handed her several leaves of

paper from his folder and she spent the next half hour quietly reading undisturbed.

CHAPTER 48

THE CHASE

As friends and neighbors started rushing out of the building, they stopped to care for the two obviously hurt women. One of the first on the scene was Maria DeFrancesco and her husband. Their apartment was directly over the Amatos and, with the open windows, the argument was followed. No one wanted to chase after Amato. After all, he had a gun and could hurt someone. The fact that the magazine was empty was not known. Lights from the apartments at the front of the building were flickering on when Butler came around the corner of the railroad station. He had heard the screams all the way from the other side of the station, on Union Place, and, as athletic as he was, got to Spruce Street within a minute or two of Giuseppe's escape.

Immediately, men and women gathered around him. In a combination of English and Italian they told him conflicting reports of what they saw. Some said Giuseppe had crossed the street and ran down along the tracks. Others said he had turned the corner and ran towards Church Street and into the train yards that way.

Within a minute, Butler was joined by Policeman McGrath who had been on Asylum Street

"What's going on here, George?" McGrath asked as he ran up. "Did I hear shots? Who was screaming like that?"

"It's Joe Amato! I think he went nuts! Call headquarters!" McGrath, too, had missed Giuseppe by only a minute or two and he had no idea which path had been taken. He went to the nearest police call box and called headquarters.

"This is McGrath. I am on Spruce Street. There's been a shooting. We need assistance and an ambulance. Two victims. 23 Spruce Street" He listened for a moment, then, hung up. He rushed back up to Butler and said, "They are on their way!"

"Pretty uncommon occurrence, McGrath," Butler commented. "This murder business. You just don't see this stuff much." McGrath was new on the job. Butler was an 11-year veteran. "Two years ago we only had five murders for the whole year. And it looks like two right here. But Chief Gunn always gets the guys in the end."

Dominick DeFrancesco came out from the crowd. "*Scuzi*, please, sirs. I think there is someone dead upstairs. This lady's husband." He pointed to Rafaella, half sitting up on the sidewalk, leaning against one of the female neighbors as friends tried to stave the blood. She had told anyone who would listen what happened to her husband.

"Crap!" swore Butler. "Show me!" he directed Dominick and followed him up the gangway and into the hallway of the building. They climbed one set of stairs and walked down the hall to an open door. Butler knew this was the place. The ammonia and blood smells were overwhelming.

As he and Dominick walked into the apartment, there were two little girls in their chemises, Anna and Teresa, standing by their bedroom door, looking at the bloody mess that had been their playmates' father. His clothes were torn and his hair was matted with blood, looking dirty, like the raggedy peddlers seen on the streets. These two men were the first into the apartment since the shooting had taken place. The girls, both seemingly in shock, could have been there, alone, for almost three minutes.

Dominick ran to the girls and, standing in front of them, blocking the view of the dead body, he turned them around and took them back into the bedroom where the younger ones had slept through the whole scene. He knelt in front of them and held them both tight, praying that the inevitable would not happen. Then he stood, knowing he had much to do.

"Get back into bed, both of you," he ordered, pulling back the sheet under which Dora and Nunziata still slept. "And stay here until I come for you. Do not go into the kitchen, you understand?" He tried to sound stern but tears were coming down and his voice cracked.

"*Si, Zio* Domenico!" the girls whispered softly. He left, closing the door quietly behind him, leaving the two little girls to huddle together in fear.

"What a mess!" Butler commented. He had taken the minute to assess. "That guy is dead, for sure. Bet he never knew what hit him. That's John Tassone, right?"

"Yes, it is."

"Whose place is this? Joe Amato's?"

"Yes, sir."

"Those his kids, I imagine."

"Yes. Six in all."

"Well, see what you can do about getting the children out of here. There will be investigators coming in soon. They won't have time for dealing with kids. And you don't want the other children looking at that mess."

"I will get the neighbors to help," responded Dominick as they walked out the door, closing it behind them.

They walked back outside just as the ambulance arrived. Police Surgeon James C. Wilson hopped out of the passenger side, followed by Policeman Charles F.

Daley, the driver. Wilson was a young man, out of medical school only a few years. He had left his wife and young son to answer the call immediately. His duties were primarily patching up victims and perpetrators before taking them to hospitals or jails. He rarely had seen shot and dying women in the streets at night; never had he seen shot housewives.

He saw Rafaella first. She was weak, but able to sit up on her own, chattering with friends and Officer McGrath, trying to make sense of things.

"Doc, you'd better look at the other victim, first," advised McGrath.

Carmela was going in and out of consciousness. Her sister, Maria, was with her, crying and holding her up. Friends were tearing their own nightgowns and Carmela's petticoat into strips of bandages, trying to stave the bleeding.

"Let me look, please," Doctor Wilson demanded, patiently pulling the women off his patient. He was shocked by the condition. Three bullet holes, one larger than the other two. An exit wound. So, one bullet had gone in and come out. She was not likely to make it.

Carmela opened her eyes at the sound of a male voice. "My husband, Joe Amato, did this. And no one else," she said with effort. She closed her eyes again. *"Mio marito*! He did this!" Then she said nothing more, just incoherent muttering.

"Daley!" Wilson called. "This one first!" Daley brought over a board and enlisted the help of a few of the men standing around. They lifted Carmela onto the gurney and wrapped her in a blanket. Despite the summer night's heat, she was going into shock and had started to shiver. They carried her into the ambulance where Daley covered her with blankets.

Then they went to Rafaella and put her on the second gurney. She wanted to tell everyone what happened and kept sitting up to keep the discussion going. Her English was very good and she had no trouble making herself understood.

Butler came up to Wilson. "Doctor. There's another one inside."

"Is he moving?"

"No. Dead. A bloody mess!" was the response.

"We'll leave him for later," returned the doctor. He was going to have enough to do trying to save these ladies and getting them to Saint Francis Hospital before they died.

Police Officer Daley sped all the way to the hospital, fearful of death occurring in his ambulance. Wilson stayed in the back with the ladies, doing what he could for their comfort.

At the hospital, the doctors were not at all optimistic. Carmela was losing blood from too many wounds. Rafaella was starting to have difficulty breathing and was spitting up blood, indicating lung damage. And to top it off, both women were suffering from abdominal cramps, indicative of miscarriage.

Meanwhile, George Butler, police officer and younger brother of Lt. John Butler, one of the current heroes of the department, had taken responsibility for finding Joe Amato on his own. No other officers had yet arrived and the perpetrator had several minutes head start, now. He ran to the corner of Asylum and Spruce Street and flagged down a taxi which was on its way to find a fare at the train station.

"Hey, you! Stop!" he yelled as he almost ran into the path of the car. "I am commandeering this taxi in the name of the police department!" he said to the chauffeur through the open window.

"Get in, officer!" the chauffeur responded. "Where to?"

"Huntly Place!" Huntly Place was the railroad yards some three blocks away. Butler figured that was where Amato would go first to hide.

They were there in a minute. Butler let the taxi go and he began to walk through the railroad yards, looking into freight cars, using the precaution of taking his gun out of its holster and having it ready. He found no trace of his suspect. But, with few lights in the yards, one man could easily evade another. Once, Butler thought he saw lights flash, but at second glance, he could not find the source. Finally, Butler decided that Amato was too far ahead of him and he went back to the scene to meet up with the officers who, by now, had gotten there.

Detectives Henry L. Hart and Frank Santoro and a few officers were on the scene within just a few minutes of the initial phone report. McGrath met with them.

"The ambulance just left, sir," he reported. "And George went to Huntly Place to see if Amato is hiding in the freight cars."

"I wouldn't have thought of Joe being in this business," commented Santoro. "He doesn't seem to be the type. He's a social fellow, not a perpetrator."

"Looks like a domestic dispute gone bad," said McGrath. "The women don't look too good. Dead guy upstairs."

"Frank," ordered Hart. "You know this Amato. Give these officers a good description and send them out." Then he moved away from the group. "I'm calling for backup," he called as he jogged down the street to the call box. He rang up the desk sergeant. "Get all available officers and supernumeraries to this scene immediately.

And let me talk to Lieutenant. Butler."

"Butler, here," John Butler answered the phone a minute later. He listened as Hart described the scene.

"Henry, get all the supers over to the train yards and cover every inch of the place. I will call the trolley companies and get them on the lookout. We'll get officers to the main outlets of the city and shut off every avenue of escape!" He paused for a moment. "Give me a description of this Amato. And I will call around to the nearby cities and ask them to arrest him on sight."

"He's about five foot, eight inches. Slight built man. He has a mustache. Dark straight hair, balding on top. He combs his hair over the bald spot. Last seen with a dark suit and a straw hat. His English is good. Real personable fellow, from what I hear. He is a barber. Some of the officers see him regularly."

"Thanks, Henry. I am going to call a few places right now. Keep me up to date." They hung up and Lt. Butler immediately started his phone calls. He called New Britain, Meriden and spoke directly to Chief Quilty in Springfield. The chief promised to give his patrolmen a description in the morning at roll call.

Hart walked back to the command center in front of 23 Spruce Street He spoke to the remaining officers for a few minutes, planning their actions when the police phone rang. Hart ran to answer it.

"Hart! This is Butler. There's a report that a man believed to be Amato was seen at the railroad tunnel on the north side. Send some officers out that way and look in the district above the tunnel."

"Sure, Lieutenant! I've got a few men I can send." Hart went back to the group of men and sent two detectives to go watch the trains. Meanwhile, he and Santoro headed back to the police station, leaving

McGrath and George Butler to keep an eye on the crime scene.

CHAPTER 49

HARTFORD, JULY 23, 11pm

After Carmela and Rafaella were put into the ambulance, Dominick found his wife, Maria, standing by the stoop, crying softly. He put his arms around his plump little wife and held her tightly.

"We will make it through this, just like we have made it through every other problem. Just pray, *mia cara*. Pray for the strength. We need the Blessed Virgin's help tonight. And that of the Guardian Angels."

Maria nodded, comforted by her husband's words. The whole thing was so terrifying.

"Oh, *mio Dio*!" she exclaimed. "The babies!" She looked up at him.

"I went up. Anna and Teresa saw! I put them back to bed and told them to not come out until I came back. That was ten minutes ago."

"Oh, the poor babies!"

"We have to get them to our apartment. But the body is still there. It is a mess. Can you handle it, *mia cara?*"

"For the babies, I can do anything," his wife said staunchly. They walked up the stairs together and down the hall to the door, waving off the neighbors who were still in the hallway, talking.

When they got to the door, Dominick put his hand on the knob and turned to his wife. "It is bad, I warn you." She nodded and he opened the door. The sight was overwhelming to Maria. Due to the warm humid air coming through the open windows, the stench had remained thick. They did not look at the floor, but walked up to the bedroom door and opened it.

Anna and Teresa immediately sat up in bed, holding on to each other, wide eyed and tear-stained. At the sight of Zio and Zia, the little girls jumped up and ran to the two adults and hid their heads in their clothes. No words passed between the children and the overwrought adults, but each lifted one of the little girls and carried them, silently, upstairs to their own apartment.

"Nickie!" Dominick called as soon as they walked in. Nickie walked in from the bedroom he shared with his brothers. He had not been asleep. He had been watching out the window ever since they had heard the shots earlier. He had been told to watch his siblings and not leave the apartment.

"*Si*, Papa!" he was instantly on alert. He saw his little cousins and crouched down to wipe the tears from their eyes. "Don't worry. We are here." They nodded and tried to smile.

"Nickie!" Dominick repeated. "Come with me." They walked out the apartment door and Dominick shut it. He eyed his oldest. "It is bad. *Zio* Giuseppe shot the Tassones and *Zia* Carmela." Nickie gasped.

"Signor Tassone is dead. *Zia* Carmela and Signora Tassone have been taken to the hospital. But we must get the children out. Anna and Teresa saw it. The others have slept through."

They walked down to the apartment. Dominick signaled Nickie to be quiet and opened the door.

"Oh, my God!" Nickie blurted when he stepped in. Dominick hushed him and cuffed him. Nickie looked up to his father in apology. He was truly shocked. They walked into the children's bedroom and went to pick them up.

As Nickie picked up Julia from her crib, he gasped,

again. There was a bullet hole in the wall a foot above her bed. He quickly lifted her and Nunziata and left the apartment, while Dominick followed with the baby Giuseppe and three year old Dora.

There was no horizontal surface in the DeFrancesco apartment that was unoccupied that night.

Meanwhile, after not finding Amato at Huntly Place, George Butler had returned to the scene to report in. "What is happening with the children?" he asked Chief Detective Hart who had arrived in his absence.

"The Amato children are going with their aunt and uncle who live in the building, too."

"How about Tassone's children? Didn't he have some?" asked Butler. He thought he had seen Mrs. Tassone with children once or twice.

"Go find out what you can," Hart ordered.

Butler went into the building and asked a few of the people in the hallways until he found which one was the Tassone apartment. He walked up to the third floor and went in. Flipping on the ceiling light, he looked around. It was a tidy, well decorated little place. The sitting area had lace curtains at the windows and a deep green sofa with matching chair. Over the bedroom doors were two small crucifixes. He heard crying from one of the bedrooms. He opened the door carefully and found three little children sitting, huddled together on their bed. The oldest seemed frightened and the two youngest, Bruno and Teresa, were wet-faced and wild-eyed, crying "Mama! Papa!"

Butler tried to calm them down. "Hello. I am Officer Butler. I am going to help you. Mama and Papa cannot be with you right now." It didn't help much. He left the bedroom and started knocking on doors asking for help with the children.

The first door he tried was the DeFrancesco's. Dominick answered the door. "Do you think I can take more children? I have twelve with me tonight. There is no more room!" Other doors he tried claimed to have no room, also. One said there was an uncle in town; try him. In the end, Butler called for the patrol wagon and sent the children to the police headquarters where they were handed over to the care of Matron Katherine Farr. The Matron's apartment in the station had two bedrooms, one for the matron and one for her "guests". The little children fell asleep, still crying, on the double bed in her spare room.

CHAPTER 50

HARTFORD, JULY 24, MIDNIGHT

After midnight, Amato still had not been found. So, Hart, Santoro and three supernumeraries, John Sponza, William Gunn, son of Chief Gunn, and W.C. Bunce, started out in a touring car. All three supernumeraries were young and energetic. Gunn, the chief's son and having just graduated from Yale, was there for the fun. They were ordered to tour over the countryside, both north and south of town. The car was kept in service until the following morning at 8 am. They found nothing.

The police department kept supernumeraries Antonio Clementino and John Sponza on the job overnight. The hope was, since they knew Giuseppe personally and were fluent in Italian, they could more easily search for and, perhaps, capture him. The east side was thoroughly gone over. All the haunts known to have been frequented by Amato were gone over several times.

About midnight, Police Officer Albert G. Plant walked in the main police station downtown. He greeted the desk sergeant on duty.

"Hi, Jake! What's cooking?"

"Haven't you heard?" Jake had a surprised look on his face.

"Heard what?"

"There's been a triple shooting on Spruce Street. About 10:00 tonight."

"Really? Have they caught the perpetrator yet?"

"No. There's a city-wide man-hunt set up."

"Who are they looking for?"

"An Italian. Joe Amato."

"Amato? Are you sure?"

"Of course, I'm sure. Why?"

"I could have sworn I saw him tonight. About eleven thirty."

"Where?"

"I was getting on the Wethersfield trolley to come in to work. I'd swear I saw Amato getting off the last southern-bound trolley. I know Joe. I know what he looks like. I was too far away to yell hello, but I'd swear it was him."

"Too bad you hadn't heard the news yet. We could have put this perp behind bars and be done with him by now." He shook his head then picked up his phone to call the lieutenant.

When Lt. Butler heard the news, he called in Detective Sergeant Lewis Mulberger and Sergeant James D. Flynn. Mulberger, 41, was well-known as an expert bicyclist for the Hartford Police. He was a hero, of sorts, having been written up in newspapers for his abilities at catching thieves and other criminals. Sergeant Flynn was a 15 year veteran of the regular police department. Both men were well experienced in their jobs.

"Lewis, James, we have had word that Amato may have gone south from here. We have one squad combing north of here. I want you to go south as far as Middletown and scour the countryside in a northerly direction. Come north as far as Wethersfield. That's where Plant saw him last."

"Sure, boss!"

"I want every inch of the ground along the road from Middletown and Cromwell to Rocky Hill gone over on foot. Report to me in the morning."

The men took lanterns and guns with them.

After the children were taken from the Tassone apartment, McGrath and Butler did an extensive search of the two apartments and the basement of the tenement building. The two walked into the Tassone place, admiring the décor.

"You take the living room and I will take the bedrooms," Butler instructed the younger man. "We are looking for any kind of weapon or paperwork to prove the guy was dangerous." In a small apartment it did not take long.

"McGrath!" yelled Butler from the parents' bedroom. "Look here what I found!" The younger officer stepped into the room as Butler was picking up a .38 from the top drawer of the bureau.

"Is it loaded?"

Butler dropped down the cylinder. "A bullet in every chamber!" he announced. "Ready to go! I guess the poor guy didn't know he was going to a gun fight. He might have had a chance if he'd brought it with him."

"Guess we found what we were looking for," said McGrath. "Think we should look in the common areas, too?"

"No attic in this building. Hallways always too crowded to hide anything. But I think we should check the basement," suggested Butler.

The low ceiling of the basement caused the big men to duck their heads slightly as they roamed around, pushing cobwebs away from their hats.

"Look here!" exclaimed McGrath. "By the window!" He picked up the paper target where it was still leaning on the chair. Looking around the floor, they also found seventeen spent cartridges. "What kind of a gun did Amato have?"

"I'm not sure," answered Butler, picking up one of

the cartridges and inspecting it. "Looks to be one of those new semi-automatics the lieutenant was talking to us about. I've never heard about finding cartridges like this at a crime scene in Hartford before." He looked around, trying to figure out where else something could be hidden.

"Follow the rafters. Something could be hidden up there." They silently walked along, ducking beneath the rafters, looking for something that did not belong. They found two suitcases full of moth eaten blankets and a box of old love letters dated two years earlier. But nothing for the first hour. *(a box not old)*

"Got it!" announced the younger man as he just managed to get his large hand into a wedge and pull out a cardboard box. "It looks like the box the gun came in." Butler came over and took it closer to the window to read the label.

"I was right about that gun! It's a Colt .32 semi-automatic! And it has the serial number stamped on the outside. Should make identifying the weapon easy." He took out his notepad and recorded the number immediately.

Newspaper reporters were on the scene by midnight. This was sensational news and they were going to make the most of it. Newspaper headlines appeared in the morning papers. "Triple Shooting on Spruce Street" they read. Conflicting reports occurred about the causes of the shooting and doubts of the ability of either woman to recover were detailed. When the police officers finished their inspections of the apartments, they had allowed the reporters in to inspect the premises of the victims. The Amato apartment was unkempt, with diapers and dirty dishes needing to be cleaned. It was reported that this was the type of place social workers would have a time with.

"Of course," commented one reporter, "Perhaps it is

* Did they have social workers back then?

because the housewife is lying in a hospital, dying and just hadn't gotten around to finishing yesterday's chores." The others laughed knowing that the Italian race was known for being dirty. But they were much more sympathetic to the Tassone place, where the furniture quality was better and neatness was more evident.

Within hours, police had tracked down Bruno Tassone, Giovanni's brother. Antonio Clementino, one of the supernumerary officers, was sent to interview the man. Clementino spoke Italian, just in case Tassone's English was not good. The brother had a small room on Front Street, several blocks south of Spruce, and lived alone.

When Clementino knocked on the door, Bruno Tassone answered slowly, as if he was just getting up. He had already heard about his brother. There was no love lost between the two. He was not in mourning.

"I suppose you are here about my brother," Tassone said on opening the door and seeing a uniformed officer. "There is nothing I can tell you."

"You make my job easier," Antonio Clementino responded in Italian. "May I come in? I do have a few questions."

"Sure, sure!" Tassone backed away so Clementino could enter. He picked shoes and a shirt off a chair and put them on the floor. "Sit!"

"You know who killed your brother?" Clementino asked. Tassone cleaned off another chair and balled up the pants on that chair, tossing them into a corner.

"Sure. Joe Amato!"

"Do you know any reason why Amato would want to kill your brother?"

"Giovanni was a hot head and a little nuts, if you ask me! Terrible jealous of his wife. He went off easily. Like when Concetta died. Giovanni was screaming and crying like a girl, for days. Rafaella didn't even cry like that!" He shook his head at the memory.

"Who is Concetta?"

"Their first child. She died when she was a baby."

Clementino recorded Bruno's words in a notebook.

Bruno went on. "Giovanni was a controlling man. I guess Rafaella couldn't stand it anymore. She took off. Amato's wife was her friend. So Giovanni decided that the Amatos had helped her to run off."

"He blamed the Amatos for his wife leaving?"

"Yes. And when he paid the private investigator to find her, he blamed them for making him lose his money."

"Where did he find her?"

"Ah! She had gone home to her parents! In Providence."

"But why did Amato kill him?"

"My stupid brother! He kept saying he was going to kill Joe for what he did."

"So, it was a matter of kill or get killed?"

"I guess." Tassone shrugged but had nothing more to say about it. Clementino left.

CHAPTER 51

SEVENTH SORROW: JESUS IS BURIED

HARTFORD, WEDNESDAY, JULY 25

Wednesday morning, the nurses thought they were going to lose both women. Dr. Wilson checked in on them at 8:00 am. Carmela was in and out of consciousness. She had lost much blood, as well as the baby she was carrying.

"The patient is in need of a blood transfusion," Dr. Wilson commented. "Have any neighbors offered to donate?"

"No, Doctor," responded the day nurse, Miss Kent. "Orders went out to ask around the neighborhood but none would do it."

"They think we are going to take their lives if we take their blood, I am afraid!" the doctor responded. "I know there is something in the blood that makes people react badly sometimes. We need transfusions from people of the same race."

"But, Doctor, several of the nurses have offered to donate their own blood."

"No. That will not work. The nurses couldn't work for a few hours afterwards. Besides, there are no Italian nurses. How do we know the Irish blood would work?" Wilson sighed. "And we know she will die without it."

He shook his head and turned towards the other shooting victim. Wilson took her wrist to check her pulse. It was slow. He took out his stethoscope and listened. Her lungs were not operating well and her breathing was labored. Wilson muttered to himself and quietly addressed

Miss Kent, "Her prognosis is touch and go."

To get eyewitness reports as quickly as possible, the assistant coroner and the prosecuting attorney decided to visit the hospital and question the two women.

Deputy Coroner William H. Leet of Thompsonville was a lawyer and had dreams of a political career. That's why he had taken this position. He didn't know the first thing about medicine despite his title. Edwin Dickenson, prosecuting attorney for Hartford was a young, imaginative lawyer and a short story writer. He also had expectations of an active political career and, within a decade would become a published author, an associate judge and an entrepreneur. From the point of view of these two men, this visit was a minor, unimportant moment in their lives, a simple data collection.

They walked into the large hospital ward, with the day nurse, where the two women lay, across from one another. It had been only twelve hours since the shooting and the two friends were both asleep. There were six other women lying on the white-painted brass beds, lined up against the walls. Each was covered with white muslin sheets up to their chins. Some were awake, watching the two men, who obviously were out of their element. The nurse, crisply professional looking in her whites, walked down the center of the room to a bed where a woman with long auburn braids lay.

"Mrs. Amato," whispered the nurse. "Can you hear me?" Her eyelids fluttered but that was the only response she gave.

The nurse, Miss Kent, looked at the two importantly-dressed men and shrugged. She felt uncomfortable in their presence.

"How about the other woman, uhm, Mrs. Tassone?"

asked Leet. He looked around the room, spying the large crucifixes on the two opposing walls. As a Protestant, he felt such a display of Catholicism had no place in a room full of sick women. But the Catholic Church was paying for it, he thought. Let them do what they will with décor.

"Across the room, here, sirs," Miss Kent replied as she moved over to Raffaela's bed. "Mrs. Tassone?"

Rafaella looked like a child as she lay there, with her dark hair splayed out around her head. She opened her eyes after a few moments. But she did not seem to know where she was.

"Mrs. Tassone, I am Edwin Dickenson and I am the prosecuting attorney in the city. I would like to ask you a few questions."

Rafaella tried to sit up but fell back on her pillow immediately. Trying to talk only made her cough, painfully. She looked at them, mutely, and started to tear up.

"I am sorry, sirs," insisted Miss Kent. "This is obviously too much for Mrs. Tassone. You need to leave. Maybe in a day or two she will be able to answer your questions."

Her patients were her first concern and she wasn't going to let two big-wigs push around any weak little thing like this girl. The men with their fancy leather briefcases left with no information.

A few hours later, a middle-aged, red-headed man walked into the ward during regular visiting hours. He had some papers with him and another, smaller man followed behind. The red-headed man walked up to Carmela's bed and sat himself down on the straight-backed chair next to it. His red hair was matted from the humidity outside and he had the look of a man who was overwhelmed. He had hardly slept the night before, comforting his darling Maria as best he could.

"Carmela," he whispered. "It is me, Dom."

She opened her eyes for a moment then shut them again.

"Look, *cara*. I don't think you are going to make it and neither do you. Maria sends her love. She has the children. They are going to be fine." He paused. "Look, *cara*! I want to talk to you but you are so tired. Every time I ask a question, all I want you to do is raise your finger." He touched her pointer finger. "You raise it every time you mean yes." He looked at her face, ashen and in pain. "Do you understand?" The finger went up slowly then down. "Good."

"I have a man with me. He is from the courts. He is going to help us. Do you understand?" The finger went up and down again.

"Look, Carmela. The children are going to need money. I think you need to sell Joe's shop and get some money." He stopped for a minute to see if she would react. She did not.

"I want to buy the shop from you and then sell it for the money. I have checked that account you have in your name and know how much money is in the bank. We will take that out, too. Do you know what I am saying?" The finger went up and down again. Carmela's eye remained closed the whole time.

"We are going to write you out a will. You will leave everything to the children. And I will take care of the finances. It will have to go through the courts but we have to get this done right away. I am so sorry I have to make you do this today." He choked on his words as he got tearful.

The little man, so far having said nothing, pulled out papers from his briefcase and handed them to Dominick.

There was an inventory of all the things in the shop including their values. Dominick picked up Carmela's hand and put a pen in it. Her eyes opened. "You must sign your name, Carmela. I will help you." He guided her hand as he signed her name. She immediately closed her eyes again, as if exhausted. Then he handed the papers back to the little man who signed his name as witness and put the papers back in his briefcase. Then he walked into the hallway to wait.

"The children send you their love." At that, Carmela opened her eyes one more time, looked at him and smiled faintly. "I will take care of things. Do not worry." He bent over to kiss her forehead. His tears fell on her face. "Until we meet again. *Arriverderci!*"

She closed her eyes and he left to join the court officer, who was wiping his sweaty face with a large cotton handkerchief.

Alone, Carmela balled up her hand a little, gripping the sheets. Tears appeared from under her lids. If someone had bothered to listen to her whispers he would have heard her words, "Dear Lady, my Mother in Heaven, this is the last one of my seven sorrows."

CHAPTER 52

WINDSOR, CT. JULY 24

Wednesday, July 24, was a lovely summer's day. Outside of the hospital, most were enjoying the warm weather. Children who had the advantage played in any body of water around.

Outside the little hamlet of Windsor, just north of Hartford, several children were playing in the shallow waters of Stony Brook. The boys had rolled up their overall pant legs and were splashing around to cool off.

"Hey! Look at this, guys!" Mike Tuttle yelled. He saw a shiny object and bent over to retrieve it. It was a gun. The boys, all ten to twelve years old, gathered around to admire it. The gun was much smaller than anything they had at home. And it did not have a bullet chamber like the ones their dads and brothers used for hunting. They took turns pretending to aim with it and shoot with it.

There was a bridge across the little creek for a farmer's cows to cross. It was not very sturdy nor very large, but it did the trick when the grass got low on one side. Tim Parry's dad owned it and the children were allowed to play there. However, this afternoon, there was another person sitting by the bridge. He was a poorly dressed man of about 50 years of age, obviously not fastidious in his use of soap and water. He was the typical homeless vagrant. And the vagrant was watching their every move.

"Hey, boy!" he yelled. "That there is my gun! Give it back!"

The boys stopped in their tracks. Mike yelled back, "So why is it in the water?"

"I dropped it last night and couldn't find it in the dark. I slept in this morning or I would have gotten it back by now." The older man had gotten up and was walking slowly towards the boys with his hand held out. "So, now, you be good boys and give me back my gun!" His voice was menacing to the four and they began to slowly back their way out of the creek and onto the grass.

"So, if it's your gun, what is the make?" Mike called again, gathering some courage.

"Give me that gun, you damn kids!" the man yelled as he broke into a run towards them. The boys, all light on their feet, could easily outrun a down and out vagrant.

They arrived at the Parry farmhouse, not a quarter of a mile off, without losing their breath, Tim went running to the barn, calling for his father. Mr. Parry, having been resting in the cool of the shade, walked quickly out of the barn when he heard his youngest yelling his name.

"What is it, boys?" Mr. Parry asked, looking at the four anxious, flushed faces. He squinted into the sunlight and saw the disheveled stranger who had walked boldly up to the barnyard, with his hand out.

"Who are you?" Parry asked, turning to the man.

"They got my gun! I want my gun!" the fellow responded.

Parry looked at the boys and back at the man. "Tell me the truth, boys. Where'd you get this gun?"

"We found it in the creek!" all four replied.

"What kind of a gun you got, Mister?" Parry asked the vagrant. The man could not answer and turned away. He knew he was not going to get that gun. It would have given him close to ten dollars at the pawn shop.

"How much did you pay for this, Mister? This looks

a little pricey for the likes of you!" Parry called to him. The vagrant kept walking.

"Now, boys! You can't keep this gun. It belongs to someone. It's new and a lot of money." Parry said, turning to the boys.

"What'll we do with it, Pa?" asked Tim.

Parry stood still for a moment and turned the matter over in his head. "I think we ought to turn it over to Sheriff Welch. You boys run into town and find him and get him over here. I will hold on to the gun in the meantime."

The four barefoot boys were off at once. It wasn't half a mile into the hamlet and the sheriff could always be counted on, this time of the day, to be reading the newspaper on a seat in front of the general store.

Edson S. Welch was getting on in years. He had been deputy sheriff, and then sheriff, of Windsor for twenty years. His wife, Mary, and he had been married for 37 years and she could best describe him as comfortable as an old glove. They had spent most of their mature years caring for poor folks and lost souls in their home in Windsor. He was a most honest man.

The two Hartford papers had screaming headlines about the shootings and Welch was absorbing the stories as the boys ran up, excited about a fancy gun. The sheriff put two and two together real fast for a countryman. Welch was not going to get involved with taking possession of a murder weapon. He took the boys over to his office where he rang up the Hartford police.

"This here is Sheriff Edson Welch of Windsor. I got to talk to some detectives. Sure, I'll wait." He paused and motioned to the boys to help themselves to the big jar of penny candy on his desk.

"Hello? Detective Santoro? This here is Sheriff Edson Welch up in Windsor. I got me a gun found in Stony Creek about an hour ago. It sounds like it might be something you are looking for. New. Sounds like a semi-automatic. Nope. Haven't seen it yet. But it is a Colt." He listened for another minute then closed with, "That's fine. I'll be waiting on you."

After the phone call he turned to the boys.

"You go back to the farm and stay put. The police from Hartford are sending out some detectives to meet me. They should be here in an hour or so. Go tell your pa to put that gun someplace safe and we'll be over soon's they get here."

The boys turned to leave the office and one of them remembered to say thanks to Welch. He smiled his old man smirk and they left.

True to his word, about an hour and fifteen minutes later, one of the Hartford police touring cars was seen rumbling down the rutted road to the Parry farm. The boys came running out of the barn at the sound. They had rarely seen a car, much less a police car. They surrounded it as soon as it came to a stop. Policeman John F. Flanigan got out of the driver's side and Detective Frank Santoro got out of the passenger side, with Welch pulling himself out of the back seat. Mr. Parry walked out of the barn right behind the boys and was there to greet the three officers.

"Edson," Parry nodded to the sheriff. "Gentlemen," he greeted the representatives of Hartford. "Please, come in the house." He led the way into the kitchen. It was a big room in a hundred year old house. There was a fireplace, although Parry had bought a new wood-burning stove for his wife a few years back. There was a large table in the center of the room with a well-scrubbed gleam to the wood and a jar of wildflowers in the center. The boys and men had plenty of seating at the table.

"Have a seat at the table, gentlemen. I'll get the gun," Parry said and he walked into the pantry. Returning with the prized piece, he set it on the table, in front of Santoro.

Santoro pulled a piece of paper out of his vest pocket and compared the numbers on the paper to the serial number etched into the gun. Then he looked up. "This is it. I have the serial number from the box Amato left in the basement of his building. This matches." He put the gun in his pocket after checking to make sure the clip was empty. The boys watched his every move. But they knew better than to ask to handle it again.

Santoro then turned his attention to the boys. "I want you to show me where you found it." The boys, all too anxious to be involved, jumped up and led the way out the door and down the slight incline to the creek. Santoro followed, leaving Flanigan and Edson up at the house with Mr. Parry.

"Right there, mister," Mike pointed. "It was in a foot or so of water, next to that rock." The detective took notes on a pocket-sized sketch pad.

"Thanks, boys," he said. "You did some fine detective work." He smiled broadly enough to show his teeth beneath his ample mustache. The boys, excited about a compliment coming from a real live detective, would daydream for days about joining the Hartford police department and be detectives themselves, some day.

Meanwhile, the Springfield patrolmen and several members of the detective bureau spent most of Wednesday in the Italian quarter searching for a man who met Giuseppe's description. They even ran into a man who seemed to be the culprit, until they noticed that he had curly hair. They let him go.

Assuming that Giuseppe had headed north, Hartford officers Sponza and Santoro went to Thompsonville on the Connecticut- Massachusetts line on Thursday afternoon. A holiday excitement permeated the population in the little village as the officers searched faces, looking for the murderer in disguise. Everyone had read newspapers or heard talk of the events of Tuesday night and were anxious to be involved. A reporter from the *Springfield Republican* showed up and questioned the two.

"Have Quilty's men found any clues yet?" the reporter asked.

"No. He is pretty sure that his men have combed the area and would have found him if he was there. We think he is either hiding in a small town or headed further north," responded Santoro. He was beginning to wonder about this elusive man. He had always been involved with investigations that got their man! But this time seemed so different.

CHAPTER 53

HARTFORD, THURSDAY, JULY 25

Giovanni's body had no mourners on Thursday morning when Joe D'Esopo's place on Temple Street had a burial service for him. Not even his brother, Bruno, showed up to view the closed casket or participate in the service. No one had loved him. Even his wife, who was too ill to worry about it, was not sad when she was well enough to visit his grave. Only D'Esopo, his wife, Mary, and a reporter from the newspaper were there to observe the last of Giovanni Tassone's life journey.

The Thursday morning papers also announced the death of Carmela Amato. She had succumbed to her injuries about midnight, having suffered for over twenty-four hours. Dominick took responsibility for having her sent over to D'Esopo's and to arrange a funeral Mass for Friday morning.

Maria, as traumatic as her life seemed to be at the moment, held the family together. She did what she could to feed the 12 children on one barber's salary although, creative as she was, there was little enough to go around.

After the announcement of Carmela's death, the mourning in the tenement house became obvious. It was not even 7:00 am when people started knocking on the door of the DeFrancesco apartment. Every hour, all day long, more food was brought. The Italian custom of bringing food to the family of the deceased was never more welcome.

The children's eyes bulged as they saw trays of prosciutto, provolone, peppers and olives. There were baskets of oranges and bananas, rare, indeed, in an era before refrigeration. There were deliveries of casks of wine and cakes. The younger children could not comprehend the party atmosphere. Nor had most of them seen so much food at one time. Even the older ones oohed and aahed as each dish was uncovered to reveal items they had only seen in the store windows on Asylum Street.

Thursday night was another warm night. Dominick and Maria went out of the building after the little ones were settled. Nickie and Maria's Teresa stayed in to keep an eye on things. It was almost 9:00 pm and the last glow of the summer sun was waning. The couple went for a walk in Bushnell Park. The past 48 hours had exhausted them to the point where they could not sleep. So, they walked quietly, his arm around her, along the fragrant pathways until their jangled nerves relaxed.

"Maria, *mia cara*!" Dominick began. "We cannot continue like this very long. We cannot afford to feed so many on my salary."

"I know that. I just cannot stand the thought of tearing the children apart, like we must."

"I have a surprise for you. I sent Ciro a telegram last night, before Carmela died. I did not want him to see something in the newspapers. And I received one back from him this afternoon. He and Emilia are coming on the train and will be here in time for the funeral. But your brother Joe cannot make it."

"Oh, Dom! How wonderful and thoughtful of you!" Maria turned towards him and gave him a hug. "I am so glad he is coming. He will help us decide what to do with the children. They will see how impossible it is for us to keep them all."

"Ciro is a good man. He will help us with this

284

problem. We will come up with a plan." His relieved smile was genuine. He hated to see Maria overwhelmed and was glad that something he had done had helped. For at least a few hours, she would be able to catch some sleep in the hopes of a solution forthcoming.

They were up with the sun in the morning. There was much to do. The neighbor ladies had volunteered to scrub the Amato apartment after the police had finished their investigation. The blood and other stains were much faded and the place was picked up, fresh linens on the beds. Maria called her two daughters to her side, after an early breakfast. At 13 and 12, they were so grown up, now.

"We are having guests, like I said this morning. We have to use the other apartment. You girls will spend the nights downstairs in Zia Carmela's place. You stay in the children's bedroom. Zio Ciro and Zia Emilia will sleep in the other bedroom. You take care of the place and keep it clean, like here. And you cook them breakfast in the morning. They will eat here the other times. You understand?"

"Si, Mama!" the girls responded. They were a little squeamish about sleeping in that apartment, but they knew better than to argue with their mother. They went to their room and got their night clothes and brought them downstairs. The two girls walked the long way around the kitchen table to avoid the stain still somewhat evident on the floor. They looked at the walls which the chlorine bleach still hadn't cleaned completely and shuddered. Going into the bedroom, they threw their things under the pillows on the bed and dashed out of the room, through the kitchen and out the door as if chased by ghosts.

Coming back into the upstairs apartment, Nickie was already dressed for the funeral.

"Don't eat anything with that suit on!" warned Teresa. "You might break a button! Look at you! The pants are inches above your shoes! And you better not bend your elbows! They will split!" The girls laughed, glad of something to laugh at. Nickie was self-conscious but grinned at them, all the same.

"It is all we have. It will have to do," sighed Maria. "Now, Nickie, you go to the train station and get your *zio e zia*! You do not want them waiting. They haven't been here in years. They won't remember which house is ours."

The girls helped get the little ones ready, trying to mix and match ribbons and dresses and petticoats until everyone had enough to look presentable at the funeral.

Carmela's Teresa and Anna were understandably quiet. They had not spoken much since the night of the shootings. They clung to each other and whispered words no one else heard. Anna stared through people with her big blue eyes and Teresa looked down at the floor except when being addressed. They sat on the floor where they were instructed and held their own siblings tightly as each was declared dressed and ready to go.

An hour before they had to leave for the funeral, Nickie, Ciro and Emilia came through the door. Maria, already dressed in her old black satin dress, was so very thrilled to see her brother after several years that she ran across the room to greet him and his wife. Then she burst into tears as the emotional weight overcame her.

"There, there, Maria," Ciro crooned, holding her tight. He noted the grey hairs on her head and the care lines in her face. But she was still his darling older sister. He thought of Carmela, how she was often a little reckless and how lovely her auburn hair would glint in the sunshine. And he teared up at the thought that he never was able to say goodbye. Then he looked around the room at the ten pairs of eyes staring at him. Many had never even met him. He patted Maria on the back and released her. He knelt to get to the children's height.

"Ho! What's this? Look at all these little people!" He felt he could at least have an attachment to his dead sister through her children. "Nickie! You have to introduce me to all my nieces and nephews!" He did what he could to sound upbeat. Nickie pointed to each in turn, running through all the names for his uncle as Ciro had something to say about each one. Carmela's two oldest were unresponsive but her others, too young to understand, were happy to meet another uncle.

Soon it was time to leave for Street Joseph's Cathedral. As Maria explained, the pastor at the little Street Anthony's had advised the family to have the funeral at the bigger church, being as there would be many people coming to see the curiosity. He did not think that the little building would hold the expected crowd. But the cathedral was only a few blocks further away and they would walk. On the way, Dominick walked with the dry, silent Emilia. He could think of very little to say to her. Ciro walked behind, right next to Maria so they could talk.

"Carmela's two oldest saw what happened? They are not in mourning. It is something else."

"Oh, Ciro! They saw the dead man's body! It was, it was….awful. He was shot in the head and other places, too! No one thought of the children for a few minutes. When Carmela and Rafaella were shot we all worried about them! Dom found Anna and Teresa alone with the body."

"*Mio Dio!*" Ciro exclaimed as he made the Sign of the Cross.

"We think it is best if we don't talk about it at all. The girls are in shock. No need to talk and wake up the memories."

"I will remember that. I will say nothing about the deaths." Ciro responded. "Did they see their mother after?"

"No. Dom put them back to bed and then the ambulance came." Maria shifted the baby, Giuseppe, so that she could wipe her eyes. "The man's body was right in the kitchen! How awful!" She blew her nose and startled the baby who sent off a shriek. She laughed tearfully and murmured, "Don't worry, *mio bambino!*"

Ciro put his arm around his short sister and continued the walk in silence down to Farmington Ave. When they got to the church, Joe D'Esopo's hearse was already there with the coffin in the back. They eyed it as they walked past it on the way to the steps of the impressive church. At the top of the stairs, before opening the large wooden door, Maria checked each girl to make sure she had a proper head covering. She checked her boys to make sure that dirt had not mysteriously appeared on their best clothes. Dominick smiled despite the seriousness of the occasion. Maria did the same thing every Sunday.

The children filed in between the adults and walked to the front of the church. Those who were already seated looked on the six Amato children with sincere sadness. Maria and Dominick kept control with the help of their three oldest, dispersed amongst the younger ones to help. Most of the children did not understand the Mass, the Latin or the coffin sitting at the front of the church, but they knew to sit still. And Maria was proud of their efforts.

After Mass, only a few adults went on to Mt. Saint Benedict Cemetery to watch Carmela's remains buried.

Maria and the children went back to the apartment.

All afternoon, wave after wave of well-wishers and mourners came and went. Children got tired and ornery and Maria prayed it would end soon. The visitations finally ended at nightfall.

After the younger children were put to bed, the four adults were able to sit down and discuss what to do with the children.

"Have you heard anything about Giuseppe?" asked Ciro.

"Only what we read in the newspaper," Dominick responded, pouring himself and his brother-in-law some wine.

"Is there any way that it was an accident?" Ciro asked, again.

"No. And I do not think it was, as they say, a domestic dispute."

"Why do you say that so strongly?"

"Joe has been having financial problems for a long time. I think he used the problem with Tassone's wife as an excuse to get out of them."

"What do you mean?" Maria piped up. She had no knowledge of Giuseppe's finances. She thought his difficulties were the same as other immigrants.

"He was in with the wrong crowd and couldn't get out. They pressed him for money and he gave it to them. Then he started handling an illegal lottery and cheating on the leaders." The women gasped.

"What did I tell Carmela years ago!" exclaimed Ciro, slamming his hand on the table.

"Please, Ciro! Don't start talking ill of the dead!" Maria put her hand on his arm, pleading. Ciro sighed and looked with pity on his sister who was so sad at the death of her best friend.

"Ciro," Dominick continued. "You remember a fellow named Tony the Mule? He was a funny looking one. Had a crooked finger. He always seemed to have money but no one knew where he got it, since he didn't seem to have a job."

"Yes, yes. Now that you mention it, I do seem to remember him. I did not have anything to do with him. He had the mark of the devil in him. Remember he had the one pierced ear and the bandana around his neck. Always that bandana! But, what of him?"

"He has been here in Hartford. I haven't seen him, but he would stop in and see Giuseppe from time to time. He sold insurance, or something he said was insurance."

"Extortion! So that is what he is into! I am willing to bet he had the same line of work in Serra! Although, no one talked about that up on the mountain. He probably went down to Tropea and other places on the coast where the businesses were more profitable."

"So, Giuseppe was found by Tony a few years ago and has been paying money to him ever since." Dominick shook his head sadly. "Once you associate with that type, they have you in their grip!"

"That is so common in the City," commented Ciro. All the New York papers cried volumes about the Italian gangs. "The Morello gang was doing that extortion work. But they got jailed on counterfeiting."

"*Stupido Siciliano!*" Emilia added, her grim mouth in a lipless frown. She worked in New York and heard much. Ciro worked in Newark and read the papers.

"Now, Ciro," Dominick began, again. "We cannot keep all the children. That is out of the question on a barber's salary. I think that the children will have to be sent out."

Maria let out a teary sigh. She was very attached to her nieces and the baby.

"Maria," Dominick tersely said. "You and I have already discussed this. It is too much to expect."

He turned back to his brother-in-law. "I figure Maria and I will keep Julia and Giuseppe. They are little and need us. We will send out the four oldest. We are just not sure how to do this."

Ciro knew his wife's mind. After the loss of their baby, she was going to have nothing to do with children. But he also knew the children could not go to strangers. He was the head of the household and she had to do as he said. "Maybe we could take one of the older ones, Anna or Teresa. And maybe Joe could take the other. He and Serafina have several but just one wouldn't hurt. Serafina would not be able to handle a little one, but an older one, I am sure that they could take."

"We will send him a telegram and make sure," Dominick nodded agreeably. "See how easy this is, Maria? And they will still be with family." He looked at her reassuringly.

"Now, what shall we do with Dora and Nunziata? The sooner we decide, the sooner our lives will get back to normal."

"Are there no neighbors who can take one or both?" asked Emilia.

"Well, one of the neighbors down the hall from Carmela, her daughter plays with Nunziata and Dora often," pointed out Maria. "They are friends, even though they are so little. Mrs. Morgani said that if worse came to worse, she would take Nunziata. She is already trained and needs less supervision than Dora. It would not be too hard for the Morganis. Her husband makes good money over at the meat packing plant."

"So, then, that leaves Dora," Dominick said.

The adults were at a loss. There was no spot for Dora. Then, Ciro suggested, "My mother has lost two daughters, now. She should, perhaps, have another to take their place and give her joy in her old age, now that all her children, but Stella, are gone from her."

Maria looked at him, stunned. "A little one go across the ocean with no mama or papa to care for her?"

"I helped you when you came here. I am sure there is some neighbor going back who can help us with her. And, when she gets there, Stella is still home. She will never get married, I think. She can help Mama raise the child."

"It makes sense, *mia cara*!" Dominick said softly. "We do not have many choices."

Maria cried softly as they discussed who they knew going back shortly. Maria would never see Dora again, she knew. And letters were not the same. At the same time, adding two to the family would put enough of a strain on the resources, so much more three. After a few minutes, they decided that Ciro and Emilia would take Dora back to live with them and Anna and Teresa temporarily until they could find someone who lived near Serra and was heading back shortly..

"It is late," announced Ciro. "We have had a very long day. We all need our rest. I will think of these ideas overnight."

"We can go over the details in the morning," Dominick reassured him.

Ciro and Emilia left to go downstairs. When they got out of earshot, Emilia turned to her husband. "You just volunteered me to raise another woman's brat? How could you, without talking it over with me?"

"This is my sister we are talking about. I do not need your permission to help family. We will take one of the older girls and you will raise her properly and you will not counter my decisions. Do you understand?"

"But the money! We are finally doing well! I would have to stop working!"

"We will manage just fine without your money. And in a few years, when the child is old enough, we will put her to work, also. Then there will be even more money. I know what I am doing." His was the final word.

CHAPTER 54

HARTFORD, 1930

"Can you talk again?" Santoro awakened Anna Amato from her reverie. He saw that she had completed reading the reports and assumed that she was remembering bits and pieces of those few chaotic days. She half smiled at him.

"I am ready." She handed the sheaves back to him.

"We lost track of your father. We figure there was a professional involved in this. Too neat. No one reported a man in bloody clothes on the public transportation. So we assumed either he changed, meaning someone had to help him by holding on to the clothes, or he had some private transportation, which means someone with an auto. Either way, there was an accomplice. With the info you gave me, I assume it was Tony and DiNitto and that crew."

"I can see that."

"We heard a few years later that he was in British Columbia but we did not know where. Now, I have an idea on how it all went down. I will tell you what I think. And then I will write it down and give it to Chief Farrell. That will wrap up the case as far as we are concerned. And you will not have to worry about all this mess again."

He leaned back in his leather chair and drank his second or third sip from his own glass of whiskey. The old detective then placed his glass down and began his hypothesis.

CHAPTER 55

THE ESCAPE

Giuseppe had run down the stairs, onto the gangway and to the public sidewalk before he knew what he was doing. Gun still in his hand, although empty of cartridges, he screamed at the few people on the sidewalk, "Leave me alone or I'll shoot!" He heard the shouts of Carmela and Rafaella coming behind him and he ran across the quiet street and along the rails towards the freight yards.

His head was spinning, his clothes damp with sweat. Giuseppe knew he had just a few minutes to get to Hanly Place before the police would be pursuing him. That damn giant George Butler could outrun him out of sheer size, he thought. He hadn't run three blocks since he was a kid, but the fear in his heart kept his legs moving.

Finally, he saw the freight cars parked on the side rails. He climbed into one and leaned against the interior wall, panting, sobbing, and listening to his heartbeat. As he slid down the wall into a sitting position, his hat fell off and rolled a few feet away. He reached for it, looking down at his pant legs. They were covered with spattered blood. So were his jacket and shoes. Even his hat had a few drops clinging to the brim. He began to cry in earnest.

"Why did I do it? Why couldn't I control the gun better? I didn't mean to kill them!" As his heart rate and his crying subsided, he pulled himself together. The alcohol haze seemed to have dissipated.

Getting up, he grabbed the gun, shoved it in his pocket and peeked outside the open car, checking for anyone's whereabouts. He was to meet the men on the side of the tracks closest to the park. He was to wait in the shadows until he saw the car lights. After that, he could not remember all of the further instructions. It looked clear so he carefully jumped down from the freight car and quietly moved west through the yards, moving quickly through open spaces and gliding along cars as often as he could. There were no guards seen walking around and no lights to brighten the yards. It was easy to keep in the shadows.

Once he thought he saw a lantern on the east side of the yards, slowly moving between the cars. Then he did not see it anymore. Perhaps someone looking for a lost dog? Or a murder suspect? He did not want to wait to find out. Finally he got to the farthest point in the yards. He leaned against a fence post and looked around. He saw no auto waiting for him and he panicked. To settle his nerves a little, he pulled out a cigarette and lit it.

Suddenly, from down the street, an auto flashed its lights. Once. Twice. That was the signal! Giuseppe walked towards where the light had originated and he heard a motor turn on. With relief, he ran the last half a block to the car, jumped on the running board and let himself in the back.

"Joe! You look like you saw a ghost!" Tony laughed from inside the auto. Giuseppe did not look at the others in the back seat.

"I don't never want to do anything like that again. I don't think I will ever sleep again!"

"Anything go wrong or do you just have the first time jitters?" DiNitto asked.

"I killed her! I killed both of them!"

"Killed who?"

"I killed my wife and Tassone's wife." The auto was

296

silent for a mile before anyone dared speak.

"That's a shame, Joe. A dirty shame." DiNitto didn't care but he had to act the part. "Did you get Tassone?"

"Yes. That's why the women they started to scream. He just popped blood. It was awful."

"Well, you got the job done. That's the important thing." The car pulled over to a dark building. It was a small house on the outskirts of town.

"Here, Joe. We are gonna to stop here. You got two minutes to change clothes. I got you a suit and a new shirt. You can't appear in public like that!" DiNitto chuckled at the blood-spattered pants and jacket. "And a new hat. You can't wear a straw around here no more. The police around here probably all know about you straw hat by now."

Giuseppe climbed out of the car and looked around, lost. He took off his hat and smoothed down his sparse hair. "Joe! Go to the door and you knock twice. Someone will answer. You tell them you are Joe and you need to come in for a minute. Say it just like that." Giuseppe repeated the words, nodded and went to the door. A minute later he was let in. When he came out he looked somewhat refreshed and certainly cleaner. His straw had had been exchanged for a bowler. His dark suit had been exchanged for a light tan summer wool. He climbed back into the car and the driver pulled out into the road and proceeded in a south-westerly direction.

DiNitto pulled out a box from under his seat and opened it. He took out a few glasses and a bottle of whiskey. "You need this more than I do, Joe," he winked at Giuseppe. "Tony, open this bottle." DiNitto held the glasses as Tony poured. "I'm better than those peasants who don't know the finer things in life. We drink from glasses, like the gentlemen." He smirked. "A toast to our good friend, Joe Amato. Thank you for helping us out. Now, it is time for us to repay the favor."

He handed the glasses to Joe, Tony and a fellow Giuseppe did not know, named Minicone. And they toasted their success. The driver did not get a glass. "Not because I don't love you, Pasquale, but because you got a long drive ahead," explained DiNitto.

"Sure, Boss," Pasquale answered and drove on.

The car drove, then to the south side of Hartford, to a trolley stop. "Get out, Joe," DiNitto ordered.

Giuseppe looked at him blankly.

"I know what I'm doing. Give me the gun and get out of the car."

Giuseppe slowly handed him the gun and edged his way out of the car, wondering if one of them was going to shoot him. He shut the door and started to back away.

DiNitto started to laugh. "Come here!" He laughed more. "You just kill me! Don' you remember what we are doing?"

Giuseppe shook his head slowly. The alcohol and the shock had muddled his thoughts and he could remember none of the plans.

"You got a few nickels in you pocket," DiNitto said. "You take the trolley to Wethersfield. This way, when the police start investigating, someone sure gonna say they saw you on the trolley going south away from the city. See? Easy!"

Giuseppe nodded. "We will meet you two block from the trolley stop in half an hour. Now, go before you miss it. This is the last trolley south tonight."

Giuseppe walked to the stop and waited a minute or two. Then he heard the distinctive screeching of the metal wheels as the trolley went around a slight curve just before it came into view. Once it came to a stop, he mounted the steps, dropped his nickel in the box and found a seat. He pulled his new hat down over his eyes, crossed his arms and pretended to nap. It was not ten minutes before the conductor called the Wethersfield stop. All the riders got off. It was the end of the line. As he was getting off, he glanced at the north-bound trolley, standing as it picked up riders. He thought he saw a fellow he knew, one of the police officers he had befriended. Turning his head, quickly, he headed out to the streets to find DiNitto's car.

"You follow instructions good, my friend," DiNitto said when Giuseppe climbed back in. "Now that I'm sure someone seen you go south, we go north. This is gonna take a while, so, you can take a nap. I'll wake you when I need you." DiNitto tapped the driver on his shoulder. "Take it easy. Don't go fast. I don't want no questions from nobody. You pull over in an hour and get Minicone to drive. Understand?"

"Sure, Boss," responded Pasquale. He pulled the cigar out of his mouth, sent a wad of tobacco stained sputum over the door and replaced the cigar. The three in the back seat and the two in the front seat were quiet for the next hour as Pasquale drove around city streets, headed to the north side of Hartford. Finally they left the lights behind and were driving slowly on country roads towards Springfield.

After an hour, the car came to a stop under a grove of trees. DiNitto was instantly awake. "Where are we?" he asked.

"Near some hamlet called Windsor," replied Pasquale.

DiNitto sat up and looked around. He noticed a thin silver line reflecting the moonlight. "There's water. Go follow that creek a little way. We gotta get rid of this gun."

Pasquale got out of the car and reached in over the back door to receive Giuseppe's gun from DiNitto. Then he began to walk down to the water. A few hundred yards from the road, he noticed a little bridge. Seemed like a place to hide something you didn't want anyone to find any too soon. He walked down to the creek's edge, looking around to see if anyone was watching. Then he walked to the bridge and threw the gun under it. The gun hit a rock, flew a few feet into the air and fell five feet from shore. That was good enough. Then, Pasquale started walking back up to the car. That's when he noticed a man under a clump of trees. He was fast asleep and seemed to have never noticed the sounds. Probably due to that wine bottle near his feet.

Minicone was in the driver's seat for the next two hours. They kept spotting each other all night and followed the road along the Connecticut River. By sunrise, they had crossed Massachusetts and were in southern Vermont. The roadster pulled into the village of Brattleboro and drove around looking for a diner that was open.

"There's one!" Pasquale pointed out. Minicone parked the auto and the five stepped out onto the dirt road and stretched.

"The bumpy ride kept me awake most of the night!" DiNitto grumbled as he tried to smooth down his rumpled jacket.

"No one has gotten a good night's sleep," growled Tony. "I think we are all ready for breakfast."

The five men walked into the little diner and looked around. It seemed safe enough, not that any news of the murders would have gotten into this morning's newspapers or to the local constabulary, yet.

They sat at a booth and silently read the menu on the wall, not wanting to talk about the last 12 hours or anything else. After a few minutes, the waitress came over.

"I am Edith, your waitress. What can I get for you gentlemen this morning?" she asked.

"My treat," DiNitto said with feigned cheeriness. He was not used to a bad night's sleep. Pensara was going to have to pay him more for his uncomfortable night. "Coffee, all around. Then come back in a minute." The waitress was used to gruff attitudes first thing in the morning. But five rumpled suits? There were no trains arriving this early to explain that. She left and returned with five mugs of steaming coffee. After taking the order, she left again, somewhat suspicious of the men.

"So," began DiNitto. "Here is how we play out the rest of this little adventure. Joe, you are taking the first train out this morning. It will take you over the border into Canada. Here are a few things you gotta have." He turned his attention to Tony. "Give him those papers."

Tony took a package out of his inside jacket pocket. He laid them out on the table.

"Here is your passport," DiNitto continued. "You are a US citizen named Joe Pace. You were born in Gioia Tauro, Italy. That way, if they hear your Calabrese dialect they can't question it. You never been to Serra San Bruno, a little village in the mountains. You understand?" Joe nodded, realizing he was taking on a new identity. He was uncomfortable rejecting his past. But what else was there?

"Here is 200 dollars. Pensara was pretty generous, you think?"

Guiseppe's eyes opened wide. Almost half a year's salary! Between that and the money in his pocket and the new suit, he was set!

"And here is the ticket to get out to Fernie. All the connections are written down. It will take a week to get there. After that, you are on your own. You don't know us. We don't know you. We haven't been in Hartford in a few years. You never been there. You got off the boat in New York. Understand?"

"Sure, sure, DiNitto. I got it." Guiseppe's brain was starting to calm down after some sleep and this strong coffee. He was mostly thinking of Carmela. Was she going to recover? Was she dead?

Edith quickly returned with five earthenware dishes of American breakfast food, ham and eggs. The men said not a word as she distributed the plates.

"Okay, then," continued DiNitto after she left. "After we finish breakfast, we go to the car. I got a package of clean linen for you. Then, we will go drop you off at the train station. And it's *arrivederci* from there. Good luck and all that."

Giuseppe swallowed his eggs without tasting them. He was anxious to be away from these men. He did not participate in their conversation. They were nothing to him compared to his Carmela and the children. And he had ruined that!

The men left the waitress a hearty tip and left the diner. Within a minute or two, the newspaper boy brought the morning's papers in to put on the display rack. Edith picked up the Hartford Courant to peruse the front page. The headlines shouted out Amato's deed. She thought about the very Italian look of the men she had just served and of their wrinkled dress. Then she shook her head, laughed at her imagination and placed the paper back to go help more customers.

Minicone went into the station first, looking for a

newsstand. The Wednesday morning Courant was already on the stands. He bought a copy and handed it to Giuseppe. "Here. A going away present," he chuckled.

Giuseppe bade farewell to the four others, mounted the steps to the train, found his seat and settled in. Anxiously, he opened the newspaper to read about the search.

On the bottom of an inside page was the news he needed to hear. Carmela was in the hospital, as was Rafaella. She was not dead! He silently prayed for her as the train left the station. Maybe, just maybe, things would go right, after all, and he could have her back in his life, again. He would check again in a few weeks. After he had a place in Fernie. He was sure that Concetta and Raffaele would help him. With that he settled in for a very long trip.

CHAPTER 56

HARTFORD, 1930

"So, we know he ended up in British Columbia. We've known that for at least ten years. But we did not know where. So we could not notify the Mounties to pick him up. I guess it's a cold trail."

Santoro shrugged his shoulders. "Now I have to ask you, same as with your other family members . . . Have you seen Joe Amato in the past 18 years?"

"No, sir."

"Has he tried to call you or write you letters in the past eighteen years?"

Anna Amato's eyelids fluttered slightly, but he took it to mean she was tired. After all, five hours of questioning, with just coffee and water, would do it. "No, sir."

"All right, then. You can go. Here. Use my phone to call your husband and he can come down and get you."

Miss Amato quickly made the phone call. "He will be right down. He was getting worried." She put on her mink coat, adjusted her hat, and pulled on her gloves.

Putting both hands on his desk, Detective Santoro pushed himself up out of his chair. He walked around the desk and extended his big hand. Her small one was lost in his handshake.

"I am sorry I had to make you sit here so long," he apologized. "I wanted to end the file for the Chief. He and I are retiring soon. I thought he would like it complete."

"I am glad I could help."

"I have never met a woman with such a memory for

detail! I am impressed. Honestly." He released her hand. "Let me walk you out to the front." He took his witness's arm and put it through his own, walking her past the office door and through the detectives' room in that manner.

Anna Amato's husband, Joe (an awful coincidence, thought Santoro) was just driving up in his well-polished Ford when they reached the front door of the police building. He jumped out and walked over to the two.

"Are you finished?" he asked in an annoyed voice. "It took you five hours?"

"Yes, it did!" Santoro was easily annoyed with this skinny young man. "I wanted everything I could get out of her. Now take her home and give her some food."

"Mary's got some dinner for you," Joe's voice got more accommodating towards his wife. Then he turned back to the police detective. "Do you need her anymore?"

"Got it all wrapped up. You go finish your holiday in peace and quiet."

"Thanks," said Joe. He took his wife's arm and led her to the car, opening the door for her and helping her in.

When he had gotten into his side of the car and shut the door, he turned towards her. "Did you tell him you have spoken to your father, Anne?"

"No. He asked if my father called me. He didn't ask if I called him. And he didn't ask about the phone number Mary gave the police. But it is just a library number."

"So, he doesn't know about the phone call you made to him yesterday?"

His wife shook her head.

"Good," responded Joe. "Let sleeping dogs lie. Your father quite obviously doesn't want anything to do with your family, anyway."

With that, Joe started the car and headed off to his

sister-in-law's house.

THE END

That's the ending?!

Disappointing!

ELIZABETH A MARTINA

Elizabeth is an amateur genealogist, a writer, a voracious book collector, and a gardener, though not necessarily in that order. Her addiction to travel has brought her to Europe, Japan and Canada. Most of her writing inspiration came from listening to her grandmother's stories and her lifelong reading habit. Elizabeth lives in the mountains of northern New York with her husband and their dog, Max. You can read some of her short stories at

www.lanternariuspress.weebly.com/elizabeth'sstories

Laternanins Press
707 Utica St.
Oriskany, NY
13424

Made in the USA
Middletown, DE
27 October 2015